EVA CHASE

# GRIM WITCHERY

ROYALS OF VILLAIN ACADEMY #7

Grim Witchery

Book 7 in the Royals of Villain Academy series



First Digital Edition, 2019



Cover design: Fay Lane Cover Design

Ebook ISBN: 978-1-989096-54-3

Paperback ISBN: 978-1-989096-55-0

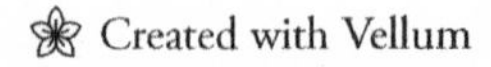
Created with Vellum

# CHAPTER ONE

*Rory*

I'd figured that once I started spending more time with my birth mother, there'd be a certain amount of family bonding. I hadn't expected any of that bonding to take place at a shooting range.

"The original owner was a retired blacksuit," my mother told me as she parked her gold Lexus outside the dark gray face of the building at one end of the strip mall. "Other fearmancers have taken up the business since. They accept Nary customers, of course, to sustain their income, but they have a separate bay for mage clients."

She fell silent as we stepped out into the crisp October air. A couple of young men were just heading into the building with eager smiles. We strode in behind them.

A faintly metallic scent laced the air just inside. The woman at the front desk caught sight of us with a twitch of her expression that told me she knew exactly who we were. "Just a moment," she said to the other customers, and came over to serve her current and future Barons Bloodstone.

"Here you go," she said, handing a keycard to my mother. "Everything's set up in the bay for you. We're so glad to be of help." I suspected she'd have been even more effusive if the presumably Nary guys hadn't been looking on. As ordi*nary* human beings, they had no idea magic even existed, let alone that we were one of the ruling families over a community that worked spells fueled by fear.

We headed down a narrow hall, having to brush past a small group that was just leaving one of the regular bays. The doors and walls must have been soundproofed, because the crack of gunshots barely penetrated them, sounding as far off as if they were being fired miles away.

I wouldn't have thought mages would bother much with regular guns—I'd never seen even the blacksuits, our law enforcement officials, wield one—but I stayed as quiet as my mother was. One of the longest held rules of our society was to avoid making any show or mention of magic in the presence of those who had none.

The baron waved the keycard in front of a panel on a door at the end of the hall, and the lock clicked open. As soon as we'd walked into the eerily quiet space, her shoulders came down. She let out a sigh with a little shake of her body as if shedding something distasteful. My mother was no fan of the Naries—or as she'd have called them in her harsher moments, "feebs."

A glance around the bay told me immediately that this

wasn't the kind of shooting range I'd have pictured from the movies I'd seen. Our end of the room held no weapons at all, the one rack mounted there empty. At the far end, against a black wall, a beige sculpture of a vaguely rendered, androgynous face and torso was posed where I'd have expected to find a paper target hanging. Apparently *we* weren't going to be using guns after all.

My mother set her purse on a table in the corner, so I did the same with mine. My eyes lingered on her leather bag for a moment before I turned back to her.

I'd started coming to her more, acting as though I wanted to follow in her footsteps, because I was hoping to uncover more about the plans she'd been making with her fellow barons—so that I could intervene before they caused any more damage. So far she hadn't offered much though, focusing more on what she talked about as my preparation in my role as her scion. I couldn't help wondering how much I might find out from the contents of that purse.

My mother motioned to the sculpture. "The targets are created with magical enhancements. If you strike a potentially fatal spot with enough magical force, they'll shatter. Otherwise they merely crack at the points of impact. The most vital points are the center of the forehead and the heart. Let's see how you do."

An uneasy laugh escaped me as I moved to the spot marked on the floor. "Not a skill I'm going to have to use very often, I hope." I was aware that my mother had killed at least one fellow mage in a dispute during her university days, so she'd obviously made use of this kind of magic before.

And the barons and their scions did have to be more vigilant when it came to self-defense. "I hope so too," my mother said, her mouth tightening. Just last month, I'd joined a squad of blacksuits in rescuing her from the other faction of mages in this country: the joymancers. As mages who drew their power from encouraging happiness in others, they looked on our fear-driven magic with horror.

Seventeen years ago, a bunch of them had attacked my birth parents, another baron, and various other fearmancers who'd been on a business outing. Everyone other than my mother and I had been killed, and the joymancers had made it appear that my mother had died in the assault too. She'd spent the past nearly two decades imprisoned in secret, and I'd been set up with a joymancer family who'd raised me with love while concealing my heritage and my magic from me.

I guessed if the fearmancers present had been better at magical combat, the outcome might have been rather different.

And it wasn't just the joymancers I had to be wary of. Many fearmancers lived up to the awful impression our enemies had of us, not least of all the barons. I'd faced bullying and challenges to my authority from my classmates ever since arriving at Bloodstone University, and the older barons, unhappy about the joymancer attitudes I'd grown up with, had made it their personal mission to crush me and the people who'd supported me in every way possible.

So, yes, I hoped I'd never have to hit someone where it hurt… but it wasn't totally out of the realm of possibility that I'd need to if I wanted to make sure they didn't kill me first.

I drew a casting word onto my tongue as I focused on the target. Over the past several days, I'd been working with my professor mentor at the university on creating my own strings of seemingly meaningless syllables to imbue with magical meaning. Personal casting words had the benefit of preventing anyone listening from knowing what spell you had in the works before they saw the effects.

But making that mental leap also took more concentration, especially when you weren't used to it. I debated and decided that for the purposes of this exercise, I was better off staying in my comfort zone.

"Strike," I said, willing a portion of the magic that hummed behind my collarbone to solidify into a bolt of energy. With the force of the word, I flung the energy across the room. I'd been staring at the sculpture's face, meaning to hit the forehead, but the gleaming bolt glanced off the top of its nose instead. A thin crack opened up in the plaster.

"Close," my mother said without any hint of approval or derision in her tone. "You'll want to give it more power than that too."

"Right." I dragged in a breath and trained my gaze on the target again. Imagine it was a vicious attacker lunging at me. Imagine it was Baron Nightwood, about to cast a brutal spell against me—or his son.

I snapped out the casting word again, hurling the energy with all the strength I could give it. This time the bolt smacked right into the sculpture's forehead—but only hard enough to leave another crack. I grimaced even as my stomach turned at the thought of my goal.

I didn't really *want* to smash anyone's head open.

"Better, but I'm sure you can hit harder than that." My mother turned her piercingly dark gaze on me. "You can't be afraid to strike back when need be, Persephone. You need to be ready to fight with everything you have. Too many people in this world want to bring us down or see us suffer. Too many have become shaky in their loyalties. They have to know that if they go up against us, they'll regret it."

Her voice turned sharp with those last words. She spat out a casting word and flicked her hand toward the target. The air quivered, and the sculpture burst apart in an explosion of plaster shards. I had to stiffen up to stop myself from flinching.

As far as I could tell, everyone who knew Baron Bloodstone was already terrified of her. I hadn't seen any mage act against her since her return. But she'd come back to fearmancer society after her long imprisonment with wounds you couldn't see just by looking at her. She was suspicious of even our own household staff trying to sabotage her somehow, muttering spells after every interaction to double check her security.

She didn't even really trust *me*, or she'd have shared more about her plans by now.

Another target whirred automatically into place from above. As I readied myself, I took the opportunity to prod her a little more about the part of the barons' schemes I did know. They'd decided it was okay for the students at Blood U to break the rule about magical secrecy, terrorizing the Nary students who were allowed on campus on scholarship and then wiping their memories so they'd forget what they'd seen. Tormenting those who had no magical defenses gave a quick boost to the fearmancer students' power… but the trauma, even repressed, was already taking its toll on their victims.

"There haven't been any more casualties among the Naries at school," I said in as casual a voice as I could manage. The memory of the girl I'd watched jump to her death in the grips of some kind of distress made me feel sick. "How long do you think you'll keep the new policy so restricted, especially with word about it getting out?" Only select groups of students had been let in on the terror sessions so far, under the watchful eye of a few of the professors.

"You should see some changes there shortly," my mother said. "There's been no significant pushback, so it's time to extend the opportunity to all of the students. We'll be making some adjustments that should both reduce the wear on the feebs' minds and extend the benefits that the rest of you will gain."

The whole school was going to get in on the torture now. Wonderful. I kept my expression calm and sent a bolt of magic toward the new target. It broke off a chunk of the sculpture's temple.

My mother had already tortured *me* for speaking against the new policy in public. She'd amplified one of the Desensitization sessions the school used to help us build our defenses against our own fears and locked me in the chamber with those illusions. I'd been playing the part of a contrite daughter since then, but I could feel her studying my reaction for any sign of continuing doubts.

Doubts I couldn't afford to show until I knew how to actually protect all those Naries—and whoever else the barons might have their sights on.

"You must be happy to see it all coming together," I said. I'd gathered from how quickly the barons had moved on this plan once my mother had returned that some form of it had been in the works since before her supposed death. "I'm sure there were lots of things you wanted to accomplish that you're finally getting the chance to."

Like usual, my mother dismissed my nudge with vagueness. "Oh, yes. But we have to take things one step at a time. The rest will come as we're ready."

"If there's anything I can do to help—"

"You'll have plenty of chances as we move forward. One thing you'll need to learn for when you're baron is not to discuss your future intentions until you're putting them into action. Right now, you're best off focusing on what's currently happening around you. And making sure you're fully prepared for anything you might face from an opponent." She nodded to the target. "Continue."

A prickle of frustration ran through me. Maybe she didn't want to discuss schemes she wasn't totally sure she'd get to enact—or maybe she still didn't think I was worthy of sharing those ideas with.

I balled a surge of magical energy and hurled it at the sculpture with a word. It pierced the middle of the target's brow—and the plaster burst like it had for my mother. She clapped her hands with a small and only mildly warm smile.

"Excellent. Let's see you try for the heart spot now. It requires you to be a little more precise with your aim."

I didn't dare push any further about her goals—that would only make her more suspicious. But I was tired of getting nowhere. Every visit I had with my mother, pretending to agree with her attitudes, chipped away a little piece of my own heart.

Her purse was *right* there, with her phone and who knew what else that might give me a clue. If I could convince her to leave the room for a minute or two… but it had to be an urgent enough reason that she wouldn't stop to collect her things first.

I focused on the third target and formed a few syllables on my tongue that had a striking feel to them. I could get in a little more practice at that kind of casting—and it would let me cast more than just the spell my mother saw.

I spoke the nonsense word and threw my magic. A crack formed where the target's collarbone would have been if it'd been designed in that much detail. Frowning as if annoyed by my failure, I tried again with a longer sequence of sounds this time.

The next impact opened a larger crack in the center of the thing's chest. I adjusted my casting word just slightly —shortening it and adding another that I hoped would create the effect I wanted.

I tossed both out one after the other as if it were all one long casting word like I'd used just before. A splinter of plaster fell from the left side of the target's chest. And my mother's head jerked around.

It must have worked. I'd meant to strike her car outside too, just enough to put a little dent in the body. I'd seen her casting and checking the protective spells she'd woven around the gold Lexus more than once. Any magical interference would send an alert to her.

"I'll be right back," she said abruptly, and hurried out of the room, leaving her purse behind as I'd hoped. I waited until the door had thumped shut and darted to the side table.

There was her phone, but a quiver of magic surrounded it. Damn it. She had a protective spell on that too. I should have figured. There was no way I'd be able to break it and rebuild it before she got back. I dug farther into the bag's contents, sharply aware of the seconds ticking away before she'd determine there was nothing to pursue outside and returned.

I turned up a business card from what I thought was a store in the town just off campus, with a couple of names scrawled on the back. I took a quick picture of it with my own phone so I didn't have to rely on my memory and tucked it back in. Otherwise the purse held a couple of pens, a tube of lipstick, a pack of cinnamon breath mints, a spare phone charger, a tiny foldable knife with a symbol etched on it that I took a picture of too, and her wallet. I flipped that open—and the door handle clicked.

My pulse hiccupped. I shoved the wallet back into the purse, jerked over the flap, and sprang back into my spot in front of the target. Would she notice it wasn't in exactly the same position as when she'd left? Shit, shit, shit.

The hinges squeaked faintly as the door swung open, and I threw myself into the best strategy for distraction I could think of.

"Strike!" I hollered, ditching the nonliteral casting words for the moment. My attention narrowed with the rattle of my pulse, and my urgency fueled my magic. The bolt I conjured blazed through the air and sliced right through the target's chest. The sculpture didn't just burst but exploded in a firework of broken plaster.

My mother came up beside me without even looking at the table. She chuckled at the sight. "There's my girl. I knew you'd get the hang of it quickly. Let's see if you can get the next one on the first blow. The less time you give them to strike back, the better."

What a comforting sentiment. "I'll do my best," I said, forcing a smile.

After a few more rounds, I managed to blast away the sixth target I'd been faced with on my first attempt. My mother gave my shoulder a squeeze that felt downright affectionate. To my relief, she didn't pause over her purse when she picked it up for us to leave.

As we walked out to the car, my phone chimed with an incoming text. I fished it out and had to catch myself before my legs locked up at the message on the screen. Instead, I nodded at it as if it'd been nothing unusual and dropped the phone back into my own purse as I sank into the Lexus's passenger seat.

"What was that?" my mother asked in an offhand manner I didn't believe at all.

"One of the scions confirming a meeting," I lied, matching her tone. I let my arm rest gently on my purse, but inside my thoughts were whirling.

The message had been from a number I didn't recognize. *I know what you've done*, it'd said. *Soon I won't be the only one.*

Were they somehow aware of the invasion of my mother's privacy I'd just made? Or were they talking about the way I'd arranged for my Nary friend and dormmate to get out of the school to a safer haven? Or one of the many other things I'd done that a whole lot of my fearmancer peers would have disagreed with?

I had no idea. I just knew there were no shortage of possible transgressions this unknown person could be planning to reveal. And Lord only knew what would happen to my precarious relationship with my mother when they did.

# CHAPTER TWO

*Rory*

An image of my mother loomed over me in the dim space, larger than life. Her fingers turned into claws as she reached for me. My heart stuttered, but I squared my shoulders, hit by gratitude for about the dozenth time that I had no witnesses other than Professor Razeden while I tackled the fears conjured up by the Desensitization chamber.

"You're not real," I told the figure in a steady voice. "You can't hurt me. You will *shrink* and you will *fade* until you disappear."

My will shifted the chamber's illusions. After the unshakeable power my actual mother had given them when she'd trapped me in here days ago, disarming the regular version felt shockingly easy. My pulse evened out as the image of her dwindled. When she blinked out of being, the lights came on, illuminating the domed black room more starkly.

Razeden dipped his grizzled head where he was standing near the door. "Excellent work. I think that's the fastest you've subdued the chamber's effects yet."

I gave him a crooked smile. "It doesn't feel quite so intimidating when I know just how much worse it could be. Thanks for letting me have the chance to do a private session before I go back to the group ones."

"I can recognize that your recent experience in here may have left some lingering trauma. The purpose of the group sessions is to give you practice coping with other people recognizing your *regular* vulnerabilities. Adding spectators to a more fraught situation might only hinder your progress."

He walked over to join me, glancing around the room as he did. His voice dropped, even though no sound could carry through the walls around us. "I thought you might appreciate knowing, in case your mother uses this space for a similar purpose in the future… There is a failsafe word that will interrupt the chamber's magic. I trust you not to use it during regular sessions, only if there's a real need."

"Of course," I said with a rush of relief. I hadn't gotten much support from the various authority figures who'd entered my life since I'd stumbled back into the fearmancer world. The fact that any of my professors were willing to stand up to the barons, even behind their backs, took a bit of the edge off my worries. "I won't mention it to anyone."

The corners of Razeden's lips twitched upward. "It was chosen by the mages who put the finishing touches on the chamber's spells with a mind to finding a phrase that no one was likely to utter for any other reason during a session. All you have to say is, 'Bubblegum popsicle.'"

I couldn't help laughing. "Yeah, that doesn't seem likely to come up in most people's lists of fears. Thank you. So far things are going… better, but I don't know for sure it'll stay that way."

"Well, if you think there's some way I can help, don't hesitate to ask. My resources and influence are limited, but I'll do what I can with them."

"Thank you," I said again, meaning it more than I knew how to express. A lump rose in my throat.

Razeden gave me a tentative pat on the back, as if he wanted to be reassuring but wasn't totally comfortable dealing with the emotion his offer had stirred up. I gave him a quick smile to show I was okay and headed out.

I came onto the green between the campus's three main buildings to find that a squad of blacksuits had arrived during my session. I might have frozen up at the sight of them if they hadn't been clearly occupied with a bunch of students who weren't me. A bunch of students who were… all Naries. The golden leaf pins that marked them as scholarship students glinted on every collar in the afternoon sun.

A dozen of them were gathered around the four blacksuits, one of whom was beckoning a few stragglers over. Two of the other officers were holding small cloth sacks. As I circled the group to try to figure out what was going on, a Nary student at the front of the gathering dropped something into an open sack with a metallic clacking.

"I don't understand," the girl next to him was saying. "We never had to give them up before."

"It's a new school rule," the blacksuit she was talking to replied. "To limit distractions. The program here is very intensive."

Why was a blacksuit enforcing the university rules? What were they taking? I eased closer, and caught a glimpse as one of the other Naries fished an object out of his pocket to hand over. It was the sleek silver shape of a cell phone.

A prickling ran over my skin. They were collecting the Naries' primary means of communication with the outside world. I wasn't sure there were even any landlines available to students on campus, at least not that could be reached without staff permission. Were they going to restrict their internet use too? With magic, maybe it wouldn't be that hard to prevent any outgoing data.

"You'll get them back over your breaks and at the end of the school year," another blacksuit informed the students in a flat tone that wasn't at all comforting. Had the Naries realized that it was only scholarship students included in this "new rule"?

My mother had said the barons were going to give permission for the staff to open up the terrorizing of the Naries to all the fearmancers at the university. This measure had to be related to that decision.

A few of those other fearmancer students had ambled

over to watch the collecting of the phones. From the smirks on their faces, I suspected they were enjoying the sight a lot more than I was. My persuasion instructor, Professor Crowford, emerged from Killbrook Hall and stepped off to the side to monitor the proceedings as well. He'd been one of the professors involved in the initial sessions to terrify the Naries—and I had reason to believe he'd supported the barons in other malicious plans in the past.

The blacksuit who appeared to be in charge consulted a tablet she was holding as the last few Naries handed over their phones. She tapped it, maybe checking off their names on a list. Then she motioned to her colleagues with a satisfied expression. "We're finished here."

When she turned toward Killbrook Hall, she nodded to Crowford with an authoritative air that set my skin crawling all over again.

The blacksuits disappeared into the building that held the staff quarters. Were they going to leave the phones with the headmistress, Ms. Grimsworth? Or possibly the barons were so concerned about security that they wanted a higher authority monitoring them.

What if this wasn't the only way the blacksuits were going to start directing activities on campus?

I barely had time to shudder inwardly at that thought when Professor Crowford took a step forward and made a sweeping gesture with his arm toward the watching fearmancers. "Everything's taken care of," he said in his suave voice. "They're all yours."

All… Oh. Before I'd even processed the words, a

couple of the smirking students called out casting words, their expressions shifting into pure delight.

Some of the Naries had already wandered off the green, but several had lingered in conversation. Now the ground lurched beneath their feet. As a few of them let out startled yelps, an illusionary demonic creature swooped down on them from above. It gnashed knife-like teeth in its ghoulish face.

The yelps turned into shrieks. The Naries scattered, a girl near me babbling to herself: "Oh my God. Oh my *God.*" I could practically see the waves of fear they had to be giving off lighting up my fellow mages with a giddy glow.

My gut knotted. A protest rose up in my chest, but at the same moment my gaze slid back to Crowford—who was watching me.

When our eyes met, he made an encouraging gesture as if suggesting I join in. The thought made me want to vomit. But I couldn't openly argue against this assault on the Naries either, not if I wanted to keep whatever good will I'd managed to build with my mother. Not if I wanted a real chance of heading off whatever other plans the barons had in the works. Crowford had already tattled on me to her once—the time that had gotten me locked in the Desensitization chamber.

"So they've already started," said a solemn voice from behind me. Declan, the Ashgrave scion and soon-to-be baron, joined me, his slim frame tensed as he took in the scene before us.

Of the five baronies that ruled over fearmancer society,

the Ashgraves were the only ones who'd generally shown much sympathy for the nonmagical people we lived alongside, a fact that had earned them the other barons' disdain. He couldn't speak up against this publicly either, not without his colleagues branding him a traitor.

"You knew this was going to happen?" I asked.

"Baron Stormhurst helpfully filled me in just a few minutes ago. Apparently the others decided they didn't need to discuss the development with me ahead of time, since it was part of the strategy my aunt already approved of. Or at least, they know she'll say it was if they ask her to."

His voice held a dry edge without much humor. The barons had already tricked him once to ensure they could approve the new policy using his aunt, who'd acted as his regent when he was younger and still had a spot at the table of the pentacle until he graduated and could take on the full role of baron.

I drew farther back as the ground shook all the way to my feet. A few more fearmancer students had joined in, one of them tossing a Nary around with violent gusts of wind, another sending streaks of electricity crackling across the grass. Whenever one of the Naries tried to flee, one or another tossed a spell out to block them.

"Why take their phones?" I asked. "So there's no way they can tell anyone what's going on in the moment?"

Declan shook his head. "They're taking into account the damaging effects the memory wipes appeared to be having on the students. Rather than closed sessions with memories erased after each one, it's going to be a free-for-all as long as the Naries are on campus. The blacksuits will oversee their mental 'adjustments' before they go home or anywhere else. There are new wards around campus, too, to prevent them from running off without permission."

"Less messing with their memories, a lot more messing with them in every other way." I hugged myself. Not only were we torturing them now, but we were also denying them any kind of social support from their families or friends off campus. Not to mention… "How the hell are they going to learn anything when they're going to be freaking out the entire time they're at the school?"

"A good question," Declan said. "And one I'm planning on bringing up with the barons when we have our next proper meeting. If we're not turning out high-performing graduates from the scholarship programs, people will stop applying to them."

Hopefully that would be a clear enough practical problem to sway the barons. I turned away, unable to stomach the torture any longer. Declan must have given the rest of the scions a heads up, because the other three guys had just emerged from Ashgrave Hall, which held the senior dorms. We went over to meet them.

"It's a lovely day in the neighborhood," Jude intoned with a playful lilt, but his eyes widened a little as he swept his floppy dark copper hair back from his forehead, taking in the chaos on the green. The supposed Killbrook scion could turn just about any situation into a joke, but I knew he felt things deeply under that carefree exterior.

"They didn't waste any time, did they?" Malcolm's

expression turned dark as his deep brown gaze followed the same path. As the heir of Nightwood, his father's status had made him king of the campus, but lately they hadn't been seeing eye-to-eye on most matters.

Connar shifted his stance with an uncomfortable twist of his mouth, his brawny arms folding over his chest. "They can't keep this up for weeks on end, can they?" he asked, but his deep voice didn't hold much hope. Like Malcolm, the Stormhurst scion had plenty of direct experience with how brutal fearmancers could be, much of it courtesy of his own parents. "They'll get bored of harassing the Naries."

"Maybe, but even if they do, the Naries will still be pretty messed up after what they've seen and not knowing what might be thrown at them next," I said. "They were shaken enough *without* remembering the horrible things the mage students did to them."

We drew closer to the building, Declan shooting a glance around to confirm no students or staff were near us. "There have to be other families who don't feel comfortable with this approach," he said. "Whether because they see the Naries as human beings with actual rights or because they're worried about the implications for our society in the long run."

My stomach knotted. "There's not much any of us can say to encourage those attitudes without bringing the barons' wrath down on us, though."

Malcolm's divinely handsome face had gone unusually solemn with thought. "Not in a big public way. But I've got a sense of who's most likely to have a problem with the new policy." A flicker of a smile crossed his lips. "Going by which families my dad complains about the most is an easy starting point. I can work the room, put out some feelers, connect people who'll be more inclined to protest if they have someone standing with them."

Jude shrugged. "None of the barons expect much from me at this point. I can get a lot of mileage out of mocking the people who *do* think this is a reasonable use of their time." He rubbed his hands together with a sly glint in his dark green eyes.

"I can disrupt some of the spells without anyone knowing it's me," Connar put in. "Make them feel less confident in their abilities, and maybe spare the Naries a little."

His broad brow knit beneath his chestnut crewcut. He knew as well as I did that none of those measures would get the Nary students completely out of this awful scenario any time soon.

I let out a rough breath. "I keep *trying* to get more information out of my mother so I'll know where we might have some leverage… She still isn't trusting me with many details on the political side."

Declan turned his bright hazel gaze on me. "You're doing the best you can, Rory. I know how hard it's been for you as things are." He turned toward Killbrook Hall. "We might be able to at least moderate the torment for the time being. I'll go talk to Ms. Grimsworth, point out how disruptive this… free-for-all is for not just the Naries but the fearmancer students too. As long as I'm just asking for a more disciplined approach rather than to cancel it outright, the other barons can't really see that as defying them."

I hoped not. "Be careful," I said as he moved to set off.

"You know, my dad still thinks I'm on his side," Malcolm said, cocking his head. "Maybe I can make some progress right at the source. Complain to him that all they're doing is encouraging people to run around campus like a bunch of idiots. It won't be enough for them to call off the scheme, but it'll give him more reason to listen if Ms. Grimsworth tells him she's laying down some new rules of conduct."

He gave me a flash of a smile as if reading the concerns already resounding in my head. "Don't worry, Glinda. I'll be careful too."

With a wink to go with the nickname, he headed inside to make the call from the privacy of his dorm room. A scream rang out behind me, and I winced, afraid to look to see what new horror of magic had caused it.

"None of this feels like enough," I couldn't help saying. "What good am I as a scion if I can't stop something this awful from happening?"

"Hey." Connar caught my arm with a gentle squeeze. "Declan's right. You're trying everything you can. And when Declan's officially baron, he'll have more clout to go against the others."

"In three months," I said. Three months of torment for the Naries—if he could even get the policy reversed right away, which was doubtful.

"I'm sure between our five brilliant minds, we can come up with a solution sooner than that." Jude looked me over. The mischievous gleam came back into his eyes. "I think all the time you're spending with your mother is wearing you down. Let's get out of here, clear our heads, and remind ourselves just how ready we are to fight."

I raised my eyebrows at him. "What did you have in mind?"

His lips curled with a grin. "I have an outing I've been keeping in my back pocket. I'm thinking now is the perfect time to use it. Come on, both of you."

# CHAPTER THREE

*Rory*

Jude let Connar drive. He interjected directions from the back seat in between mysteriously hushed phone calls. An autumn evening was settling in when we reached a huge, pale peach cube of a building on the outskirts of a town about an hour and a half away from the university. Most of the place's windows on both floors were painted over in the same shade. The sign over the darkened front door said…

"Paintball arena?" I twisted in my seat to give Jude a quizzical look.

He gave me a sly smile. "You'll see. Let's go. I've got everything taken care of."

A sign hung on the inside of the door that read, *Closed for private function.* "That would be us," Jude announced, and opened the door with a brief casting and a twist of his fingers. He strolled right in, flicking on the lights, as if he owned the place. Which maybe he did for the next few hours, however much cash he'd needed to cough up for that privilege.

Three shoulder bags were waiting for us in the front hall. Jude lifted one and unzipped it to show the heap of paintballs inside. His were all red, a brighter shade than his hair.

"I asked for fifty each, but the owner said we probably won't get through that many." He set down the bag to reach for one of the padded black vests leaning against the wall next to them. "Since it's just the three of us, I figured a game of one-and-out wouldn't be much fun. We can each take five direct hits. The vests have a spell that'll scan the rest of your body. When you've reached five, the vest will fall off. Last one to keep theirs on wins."

"And this is going to help us stop the barons how?" Connar said in a doubtful voice, hefting the largest of the vests.

Jude rolled his eyes at the bigger guy without dropping his smile. "A boost in confidence. A chance to shake off all the dire aspects of our situation and refocus. Plus practice at honing our wits in combat and flexing our magical skills." He tossed one of the balls in the air and caught it. "For *our* kind of game, we won't use the paintball guns. We aim them with magic."

I wasn't sure this activity would lead to any useful inspirations, but I could see Jude's point about refocusing. It'd be a relief to play a game that really was a game, just for fun, with people I trusted, instead of the potentially fatal one I found myself engaged in every time I was around my mother or the other barons. And who knew—maybe it would shake something loose in my head that'd set me on a better course.

"I'm in," I said, sliding my own vest over my shoulders. A tingle of magic rippled over my skin as I zipped it up. It formed a solid but not uncomfortable weight on my chest. I slung one of the bags, this one full of blue paint balls, across my back. Connar grabbed a yellow set, obviously willing to at least give it a try.

We pushed through double doors at the other end of the hall into a space so vast I had to catch my breath as I took it in. The ceiling must have loomed at least twenty feet over our heads. In every direction, walls and boulders made of foam, plastic, and metal jutted from the slightly spongy floor. Several sets of stairs led up to platforms above us, the largest filling about a third of the space with hiding places of its own, the smaller ones no more than ten feet across, with ropes connecting them to each other or allowing an alternate escape route to the ground. A distant whirring carried from the filtration system's grates high above.

"This place used to be a blacksuit training facility," Jude explained, ambling farther into the arena. "From what I understand, pretty much everything in it has some kind of magical trick you can make use of. The current owners host regular paintball sessions during the day for people who can never make use of those extras, but they're always open to private bookings from fearmancers."

Connar let out a low whistle. "Pretty sweet." He sounded only impressed now.

Jude grabbed a couple of paintballs out of his bag, keeping one in his hand and tucking the other into the crook of his elbow. "Let's say five minutes to explore the place and come up with a strategy, then the paintballs fly?"

"Sounds good to me." I bounced on my feet, warming up my muscles with a growing sense of anticipation. Hell, yes, I was ready to remind myself what I could do when I was the one calling the shots, not trying to cater to someone else's expectations. Connar nodded.

Jude gave us a little wave, already turning to jog across the room. "Excellent. May the best mage win."

Connar chuckled and paused to give me a quick kiss on the cheek before he loped off to the left. Figuring it was better to stake out separate territory, I veered to the right. What kinds of secrets did this once-blacksuit-owned facility hold?

The landscape offered a huge variety of options, from simple walls with a few holes you could use as handholds or sniper spots to nooks with shelter on all sides and those higher platforms. I traced my fingers over the metal surface of a narrow pyramid just wide enough to block me from view and found a faint etching in the metal.

The shape of the groove sent a prickle of recognition through me. I murmured a casting word, nudging a little jolt of energy along its path.

With only a whisper of sound, the spire tipped over to provide a ramp up to a platform that had no stairs or rope at all. Not a bad spot to be staked out if no one else figured out the trick to getting up there.

I scrambled up it, finding shallow grooves in the surface to help my balance. From the platform above, I could see over most of the structures on the ground level. Connar was weaving between some boulder-shaped ones by the far wall. I caught a glimpse of Jude's copper head before he ducked out of sight to my right in the middle of a mess of twisting walls that formed a sort of maze.

This was a good vantage point, but I wasn't sure I had the aim and speed to hit either of the guys at that distance before they could dodge. I scanned the room once more and then slid down the spire.

As I righted it to remove that path until I decided I needed it again, a tone pealed through the room. That must be our signal that it was time for the battle to begin.

I grabbed a couple paintballs from my bag like Jude had and secured the rest against my back. Then I slunk through the jungle of artificial landmarks in the direction I'd last seen him. Connar was the Physicality expert—I'd rather get a little practice in before I went up against him.

My feet only made a faint rasp on the spongy floor. No other sound reached my ears now that the tone had faded out. I rolled the paintball in my hand, adjusting my grip—and a blur whipped toward me from my left.

I flinched and jerked backward, a squeak slipping form my throat, but I wasn't fast enough. A scarlet blob of paint exploded against my shoulder. I spun around just as Jude darted out of sight behind a nearby wall with a triumphant chuckle.

"You're going to pay for that," I called after him, but I had to smile. The impact hadn't hurt, and the smell of the paint was pleasantly tangy, reminding me of the plastic sculpting clay I'd shaped my little figurines out of, back before I'd known I could simply conjure sculptures out of magic. Invigorated, I crept after Jude.

I studied the structures I passed, watching for more magical symbols. There was one under a shallow overhang. I crouched to reach it and sent a whisper of magic over the carving.

The air around me blurred. Some kind of shield—or an illusion to hide me from view? Either way, it couldn't hurt to linger here for a minute or two and see…

It didn't take long before Jude slipped into sight, his head swiveling as he watched for me. He spun his next paintball between his fingers. His gaze slid right over my hiding spot. My mouth stretched with a grin. I drew back my arm and murmured a casting word to guide my aim.

The blur in the air shattered as I flung the paintball through it. Jude's eyes snapped back to me, but my ball was already smacking into his chest with a blue splatter.

He sputtered a laugh and lunged toward me. I threw myself around the structure just in time to hear paint splash against the wall I'd been standing by. Jude's footsteps thumped after me.

I dashed onward, ducking left and right in the hopes of losing him. The curve of a magical carving rippled across the floor up ahead. I pushed myself forward with a little more speed and sent a rush of magic through the etching just as I reached it.

An unexpected force flung me upward. I found myself soaring through the air, over the tops of several structures, and landing with a thump partway across the room. The breath jolted out of me—and Connar poked his head out from around a wall.

I fumbled for my next paintball. He flicked his toward me with a sparkle in his light blue eyes. A smack of yellow caught me across one side of my vest, but I managed to clip him in the shoulder just as he pulled back into shelter.

Okay, I'd taken two hits, which left three more before I was out. The guys had at least one each. Maybe I could get them to face off against each other for a little while to give me a break and even the playing field.

I scrambled in the opposite direction from Connar. Jude had probably headed this way, following my magical leap across the room. What could I find around here to make use of and maybe nudge the two of them closer together to set off a skirmish?

I ducked around a set of stairs and came up on one of the boulder-like structures with a series of lumps along its base. Interesting. Circling it, I discovered another carving on its far side.

Should I activate it now or later? As I crouched there, debating, Jude's lean form darted between two walls in the distance. He'd already caught up—and he was heading toward me.

All right, now it was. I whispered magic along the lines of the carving, and the boulder vibrated. With a sudden rattling, the lumps on the other side peeled off and rolled across the room like the start of a landslide.

They careened straight into Jude's path. I only got a

brief look at him before he yelped and swerved to avoid them. Then there was a smack of paint and a shout of protest, followed by the thump of running feet.

Mission accomplished.

I hurried after them to see if I could get a shot or two in myself, only to run into Connar, dripping red paint from his stomach, having doubled back around. He hurled one of his paintballs at me and threw himself behind a structure at the same moment. The ball burst against my side. Shit. Only two more left now.

I raced up a flight of stairs and hunched low to try to stay out of sight as I watched for the guys from the raised platform. In quick succession, I managed to fire off one and then another paintball at Connar and Jude. My cover now blown, I skidded along a rope to flee, but Jude managed to catch my back with one of his projectiles. Paint dripped down my vest to patter onto the floor.

Down to my last chance. I'd managed to get myself out of immediate danger, though. Scuffling sounds and a little shout carried from farther away as the guys must have clashed again.

I crept through the room, more cautious now that I was nearly out of the game. The sounds had faded away. Wherever the guys had ended up, they were staying stealthy too. I wet my lips, peered around a wall, and dashed from there to the shelter of a partly carved out boulder. A symbol etched on a slightly raised circular slab of floor just a few feet away caught my eye.

That might be helpful—or it might fling me right into danger. I considered for a minute, my ears perked. Hell, what was the point of playing if I didn't give every special feature I came across a try? I scanned the walls around the area one more time and then sprinted for the slab.

Apparently I hadn't been the only one debating coming this way. Jude leapt toward that spot at the same moment, vaulted by some magic from farther away. We were both moving too quickly to backpedal.

I smacked forward my hand that was clutching a paintball, and he pressed his toward me just as quickly. We collided with each other in the middle of the circle, paint popping between us and mashing into a purple mess. My feet skidded, and we ended up falling on our asses.

Both our vests popped off. Jude laughed and reached for me, drawing a line of cool paint down my cheek. "Mutual destruction," he said with amusement, and kissed me.

Adrenaline was still thrumming through my veins alongside my magic. Desire hit me harder than any of the paintballs had. I kissed him back, smearing paint across his neck, hungry for more. Jude pulled me closer to him and tipped us onto our sides on the foam-like surface.

A mildly disgruntled sound brought me out of our next kiss. When we raised our heads, Connar had come over to the edge of the slab, his eyebrows slightly raised. Four splotches of paint decorated his vest and the shirt beneath.

"Looks like you won," Jude said, beaming at him. "Somehow I don't feel as if I've lost, though." He trailed another line of paint from my jaw down to the collar of my blouse just above my breasts. My pulse skipped a beat.

"Maybe not," Connar said with a smile. He shed his own vest, his muscles flexing beneath his shirt, and an even larger wave of desire swept through me.

It was still difficult to wrap my head around the fact that I could want and care about all four of my fellow scions this much. As the only Bloodstone heir, I couldn't have anything permanent with any of them except Jude, who'd been set up falsely as a scion thanks to his father's machinations. The others would have to give up their barony to be with me. But we all wanted to enjoy the affection and passion we felt for each other for as long as we could.

Jude drew me into another kiss, and Connar knelt by my back. His solid hands eased up my blouse to run over my bare skin. Then he bent closer to kiss me there, softly charting a path up my spine.

Pleasure shivered through me. I fumbled with the silky fabric, and with the guys' help I managed to pull the blouse right off while barely needing to pull away. As I kissed Jude again, I got to work on the buttons of his shirt, paint slicking over my fingers. I streaked it across his slender but toned chest the way he'd painted on me.

Connar tugged me toward him, and I rolled over so I could kiss him on the mouth. With a rustle, Jude pulled off his shirt. He nibbled his way along my shoulder blade as he detached my bra. His nimble fingers stroked over my naked breasts, and my breath hitched against Connar's lips.

The Stormhurst scion kissed me harder but still tenderly. His fingers slid across my belly as Jude continued to spark bliss across my chest. I didn't care what anyone outside our pentacle would have thought of our shared intimacy—not my mother, not the other barons, not our classmates. Every tingle of sensation that ran through me told me being with them like this was good. Right.

Jude's hands dipped down to my pants, flicking open the button at the top. As they roamed farther, Connar lowered his head to my breasts, sucking one nipple into his mouth with a swirl of his tongue. I moaned, arching into both of them.

Reaching behind me, I felt for the fly of Jude's slacks. His cock twitched through the fabric, already so firmly erect the feel of it set off a giddy jolt between my legs. I stroked it as I tugged his zipper down. He groaned and teased his fingertips over my clit. Connar slicked his tongue over my other breast, and for a second the sensations overwhelmed me.

It wasn't enough to satisfy the ache of need building inside me, though. When Connar drew back, I squirmed out of my pants and rolled back toward Jude, nudging him onto his back. His eyes gleamed eagerly as I straddled him. With a jerk of his boxers, I freed his cock to press against my sex.

Connar sat back on his heels as if he thought his part in this interlude was over. He traced his fingers over the etching that had tempted me onto the circle in the first place and murmured a tentative casting. With a faint hum that vibrated through the surface beneath us, the slab began to rise up into the air.

My breath caught. I slipped my fingers between my legs with a whisper of the protective casting and sank down onto Jude as we all soared up together. He plunged into me with a rough sound in his throat. His hand came to rest on my thigh as I started to ride him, each flex of my hips up and down provoking shudders of pleasure from my core through the rest of my body. The other cupped my breast, his thumb flicking my nipple to even stiffer attention.

I swallowed a moan and looked toward Connar. I wasn't done with him yet either. While I braced myself against Jude's chest, I motioned the Stormhurst scion closer and reached for his pants.

"Rory," Connar murmured, sucking in a breath when I peeled down the fabric. He brushed his fingertips over my hair as I palmed his rigid erection. Jude steadied me over him, and I found the right angle to bring my mouth to Connar's length while continuing to meet my other lover's thrusts. The salty, smoky flavor combined with the pleasure flaring from my sex made me dizzy with bliss.

Connar pumped into my mouth with a groan, his fingers tangling gently in my hair. "So fucking beautiful," Jude muttered, rolling the tip of my breast to produce a deeper pulse of sensation. He arched into me as I rode him, my tongue swiveled around Connar's cock, and it was hard to think of anything except the passion we generated between us, racing toward its peak.

My body started to shudder first. My lips closed

tighter around Connar, and his fingers tightened against my scalp. Jude thrust up into me so hard it left my mind spinning.

As I tumbled into the flood of ecstasy, Connar's hips jerked. His release filled my mouth as he let out a choked breath. Jude bucked into me over and over, propelling me higher, faster, and then he came too, clutching my thigh like a lifeline.

I sprawled on the platform between the two of them, too blissed out to do anything but snuggle into their warmth. As the hazy afterglow eased back, I realized the spell had carried us up above even the other platforms, the ceiling lights twinkling starkly down on us.

Jude's and my shoulder bags were still lying on the circle near the edge. Connar pulled a leftover paintball from one of them and held it up. "Why let the materials go to waste?" he said with a shy smile at me, and spoke a few casting words under his breath.

Between his fingers, the ball shifted, the thin surface merging with the paint. Then the paint molded together into a solid blue substance that formed a small blue dragon with its wings spread. A lump filled my throat as I watched.

"Pass me a red one?" I said.

Connar handed me another ball. I turned it in my hand, the lump changing into a pang of homesickness. I used to make my figurines every week back home in California. I'd done a little conjuring since I'd come to Blood U, but there'd been so much chaos and conflict in my life that I hadn't been able to get absorbed in my art the way I used to. I hadn't even realized how much I missed it until this moment.

I might have changed a lot from the Rory I'd been back then, but I didn't have to leave every part of that life behind. I could—I *had to*—hold onto the parts that mattered to me as well as I could.

And I knew, when I met Connar's eyes, that he believed that too. I swallowed hard, abruptly wrenched by the longing to have this connection forever.

It didn't do either of us any good dwelling on that. I turned my gaze back to the paintball.

"Phoenix," I said, picturing the figurine I'd been working on when the fearmancers had stormed Mom and Dad's house, willing my magic into the paint. It shifted slower than with Connar's more practiced power, but the ruddy shape twisted and warped with another casting word and another until a brilliant bird leapt from flames between my fingers.

"Very appropriate, my Fire Queen," Jude said, with a peck to my shoulder. "I won't shame myself by trying to compete with either of you when it comes to conjuring. But I can…"

He waved his hand through the air, and an illusionary dragon sprang into being, scales twinkling with every color from red to violet as it soared over us. I tucked my hand around Jude's and leaned my head on Connar's shoulder, and wished that we could paint right over the horrors still waiting for us back in the wider world.

# CHAPTER FOUR

*Jude*

Night had fully descended when we returned to campus. Other than a couple of passing students, the green was still and quiet in the yellow glow of the buildings' outer lights—no more shrieks or terrifying illusions right now, thank God. I swiped my hand over my mouth, my skin cleaned of paint through a combination of magic and the arena's showers, but a hint of the sharp smell still lingered. I wasn't sure I wanted to completely wash that away just yet.

Rory's good mood had dampened as we came out of the garage, but her eyes were still brighter, her stride steadier, than before. I'd helped her remember herself and her power. If that was the best I could offer with the craziness rising up around us here, at least it was something worthwhile.

When we reached the green, Connar took Rory's hand

with a deliberate air. He drew his already tall form even straighter, his jaw setting as if daring anyone who happened to look to take issue with their closeness.

Rory glanced up at him, her cheeks flushing but her voice quietly hesitant. "Are you sure it's a good idea to make it that obvious that we're back together?"

He and I were the only two in our pentacle who'd been open about our relationship with Rory—and in recent weeks, Connar had turned on her in a very public way under the duress of a spell his parents had inflicted on him. The more open affection he showed for her now, the sooner word would get back to Baron Stormhurst that we'd cracked the spell. Lord only knew how she'd react to that.

"I told my mother I'm not leaving you," Connar said, low but firm. "Let her find out how much I meant that." Despite his defiant tone, his shoulders had tensed. He knew he could be in for a rough time because of that decision.

And he was making it anyway. A twinge of respect ran through me for the guy. To be honest, in the past, he'd always made me a little nervous. Between his taciturn nature, the aggression that'd sometimes burst out of him when one of us faced even a minor affront, and the rumors about how savagely he'd attacked his twin brother years ago, I'd struggled to feel comfortable letting down my guard. But since Rory had come into our lives, it'd been impossible not to see that there was a lot more to the Stormhurst scion than a violent musclehead.

I really shouldn't be surprised by that. There was a lot

more to me than the cavalier joker I'd presented myself as to the other guys, that I was only just starting to show them.

I had Rory, maybe more than any of the rest of them did. The one bright side of my screwed-up history was that it made me a free agent when it came to intimate pursuits. So I could afford to be generous now, especially when Connar probably felt he still had a lot to make up for after the way he'd acted under that spell.

"You two go on ahead," I said to them, and added a wink. "Make out in the common rooms—that'll get mouths flapping fast."

Rory opened her mouth, no doubt to reassure me that I didn't need to take off, and I cut her off with a quick kiss. "I'm good. After all that… physical activity, I could use a walk to cool down before I'll get any sleep."

She gave my hand a quick squeeze. "I'll see you tomorrow."

As they headed into the dorm building, I walked on past it, crossing the green and venturing onto the wilder field beyond. The darkness lay thicker there, but the moon was half full, casting a pearly gray light over the rippling lake beyond the Stormhurst Building. A chilly breeze drifted off the water all the way across campus. Maybe I wouldn't wander quite that far.

As I ambled closer to the shelter of the forest, an uneasy prickling crept down my back. I paused to scan the deeper shadows amid the trees and the field around me. I didn't see anyone else around—but Baron Killbrook had sent minions to spy on me under the cover of illusions ever since I'd moved out on my own.

He'd want to keep an even closer eye on me now that I'd revealed that I knew I wasn't really his son. Declan had even gotten the impression that he assumed I'd told the other scions, although I'd have expected a bigger backlash if that were true.

Maybe I was just being paranoid. If he *did* have someone watching, I didn't really want to give them the satisfaction of seeing me run back to Ashgrave Hall with my tail between my legs.

I started walking again with a casual roll of my shoulders. I veered farther away from the woods, though, figuring I'd loop around to the Stormhurst Building and then walk back to the green along the official path.

Before I'd taken more than a few steps, my ears caught the crack of a twig somewhere behind me. My nerves jumped to an even higher alert. It could have been only an animal, but I'd rather not take the chance that it wasn't.

Angling my body so the motion wouldn't be visible from behind, I carefully slipped my phone out of my pocket. Glancing over my contacts list, my thumb hesitated beside the screen.

Rory might still be with Connar. What a wimp I'd look like if I called on one of them, interrupted the end of their part of our date, and it turned out to be nothing. Malcolm and Declan were almost definitely on campus too… but, fuck, I hated the idea of summoning any of them to my rescue, especially when I wasn't sure I even needed one.

I'd admitted to them that I wasn't really a scion, and they'd accepted me as is. How long would that last if I acted like a weakling who couldn't hold his own against strange noises in the woods?

My stomach clenched. I was about to swipe the list away and turn off the phone when a faint hiss reverberated through the air behind me.

I whipped myself to the side instinctively, and my thumb jammed down on Declan's name. An instant later, a paralyzing bolt of magic slammed into my side. I managed to drop the phone into the grass as my right arm and half of my torso from shoulder to hip went rigid. With a heave of my legs, I propelled myself away from it and whipped around.

A casting word sputtered over my lips to form some kind of a shield, but that was physicality magic, and for all it was supposed to be one of my strengths, the truth was I sucked at it. Which my father well knew, since he was the one who'd interfered with the university enrollment evaluation to make sure I showed up as having the standard scion three strengths rather than a more mundane two. A shimmer of conjured energy whipped up in front of me—and smashed with a crackle a second later as another stunning bolt slammed into it.

The shield deflected some but not all of the spell's power. It caught my leg, clamping around the muscles from my knee down. I stumbled, barely holding myself up. My arm dangled useless at my side. I couldn't even see my attacker, only the empty field and the forest beyond.

If Declan had picked up, he'd be listening now. "If

you're going to pick a fight with me, at least look me in the face," I shouted. "Fucking coward! Got me alone in the middle of the east field and you're too scared to show yourself?"

A gasp of pain escaped me as the spells already clutching me dug in deeper as if they had claws. I sputtered out the words to cast another shield as quickly as I could.

The air vibrated as a volley of spells hurtled toward me. I threw myself to the ground, since there was no way I was running anywhere now, and at least one of them whizzed by over me. The others crackled against the shield, their impact diluted, but still broke through. One smacked into my other leg, locking it in place. Another clipped my left shoulder. Now I couldn't even crawl. Lord knew what they would have done to me without the shield in place.

My mouth still worked, but I didn't see what use illusions or insight would do me right now. I snapped out a casting anyway, a flash of light I hoped would blind the asshole after me. My tongue tripped with another wash of pain. I forced out another few words, scattering reflections of myself on the field around me. More targets, less chance my attacker would hit the right one.

None of my limbs would move. I sprawled back, muttering to strengthen my shield as well as I could, however long this one would last. My heart thudded so hard it felt ready to break my ribs.

A blur streaked past my vision, racing through the illusions in front of me. They held in place—my illusions weren't any joke—but casting that many, I hadn't been able to create much impression of physical presence. It'd be obvious to anyone who touched them that they weren't really me.

The blur swiveled around me, a figure cloaked in some kind of concealing spell. Magic slapped through the shield and across my jaw with a splintering of agony.

My teeth clacked together, nicking my inner lip. The metallic flavor of blood seeped across my tongue. The pain clawed down my throat to burn into my chest. I couldn't part my lips to squeeze out a single spell.

I tried to roll to the side, but the blur was on me, what felt like an elbow bashing into my skull, a heel ramming down on my sternum, sending the pain there spiking deeper in every direction as even the limited protection of my shield fragmented. Inside my head, all I could do was silently scream, *No, no, no!*

I didn't want to go like this. I didn't want to die. Not when I'd just managed to start pulling my life together into something good. Not lying helpless and useless in a fucking campus field. Please, please, no.

Magic exploded behind my collarbone like a spray of shrapnel. More seared across my forehead and blazed through my mind. My thoughts started to fracture in the wake of the agony.

Another blow sent my head snapping to the side as the shield disintegrated completely. I barely felt the graze of the grass against my cheek.

And then voices hollered out from somewhere, distant but unmistakably furious even to my addled mind. A spell sang through the air over my body and must have struck my attacker. A grunt escaped the blurred form. It lunged at me with another muttered casting, and a wave of magical force flung it backward.

I couldn't turn my head to see who was coming. Couldn't even see what my attacker was doing next. As footsteps thumped over the ground, my vision hazed, the edges of it going black. Then pain seemed to explode right in the center of my head, and my consciousness snuffed out.

# CHAPTER FIVE

*Rory*

It was funny how much your impression of a place could shift over a small length of time. When I'd first arrived at the main Bloodstone residence a few months ago, it'd been ominous and unknown. During the time I'd spent there, I'd started to see it as a new home. Now, driving through the gate to park outside the looming walls of dark limestone, I felt almost as if I were arriving at a prison.

This place wasn't really mine anymore—not to do with as I wished, anyway. It belonged to my mother, first and foremost. All the dreams I'd started to have, all the plans I'd been in the process of making, I had to keep under lock and key while she ruled over the Bloodstone domain. While she ruled over *me*.

But if Malcolm could criticize his dad's decisions after the awful punishments Baron Nightwood had put him through, I should be able to have my say too. I had plenty of reason to speak up now. By far the largest of which was currently lying limp in the Blood U infirmary while the doctor on staff and others called in for the emergency cast their spells to patch his battered body back together.

I closed my eyes for a second with my hand on the car door. Tears burned behind my eyelids. Jude had been bleeding and bruised when we'd found him in the field, unresponsive to Declan and then Malcolm's attempts to rouse him. As far as I knew, he hadn't woken up yet. We hadn't been able to apprehend the figure that'd assaulted him, but it wasn't hard to guess who was responsible.

Baron Killbrook had clearly decided his secret was too close to exposure. Destroy the key evidence, and he'd never be convicted. What did it matter to him that the "evidence" was a young man's life?

I couldn't present my mother with any of those claims, though. Who knew what would happen to Jude if the other barons found out he'd been standing in as a false scion for his entire life—and had known he was living a lie for several years? His supposed father would be punished, sure, but he might face even worse.

The least I could do was make a plea to end all the other attacks being carried out on campus.

I'd known better than to assume Baron Bloodstone would be at home, so I'd called ahead of time to make sure. She was expecting me. When I reached the door, the house manager, Eloise, opened it immediately and ushered me in.

"How've you been doing, Miss Bloodstone?" she asked

me as she took my jacket. "Have you been holding up all right?"

After everything I'd been through in recent weeks, I had no idea whether she was referring to the murder accusation I'd had to defend myself against, the battle to rescue my mother, the violent attack of one of my colleagues, or something else altogether. From the anxious creases at the corners of her mouth, I suspected she hadn't missed my mother's guardedness around, well, everyone. She might even be worried I'd said something to provoke that distrust.

"I'm managing," I said, giving her a smile I hoped was reassuring. Eloise had been nothing but attentive and considerate during the short lengths of time I'd spent at home. I didn't think she deserved my mother's suspicions. "Thank you for asking."

The manager bobbed her head and motioned me down the hall. "The baron is in the sitting room. I'll bring around some tea for you both. And Claude baked a lemon loaf this morning."

"That sounds delicious."

I inhaled slowly to steady myself as I stepped into the sitting room. The sharp smell of wood smoke tickled my nose. My mother was standing by the hearth rather than sitting in any of the wingback armchairs, her slim form bathed in the flickering light. A waft of heat reached me even from the doorway.

"I'm sorry for coming on such short notice, Mom," I said. My throat still constricted a little whenever I called her that. It was hard to think of her as "Mom" when that role had been filled with so much more compassion and love by the woman who'd actually raised me, even if I hadn't truly belonged with her. "I felt the situation was urgent." And I'd figured it'd be harder for her to dismiss my concerns in person than over the phone.

My mother turned, her penetrating gaze taking me in. I'd managed not to outright cry since I'd left Jude's bedside in the infirmary this morning, but I'd imagine the strain of my worries for him showed on my face all the same. He brought so much light and passion into the pentacle of scions and into my life... I didn't know what I'd do if he didn't recover.

"Of course," my mother said in her usual implacable voice. "You should always feel you can come to me, Persephone. I trust your judgment in evaluating what's important."

And I'd better not make her regret that trust. I swallowed hard and moved to one of the chairs, not wanting to sit while she was still standing, just resting my hand on the padded back for some sense of support.

"You heard what happened to Jude Killbrook," I said. I didn't need to make it a question. There was no way all of the barons wouldn't have been informed of an attack on one of the scions.

My mother nodded, her mouth slanting in a tight line that I thought showed at least a little genuine sympathy. "A horrible situation. I hope that the culprit is found swiftly. All the more reason for you to be honing your defensive skills."

"Yes, well, I..." I dragged in another breath and

forced myself to get to the point. "I know we've talked about the new policy with the Naries and that you've been happy with the progress made so far. I understand your points about letting us benefit as much as possible from the fears we can stir up in them. But I think opening it up in a sort of uncontrolled free-for-all might have worse consequences than anticipated."

The baron cocked her head. She could connect the dots from there easily enough. "You think the relaxing of our required secrecy is related to the attack on your fellow scion."

"Yes." My fingers curled against the fabric of the chair. Maybe that wasn't entirely true, but it was close enough. "I was there when the professors gave the okay to us yesterday. A lot of students leapt right in to harass the Naries in the most awful ways they could think of without any reservation. And then the same night, someone lashes out at Jude that violently? Relaxing that policy has ended up encouraging a lot of vicious acts… I don't think it's a stretch to think some of those students will turn that violence toward other fearmancers as well. You take away a major rule, and people can run wild."

"I think you underestimate the discipline of your peers." My mother moved away from the fireplace and sank into the nearest chair. "Most of them have been taught how to moderate themselves from a very early age. They may run wild with the Naries while they're getting used to their new freedom, but that doesn't hurt anyone. It would be a much greater transgression to risk injuring a scion. Have you seen any evidence that it was a fellow student and not an intruder?"

*It hurts the Naries*, I thought but tamped down that sentiment. "No," I had to admit. "It just seems like too big a coincidence not to be connected somehow." Maybe it was connected—maybe Baron Killbrook had hoped the attack would be less scrutinized because of the timing. "And I'll admit I found the initial demonstrations to frighten the Naries kind of… unnerving."

My mother hummed to herself. "You're still developing the right mindset for our society, Persephone. Their response is natural after so many years of having to hold back. It isn't *right* that we've had to keep our natures under wraps everywhere but in the privacy of our own homes, not even able to fully show our true selves at the school where we're learning how to best wield that power. I'm sure things will settle down once the new status quo feels less new and more natural."

But violence didn't need to come naturally to fearmancers. I was proof of that. All the scions demonstrated that fact, really, even if it'd taken some of them longer to come around to seeing things that way than others.

"I just think," I tried, "if this is the whole change you wanted for the school, considering what happened to Jude, it might be wise to scale back a little and ease people into it more gradually, with clearer standards of behavior. Unless there's something else you wanted to build from there?"

"Every piece of our society has an impact on every

other," my mother said, breezing past my question with the vagueness I was coming to expect. "I won't shame your classmates for following their instincts now that we've already gone forward with this new approach. We'll keep an eye out for other incidents among the fearmancer students and re-evaluate if a worrisome pattern does develop there, I promise you."

My heart sank. She made it sound so reasonable, I didn't know how to ask for more without crossing the line from thoughtful debate to outright resistance. "Okay. I just don't want to see what happened to Jude happen to others too." Including the Nary students, not that she cared about them.

"Your loyalty to your colleagues is commendable." A wry note entered my mother's voice, and I wondered as I had before just how much she'd heard about my relationships with the other scions. She reached to the small table beside her chair and lifted a small silver box covered in ornate etchings. "I appreciate you coming to me with your concerns rather than announcing them at the school. And this was good timing regardless. I have a gift for you."

"Oh?" I eyed the box with a mix of curiosity and dread. A gift from a baron, even my own birth mother, felt like it could easily be a double-edged sword. I forced myself to sit down on the chair opposite her just as Eloise bustled in with the tea and slices of lemon loaf.

My mother waited until the manager had ducked out of the room. She held up her hand before I could reach for a plate and murmured over the tray. An uncomfortably intense light came into her eyes as she studied the spread for several long moments. Then she reached for the teapot.

"We can never be too careful," she said, a tremor running through her fingers before she grasped the handle. "Our enemies… can strike in ways we never anticipated. And can exist where we never expected. Your experience with Lillian proved that even I haven't been vigilant enough since I returned."

Yes, Lillian. My mother's best friend from before her imprisonment, one of the leading members of the blacksuits, who'd helped the other barons in their machinations against me. She'd been helping with my mother's plans too, until I'd "innocently" let one of her crimes against me, which she'd kept hidden from my mother, slip.

I'd never seen any hostility from the woman toward my mother. From what I'd observed, I doubted Lillian would have plotted against me in any way if she'd known my mother was alive. Even if she hadn't agreed with my actions and how they were affecting the barons' goals, she'd have left it to my mother to decide how to deal with me. But having her out of our lives meant one less enemy to *my* goals that I needed to worry about, so I wasn't going to let myself feel guilty about severing their friendship.

My mother poured tea for both of us, and I nibbled at a slice of lemon loaf. It was perfectly sweet-and-sour, but my stomach was balled too tight for me to fully enjoy it. I waited while the baron drank her first sip of tea. When she lowered the cup, she held out the silver box to me.

"I have to apologize," she said in an unexpectedly pained tone. "I've been so caught up in re-establishing my place here that I barely noticed the dates, and I missed your birthday."

The regret in her tone startled me silent. I accepted the box, reining in the urge to stare at her. "It's okay," I managed after a moment. "I didn't know if maybe it wasn't the sort of thing fearmancers usually make a big deal out of."

"Not a 'big deal,' perhaps, but it's an occasion that should be marked. Especially your twentieth." She nodded toward the box. "That was mine, for the little time I had to make use of it, and my father's mother's before me, and her mother's before her. It's an honor to pass it on to you."

I didn't know what to do with the twist of emotion her words brought into my chest. I was here scheming about how to best undermine her plans, and she was presenting me with a treasured family heirloom. Rather than try to come up with something else to say, I opened the box.

A ring was nestled on a cushion inside it: also silver, with glittering flecks of diamonds and sapphires forming a spiral on the wider section at the top. I hesitated, studying it.

"It's a conducting piece," I said. Not one that could hold magic, I didn't think, like the construct Connar's parents had placed on him to hold their malicious spell, but one that could channel magical energy into a specific concentrated effect, like the etchings in the paintball area. I didn't sense any spells on it now. Of course, if my mother wanted to, I had no trouble believing she could cast a spell too subtle for me to detect.

She smiled at my comment in recognition. "Yes. It has a protective function as well as being pretty to look at. Not enough to win a battle on its own, but if *you're* ever attacked, it might be enough to turn the outcome in your favor. Try it—just be careful where you aim."

I picked up the ring without putting it on and tipped the end of the spiral toward the lemon loaf. I couldn't read the exact purpose of the spell from the design, but it gave me a physicality vibe, which would make sense for protection. Concentrating on the pattern, I rolled a couple of syllables off my tongue that gave me a sense of propelling an attacker back.

The ring quivered, and the gemstones sparked. A scythe of energy whipped off the ring and cut straight through the loaf, splitting the cake neatly in two as if I'd slashed it with a razor. When I leaned forward, I made out a scratch across the plate beneath it where the spell had scored that too.

Okay, then. Not something I'd want to activate by accident. But I couldn't deny that given the challenges I'd faced so far, it might end up coming in handy.

"Thank you," I said. There was nothing for it but to slide the ring onto one of my fingers. I tested a couple and found it fit my right ring finger perfectly. As I eased it on, I paid attention to my mental shields, but not even a whisper of magical effect touched me. As far as I could tell, the ring was nothing more than what she'd said it was.

A gift, not a trap.

When I looked up, my mother was smiling at me, small but bright.

"It's been a long and difficult road for both of us," she said. "But we're Bloodstones, and we sustain. I may not intend to coddle you, Persephone, but I want you to know I'm proud of how you've pulled yourself together despite your circumstances. You've got every bit as much strength as I could have wished for in my heir."

A pinch of guilt bit into my gut as I made myself smile back at her. Yes, I was strong—and I was going forward with every intention of turning that strength against the woman who'd just praised me for it.

# CHAPTER SIX

*Rory*

"There you go," Professor Viceport said with an encouraging clap of her hands. "You're picking it up."

I made a face at the ball of light that was glowing between my hands. It was bright orange and warm enough to heat my palms, but… "I was trying to conjure flames," I admitted.

"Ah." Viceport let out a dry chuckle. The light breeze in the Casting Grounds licked over my face and ruffled her wispy blond pixie cut. "Well, it's fairly close in form and function. Getting the exact details right is the hardest aspect of personal casting words."

No kidding. I'd been doing pretty well with more generic spells where all I needed was a fairly vague force, like the bolts of energy I'd shot at the shooting range targets—or at my mother's car—but creating a more specific effect still eluded me most of the time. I'd already attempted to shape a rock into a dragon that'd come out looking more like a lumpy-backed horse and to cast an illusion changing the color of the grass that had ended up sallow brown instead of yellow.

I dismissed the light with a sigh and a wave of my hand. We'd been practicing for almost an hour, and my head was starting to ache from the intense concentration.

"You know," Viceport said, "most of the students here develop their casting vocabulary over the course of a year or more. It's unusual to make the leap from literal words to personal ones in a matter of days. Your progress has actually been quite swift."

Even though I was frustrated that I wasn't making the leap faster, knowing that did make me feel better. Especially coming from my current mentor, who wasn't generally liberal with her praise. For most of my time at Blood U, she'd been actively hostile toward me, which I'd only recently learned was because of a horrible clash between my family and hers back when she and my mother were both attending the university—a clash that had left Viceport's older sister dead.

The professor had come to see that I wasn't looking to follow in my mother's footsteps, though. The tentative new understanding we'd reached had included her giving me this extra help to make up for the months when she'd barely mentored me at all.

I swiped my hand across my forehead, where a hint of sweat had started to form. "I've been practicing as much as I can. I just don't want to hold back my practice of the other skills because my wording isn't up to snuff yet."

"That's absolutely fair, and that's why separate practice for this element of your magic is a wise idea." Viceport studied me. "Time for a break?"

"I think I could at least use a rest before I jump into more." I paused and reached into my purse. "There was something else I wanted to talk to you about, though."

I drew out the ring my mother had given me yesterday. The sunlight steaming into the broad clearing caught on the spiral of gemstones. I'd taken it off as soon as I'd left the Bloodstone property, but if there wasn't anything about it that'd be harmful to me, I wouldn't mind benefitting from that small extra bit of protection.

Viceport's eyebrows rose. "I haven't seen many pieces like that. It's quite a powerful conducting pattern—and the styling looks quite old."

"It's a family heirloom. My mother passed it on to me." I held it out to the professor. "I'd just like to be sure there isn't any magic contained in it that could act on me… just in case. I've already checked it over myself, but I figured it'd be good to get a professional second opinion."

Viceport plucked the ring gingerly from my hand and turned it between her fingers. She murmured a few casting words, rubbed her thumb over the spiral, and exhaled, her shoulders relaxing. "I can't sense any magic imbued in it. I feel comfortable saying you're safe wearing it." Her tone turned wry. "Anyone you might get into a dispute with, perhaps not so much."

"That seems to be the idea." When she handed it back, I hesitated a moment longer and then slid it onto my finger. The metal warmed quickly as it hugged my skin. Even though the ring reminded me of all the vicious aspects of my Bloodstone heritage, having that extra power at my disposal was a little comforting.

"You haven't faced any aggression yourself in recent days, have you?" Viceport asked. "No attempted assaults or more subtle attempts to strike out at you?"

I shook my head. "Nothing like what happened to Jude, and nothing on a smaller scale either beyond what I've been used to here."

"I'm glad to hear that. There was— I wasn't sure whether it was even worth mentioning, because it may be simply a psychological attempt to unnerve you rather than a real threat, but..." Viceport frowned. "Yesterday I received a few text messages from an unfamiliar number asking for any incriminating information I might have about your actions or plans."

A chill tickled over my skin. I hadn't gotten any more strange messages since the vague threat when I'd been at the shooting range, but I couldn't imagine the incidents were unconnected. "That's all they said?"

"I tried to press for more information about who *they* were and why they were asking about you, but they didn't respond. I suppose they realized that I wasn't going to offer them anything, and I haven't heard from them since."

Someone had decided to make it their personal mission to ruin me, one way or another. Despite their earlier insinuations, they obviously didn't know all that much if they were going to my mentor to ask for more dirt. Still, I didn't like the impression that I was being monitored from afar. Could it even be my mother, testing the waters to find out what I might be doing when I wasn't around her?

"Thanks for telling me," I said. "I'll keep an eye out for any signs of trouble. If anyone contacts you again, you'll let me know?"

"Absolutely." Viceport nudged her rectangular glasses farther up her nose. "Do you think you're up for a few more spells before our time here is up?"

I was about to take her up on the suggestion when my phone chimed. After the conversation we'd just had, my pulse stuttered as I dug it out. But the text was from a totally familiar source—Declan.

He'd texted all of us scions just as he had the other night when he'd realized Jude was in danger. This time, the message brought much happier news. *The doctors have woken Jude up, and the infirmary let me know he's okay to have visitors now. I'm heading right over.*

My heart leapt in a totally different way. *I'm on my way too*, I wrote, and looked up at Viceport.

"Jude's awake."

Before I needed to add anything, she nodded and made a shooing gesture. "Of course. Go see him. I'm glad to hear his recovery is on track."

It took all my self-control not to dash through the woods back to campus. I strode along the path as quickly as I could without making a total spectacle of myself and let myself speed up to a casual lope when I reached the field. As I came around the Stormhurst Building, Declan, Malcolm, and Connar were just coming down from the green. I stopped by the front door to wait for them to reach me, shifting my weight impatiently.

"Did the infirmary staff say anything else about how he's doing?" I asked Declan as we all pushed inside.

The main hall held the sharp scent of chlorine from the university's pool. We had to pass both that and the gyms, our steps tapping loudly on the wooden floors, before we reached the health center. A couple of students coming out of a change room caught sight of us, four of the five scions as a determined pack, and darted by, hugging close to the wall with flickers of anxiety that tickled into my chest.

"The woman who contacted me said he was asking to see us, so he's at least well enough to be making demands," Declan said with a tight smile. I suspected he blamed himself for not getting to Jude sooner—he hadn't realized right away that the other guy needed help when he'd gotten the odd call. And the Ashgrave scion had a habit of seeing himself as responsible for everyone and everything that mattered to him.

"Jude's made of tough stuff," Malcolm said firmly. "He'll bounce back. I'm just looking forward to when we crush the asshole who did that to him."

So was I. Maybe I didn't approve of violence as a general principle, but the thought of turning my new ring on Baron Killbrook and dealing a little of the pain he'd caused back had a certain satisfaction.

A couple blacksuits were stationed outside the infirmary doors. I didn't know whether Jude's supposed father had felt he needed to keep up the paternal act enough to request protection for his "son" or whether their presence had been Ms. Grimsworth's initiative, but I appreciated it all the same.

They looked us over but obviously knew well enough who we were. We marched into the bright, white-walled space, and one of the medical staff beckoned for us to follow her past the reception desk.

Jude had a room to himself with a narrow bed against one wall, just enough space remaining for all four of us to come around beside it. He was sitting up, propped against a pillow, poking at a bowl of soup, but as soon as he saw us he grinned and set his lunch on the side table.

"Quite the welcoming party," he said in his usual breezy tone. "I haven't been gone that long, unless the doctor lied to me."

He could joke around all he wanted, but a few faint bruises still dappled his forehead and neck that the staff hadn't been able to fully heal. And I remembered far too well how horribly broken he'd looked when we'd reached him in the field. My throat closed up. When I reached the bed, I kept moving, sinking onto the edge and leaning over to wrap my arms around him, careful of any lingering injuries.

"Hey," Jude said softly into my hair, returning the embrace. His voice stayed light, but he gripped me harder than I'd dared to squeeze him, as if he were afraid of letting me go again.

"How are you feeling?" I asked, my head tucked against his shoulder.

"I appear to have retained all my limbs and other parts in normal working order." Jude jiggled his feet beneath the blanket. "Other than a few minor aches and pains, I'd think I just had a nice long sleep. I'm sure the asshole who came at me will be very unhappy to hear that." A slight edge crept into those last words. He knew better than any of us who must have ordered the attack.

"No more wandering off alone to isolated parts of campus in the middle of the night?" Declan suggested.

Jude let out a huff, but then he hugged me harder. "I'm thinking that might be wise. And—thank you. I know I wouldn't have gotten off anywhere near this easy if you all hadn't charged to the rescue."

"I just wish we could have caught the prick and made him pay," Connar muttered, the muscles in his arms flexing. He didn't enjoy fighting, I knew, but he was more than willing to defend any of us with all his strength if he saw the need.

"All in good time, I'm sure." Jude brushed a kiss to the top of my head. He raised his hand as one of the doctors stepped through the doorway, and flicked it through the air with an extravagant flourish. "What I'd really like right now, instead of this godawful soup, is…"

A casting word dropped from his lips with a glint in his eyes. I turned on the bed to see what illusion he might be drawing.

Nothing had appeared in the air. Jude spoke again with another twitch of his fingers and then frowned.

Before he could make another attempt, the doctor moved to the foot of the bed and cleared his throat.

"Mr. Killbrook," he said. "There's a matter I think we should discuss. In private, I think would be ideal."

Jude turned his frown toward the doctor. "Anything you need to tell me, they can hear too. They saved my fucking life."

The man wavered. "If you're sure…"

"Do I sound confused? Go ahead."

Jude's body had tensed against mine. I eased back so I could clasp his hand. The doctor looked down at the notes he was holding and then back at his patient.

"The attack you faced included both physical and magical blows," he said. "We were able to heal all the major physical damage. Unfortunately, it appears… the spells that hit you damaged the part of you that collects and holds your magical power. Some of that functioning will likely return as you continue to recover, but that will take time, and we can't be sure you'll reach the same capacity you had before."

The color had drained from Jude's face. He snapped out a casting with a jerk of his hand. An image glimmered faintly in front of him, there and gone in a blink, so brief and hazy I hadn't been able to tell what he was going for. His mouth twisted. He moved to try again.

The doctor's voice turned urgent. "Please. Putting strain on yourself will only exacerbate the injury. I assure you we've done and will continue to do whatever we can to aid that recovery."

Jude's arm dropped like a dead thing. He stared

blankly at it for a moment and then turned his narrowing gaze on the doctor. "Get out," he snapped.

The doctor all but fled the room. The rest of us stared at Jude. My stomach had sunk, an ache reverberating through my chest—through the place behind my collarbone where the churning thrum of my magic reassured me of how much power *I* still held. I gripped his hand tighter.

"He said it should get better," I ventured. "You'll get your abilities back."

"Some of them. Maybe." Jude touched the same spot on his own chest. He swallowed audibly. "I can barely feel anything there. He was scared of me, scared of how I'd react, and I caught that energy… and then nearly all of it slipped right back out of me like I've sprung a fucking leak. Well. Isn't that fitting. My father has a perfect excuse to punt me aside now, *and* he's got me defenseless."

He laughed, but the sound was so hollow and hopeless it wrenched me apart. But what could I say that would make it better when that remark was completely true?

# CHAPTER SEVEN

*Rory*

As soon as we'd walked a safe distance from the school buildings, Malcolm spun on Declan. "Is there *really* nothing they can do about an injury like that, or is this his dad's bullshit meddling?"

"No doctors could fix the damage I did to my brother," Connar said with a pained grimace. "With some wounds, even magic isn't enough."

Declan nodded, his expression solemn. "It's possible his dad is interfering with his treatment, but we can see about getting him a second opinion from an outside party once he's out of the infirmary. I have heard of other cases where mages lost part or all of their magical ability permanently. So… they could very well be telling the truth. He was pretty badly beaten up. If we'd gotten there even a few seconds later, I think he'd be dead right now."

We all stood in silence for a moment, absorbing those awful thoughts.

It was hard to remember now that I'd spent the first nineteen and a half years of my life with no idea I'd ever have magic of my own. The heady pulse of energy behind my sternum was as much a part of me as the beat of my heart and the rise and fall of my breath. During the few hours when the joymancers had held me captive as I'd tried to negotiate my mother's release with them, with the cuffs they'd put on me numbing my ability to sense and shape that energy, I'd felt so horribly empty and helpless.

And I'd at least known it was a temporary effect. Jude had no idea whether he'd recover any more of his abilities than he already had.

Malcolm let out a rough breath. "I guess there isn't much we can do immediately, but I'll figure out who best to bring around for a second evaluation. Baron Killbrook can't have that many doctors in his pocket, not when he'll want to keep his intentions secret from the rest of the barons. And as soon as Jude is out, we'll need to set up defensive spells to ward off another attack, since he won't be able to cast much himself."

"One of us should be with him anytime he leaves campus or is heading out of the dorms after dark," Connar said. "Now that his father has gone this far, the next time he comes after him..."

He trailed off, obviously not wanting to say the words, but we all understood. Baron Killbrook had crossed a clear line the other night. Jude might have kept quiet about the Killbrooks' secret for his own safety, but if he decided throwing himself on the other barons' mercy was a better bet than risking another attack, the baron was screwed. He wouldn't want to take that chance.

"We should keep an eye on Jude in general," Declan said quietly. "You know how he gets when he's upset about something. And he has a hell of a lot more reason to be upset than he's ever had before."

My stomach twisted. "He'll drink." I'd encountered drunk Jude a couple times after our brief break-up. Alcohol definitely decreased his sense of self-preservation and overall common sense. Not a good combination with having a death sentence hanging over his head.

"He's got all of us," Malcolm said. "He knows we're on his side, no matter what. That's got to keep him from totally bottoming out." A shadow of worry had darkened his eyes, though.

I looked to Declan like Malcolm had before, knowing the Ashgrave scion had studied far more of fearmancer law and history than any of the rest of us. "Is there *any* way we could stop Baron Killbrook without bringing Jude's parentage into it? This can't be the only messed-up thing he's done in his entire life."

"I'm sure it's not, but knocking a baron from their place..." Declan's mouth set in a grim line. "Generally that doesn't happen except by death. We'd have to uncover a crime on the same level of treason as arranging the conception of and passing off a false scion, along with enough proof to make it stick."

Yeah, that didn't seem incredibly likely. The only reason we knew about even the one act of treason was because Jude had overheard an argument—and the only reason we could prove it was that Jude himself served as proof.

Malcolm turned back toward the Stormhurst Building. “I’m going to lay down some extra protections for the infirmary now. We can’t be too careful.”

“Connar and I have a class to get to,” Declan said, “but after that I’ll see if I can turn up any defensive spells more effective than the ones I know off-hand.”

I latched onto that idea, one small thing I could offer Jude right now. “I’ll head to the library and start researching. I don’t have class until later.”

We split up, Malcolm heading back the way we’d come, Declan and Connar making for Nightwood Tower, and me crossing the green to Ashgrave Hall. I hurried into the library and up to the second floor where the magical texts were kept in a section warded to repel Naries.

How long would the librarians keep up those measures now that we were allowed to freely demonstrate our powers in front of the nonmagical students?

I walked down one aisle and then another, skimming my fingers over the spines of the old texts as I scanned the titles. The smell of ancient leather filled my nose. Hushed voices carried from the library seating areas, but nothing clear enough to distract me. One thing the fearmancer library had in common with those in the Nary world was the expectation of quiet.

Here, this row looked promising. I was just sliding out a text on personal protective spells when the floor by the end of the aisle creaked.

I looked up to see a young man I didn't recognize slinking toward me. He looked a little too old to be a student here, maybe twenty-five, with a trim beard shading his narrow jaw and limbs that were knobby at the joints. He was watching me so intently that my skin prickled with apprehension. I turned to face him, drawing a protective spell for *myself* onto my tongue.

He was lucky I wasn't my mother, or I'd have been eyeing the most vulnerable spot on his forehead like he was one of those shooting range targets.

He spoke a casting word, but with a gesture behind him, not toward me. The already faint sounds from the rest of the library faded even more. A privacy spell. As he stopped a few feet away from me, I stayed tensed.

"Miss Bloodstone," he said in a low voice. "I was hoping I'd get the chance to talk to you."

I eyed him. "Who *are* you? What would we have to talk about?"

He gave me a slow smile. "Let's just say I know people who are interested in your situation—and in bettering it. You could use some help in attaining your goals, couldn't you?"

I relaxed slightly, still prepared to cast a spell if I needed to. Was he from one of the families who believed Naries deserved better treatment? Or someone concerned for Jude? Of course, this could also be a trap to encourage me to admit something that'd be passed on to my enemies… or to my mother, who in some ways was my enemy too.

"What goals exactly do you think you're going to help with?" I asked warily.

His smile widened, as if we were already in on some conspiracy together. "We'd like to see you take your proper place in the pentacle. Your mother has been gone for seventeen years. Why should she steal that spot from you when you were so close to having it for yourself? She's already had her chance to revel in that power and glory, and she couldn't even defend herself when the chips were down. It's your turn."

With each sentence that spilled from his mouth, my hackles rose higher. Who the hell did this guy and whoever had sent him think I was? I'd never been the slightest bit interested in glory or lording power over the other fearmancers.

Maybe he *had* been sent by my mother—maybe our talk about the possible consequences of the Nary policy had made her more paranoid about me all over again.

Well, in a case like this, I didn't see any need to be subtle with my magic. I'd treat this offense like she'd expect a strong scion to.

I shifted the focus of the magic I'd been readying and stared at the guy hard. "I'm not interested in stealing a spot that isn't supposed to be mine yet. *Tell me why you came here and said this to me.*"

I propelled the persuasive spell with all the force I could summon. The guy had mental walls up like every fearmancer did, and they didn't disintegrate completely, but my magic split through them like an arrow. He winced, his mouth already falling open to comply. Insight might have been more my wheelhouse, but I was hoping persuasion would get me clearer answers faster.

"I don't know," he said in a vacant sounding voice. "I had to talk to Rory Bloodstone. I had to offer her a deal." His forehead furrowed. "Someone told me…"

That answer wasn't particularly clear, but his confusion was obvious enough to tell the story anyway. Someone had persuaded him into coming here, without him even knowing who. A perfect way to cover their tracks. No doubt he was supposed to report back to them one way or another, and if I'd responded in an incriminating way, his memories would have served as evidence.

"*Tell me how you were going to let this 'someone' know what I said.*"

The second persuasion spell slipped into his head much more easily than the first now that I'd opened up a path. His hand dropped to the pocket of his slacks. "I have a number. I'm supposed to send a text and wait for more instructions."

"What number?" I asked, prodding the second spell farther.

He rattled off a series of digits I didn't recognize. A creeping sensation ran down my back. It *could* be my mother trying to catch me admitting treason using a different phone, but I had also received a hostile text not that long ago, and so had Professor Viceport. I didn't think those had come from my mother. I'd been with her when I'd gotten mine, and if she'd wanted to check what my professors thought of my loyalties, it'd have made a lot more sense for her to ask someone like Professor Crowford directly with her authority as baron.

"*Text that number now,*" I said. "*Ask if they want to meet.*"

Unfortunately, this was where my spell clashed with the one already placed on him. The guy dutifully tapped in the number and wrote out a text, but the mage who'd compelled him must have asked him to report my reaction upfront. *She refused offer*, he wrote. *Should we meet?*

I watched the screen over his shoulder. The response came no more than ten seconds later. *No. Return to your work and forget about this.*

He lowered the phone and immediately turned to leave. Another command leapt to my tongue, but what was the point in questioning him any more? He didn't know anything. And the person controlling him already saw him as useless now too.

I had a direct line of contact with my mysterious harasser. Let's see if I could get anything useful straight from the source—or at least *set* them straight.

I retreated to the deepest end of the aisle and sank down with my back against the wall and my phone propped against my raised knee. The ominous text was still there in my history. I considered it for a while, composing and discarding several possible overtures in my head, and finally typed in a message.

*Whatever you think I've done, you're wrong. After talking with your "friend" just now, I can tell you don't know anything at all about me or what's important to me.*

I waited, my spine rigid, as the seconds slipped by. One minute passed, and then another. They might just ignore me. Should I say something else, try to provoke them?

As I debated, an answer finally popped up on the screen. *It's easy for you to say that, but I've seen you in action. Lies won't get you anywhere.*

Seen me in action? What the hell did that mean? *You can't have seen much at all if you've convinced yourself that I'm after power and glory*, I replied. *I've never been in any rush to become baron. I've never pushed around my classmates just to prove a point. I honestly have no idea what you could be talking about.*

*Oh, no? So you've never ruined anyone's life just to get them out of your way? You need to work on your memory.*

I frowned at that text for a long moment. Whose life had I ruined? My thoughts skittered toward Professor Banefield, my former mentor, and Imogen Wakeburn, my friend and dormmate. Both of them had *died* because of the barons' schemes against me. I could imagine someone blaming me for one or both—I'd certainly blamed myself enough times—but to say I'd intended their deaths so they'd be out of my way made no sense at all. They'd never been *in* my way.

*Can't argue against that, can you?* my harasser sent in my silence. *So spare me the innocent act. One of us wants what's best for this community, and it's definitely not you. And soon everyone else will find that out too.*

The person was so sure I'd know what she meant. When else had I come even close to—

Oh. Understanding clicked in my head with a jab of cold. Just a couple weeks ago, I'd told my mother just the right thing to get Lillian Ravenguard stripped of her career and her freedom in a matter of minutes. That'd been pretty life-ruining too.

But how was it some horrible crime to defend myself against a woman who'd tried to have *me* lose my freedom, for something I hadn't even done? Who would even have realized I'd spurred my mother's anger rather than her figuring out Lillian's treachery on her own?

The question hadn't even finished passing through my head when it hit me. One person would have known I'd prompted my mother's confrontation with Lillian. One person had been right there watching it happen—a person who'd already been acting as if she suspected me of shady intentions for weeks beforehand: Lillian's assistant, Maggie Duskland.

I looked down at my phone. I could have challenged her right now, but it'd be too easy for her to simply not reply or pretend I was wrong over the phone, and then, if it was Maggie, she'd know I was on to her.

No, I had a feeling this situation would be best dealt with face to face. As soon as I found out what Maggie was up to, she and I needed to have a *real* talk, before she tried to burn down my life for reasons I still couldn't totally comprehend.

# CHAPTER EIGHT

*Declan*

If it'd been totally up to me, I'd never have set foot in the Stormhurst residence, at least not while Connar's mother was baron. In theory, the soiree they were holding was being hosted by *all* the barons—although the other four hadn't asked my opinion about that—so it'd have made more of a statement than I was ready to put forward just yet if I'd declined to attend. Instead, I figured I'd make as much use of the opportunity as I could for my own interests.

The barons had brought in at least fifty families for the party. I suspected they were a mix of already loyal supporters and more hesitant potential allies they hoped to win over. The ballroom held a faint chill even with lights, both electric and magical, glowing overhead and the cheerful classical music piped from speakers in the corners, but the wine was flowing liberally and everyone was dressed to the nines. I resisted the urge to tweak the collar of my tuxedo jacket as I circulated through the room.

"Good to see you," I said with a smile here and a shake of a hand there. "Wonderful evening, isn't it? Glad you could make it." The other barons holding court in their finery at one end of the room wouldn't find one misstep to accuse me of. Anything they'd have considered treason, I was committing only in my head.

It was useful to note who'd decided to attend. The Warburys were here, even though Cressida's parents had generally been the aloof, standoffish type. Her mother was gripping Cressida's shoulder tightly as she bobbed her head at something Baron Bloodstone was saying, while her father loomed over her younger brother.

Professor Crowford and his wife had settled into intense conversation with a few other couples in another corner of the room. One of the junior fearmancers who'd pulled a vicious prank on my brother a few weeks back had come along with what looked like his entire extended family: parents, aunts, uncles, and cousins.

Also interesting were the absences. Not a single Blighthaven appeared to have accepted the invitation, despite how enthusiastically Victory had always courted Malcolm's favor. Rory hadn't been sure of Professor Burnbuck's allegiances, but he hadn't turned up, even though I spotted an elderly woman I believed was his aunt and her middle-aged son. Not every family stood together on every political issue.

I made careful note of who'd shown up and who I

might have expected but hadn't, of which expressions looked eager or celebratory in the face of the barons' most recent decisions and who looked more uncertain. With each greeting, I also sent out the gentlest feeler of insight magic. If I could find an ally of the barons whose shields were on the weaker side, I intended to take a peek inside *their* head and find out what my colleagues might have been discussing with them behind closed doors.

My aunt Ambrosia had come, of course, her eyes never far from the prize of the barony. She sidled over to me with two glasses of wine and offered me one as if in a friendly gesture. "They really went all out tonight, didn't they?" she said, fixing her piercing gaze on me.

"If the barons can't impress, then who can?" I replied evenly.

She tucked her silvery shawl closer around her and tossed back the slick curls she'd styled much like my mother—her sister—used to. "I'm just pleased I could be a part of it."

A gloating gleam sparked in her eyes before she sashayed off. The barons had arranged for her to weigh in on the policy change at the university, ensuring that I would be unreachable while they were taking the vote. I'd bet she was *incredibly* pleased about that. The last three months until I graduated from Blood U and could take on the barony in its entirety couldn't pass quickly enough.

I didn't bother to check the wine she'd offered me—if she'd doctored it in one way or another, as she had at least a few times I'd caught in the past, she'd have done it subtly enough that it could be passed off as an accident.

Instead, I simply meandered around the room until I passed a potted plant that wouldn't mind an extra drink.

Malcolm caught my eyes from across the room where he'd ended up chatting with the parents of a couple of our schoolmates. The slight arch of his eyebrow said he wasn't particularly enjoying the conversation. But he was still putting on his own show of loyalty too. As was Rory, standing graceful at her mother's side, laughing when Baron Bloodstone did as if on cue.

She really was something. I allowed myself just a moment to admire her poise from afar. We'd all driven up from the university together, and she'd sat tensed in the seat in anticipation of the evening. As soon as she'd stepped out, though, she'd managed to shed those nerves as if she were exactly the devoted daughter her mother would have hoped for.

It must make it harder for her that she had to go without either of the scions she might have been able to rely on for public support. Jude had the excuse of still being monitored in the infirmary to justify his absence, not that I expected he'd have forced himself to come to save face for his father anyway, and Connar… I wasn't sure what explanation the Stormhurst scion had given his parents for failing to attend an important party at his own family home. All he'd said when we'd discussed the party was, "There's no way in hell I'm giving them another chance to brainwash me."

I'd already overheard a few murmurs among the guests about where the Stormhurst scion might be or why he wouldn't have come. One woman had been so bold as to comment on his absence directly to Baron Stormhurst, who'd given a brief and vague explanation with a tightening of her jaw.

The elder Burnbuck had been hovering rather close to both Baron Nightwood and Baron Killbrook for several minutes. I hadn't felt much defense against mental intrusion when I'd tested her earlier. I ambled closer, picking up a glass of my own choice and raising it to newcomers who acknowledged me.

Rory left her mother to grab a few morsels from the refreshments table. I let myself drift in that direction. "Enjoying the party?" I said, as if in polite conversation.

She gave me a wry smile that made me want to tug her off into some secluded hallway and kiss her until we both forgot about the awful politicking happening out here for a little while. Too bad giving in to that urge would be incredibly unwise.

"I'm certainly getting to know a lot of people," she said. "How late do these events usually go, anyway?"

"As long as more wine keeps getting poured, it could be hours yet. But this is your first big gala, so you could probably get away with ducking out early if you need to."

Rory glanced toward her mother with a pensive look. I couldn't tell if she was wondering whether the baron really would be all right with that or if something else was on her mind that she didn't dare say out loud in this company.

"I'll keep that in mind," she said, and headed back with a slight squaring of her shoulders.

Ilene Burnbuck had wandered a short distance away

from the barons while Rory and I had talked, her place taken by other fearmancers eager to pay their fawning respects. I eased closer to the wall, nibbling on a cracker topped with pate. With the lift of my hand to my mouth, I disguised the movement of my lips as I spoke my casting word for a general insight spell.

I didn't push my magic hard, only encouraged it into a steady seeping through the barriers the woman had up around her mind, watching carefully for any sign that she'd picked up on the intrusion. Hazy impressions started to filter into my head.

She was awfully happy with herself to be attending this party at all. In the glimpses I caught of her interacting with the barons, they seemed more standoffish than friendly. "I can't wait to see how the rest of this chain plays out," she'd simpered at one point, here or in the recent past. "If there's anything I can do to help speed that progress along…"

Other bits and pieces had nothing to do with the barons at all. Puttering around her home, lunch with her son. There was a fragment of an argument with Professor Burnbuck, something about her accusing him of "not knowing what his family deserved."

I pulled back after a little more, not wanting anyone to notice my insight-casting daze. She didn't seem to be involved in the barons' most secretive plans anyway, more a lackey than a co-conspirator.

As the night wore on, my phone buzzed with an incoming text. Malcolm had surreptitiously sent a message asking if I wanted him to come up with an excuse for us to get back to school.

My gut said, *Hell, yes,* but self-discipline kept me in check. I was already here. I might as well give myself every possible chance to get something out of the gathering.

*If Rory is ready to take off, go ahead without me,* I wrote back. *I can find my way.* If it came to that, I'd imagine I could get away with borrowing one of Connar's vehicles from the garage here. Connar certainly wouldn't mind.

*Do you really think she'd let us leave without you?* the Nightwood scion shot back with an emoji that looked as if it were rolling its eyes. Fair enough.

The crowd in the ballroom had thinned, but only a little, since most of the attendees wanted to show they were just as devoted to enjoying their barons' hospitality as everyone else there. The guests also got louder as their alcohol consumption escalated.

Fearmancers rarely let themselves get outright drunk in the presence of others—even Jude on his worst days had usually kept himself to the scion lounge or his dorm room—and a small buzz didn't give me much of an opening. I did manage to delve into the mind of one of the younger teens who really had no business drinking at all, although she also knew nothing of importance that my foray revealed.

As I contemplated a new strategy, one voice rose even higher than the others, bouncing off the ceiling. "Fucking fantastic!" said a new senior I recognized from school, sounding overjoyed, and swept his arm and the glass he was holding in an overly extravagant arc over the nearby table.

He smacked into several wine bottles that tipped and smashed onto the floor. The guy froze, his head swaying a smidgeon with his inebriation, his eyes widening as his parents stiffened in horror. No one wanted to be the family that had caused a scene at the barons' gala.

The Stormhursts marched over, all generosity with a hint of sneer. "Never mind that," the baron said with a flex of her sinewy frame. She motioned over a couple of her staff. "Let's get this cleaned up. We've got more in the cellar." Her hand rose to her husband's arm. "Why don't we pick out something even more suitable?"

They were going to retrieve more wine themselves rather than send their employees to do it? *Both* of them, together? My nerves sprang to sharper alertness. There had to be something they were hoping to discuss apart from the crowd—something urgent.

Before they could head off, the parents of the wayward guy started prostrating with their apologies. The other guests moved toward the spectacle; I eased away. Spotting another of the Stormhursts' staff moving to clear the now-empty hors d'oeuvres plates, I directed a quick insight question at him under my breath. "How do you get to the wine cellar from the ballroom?"

Images flitted through my head like a blurry slideshow: a hallway and a sharp turn, a staircase on the left, another dim hallway at the bottom, a room with a wooden door from which a dry but sour scent wafted. That was all I needed. I slipped out of the ballroom as if heading for the main floor bathroom, but veered to follow the path I'd just seen as soon as I was out of view.

The dimness of the basement hallway worked to my advantage. I wouldn't need quite as strong an illusion to disguise me here. I wavered between staking myself out closer to the stairs so I'd hear more of their conversation and farther, beyond the cellar, so they wouldn't need to walk right past me, but I couldn't afford to weigh my options too long.

The base of the stairs held an alcove full of thicker shadows a few feet from their base. I pressed myself into that spot and murmured the words to blend myself into the stones and darkness.

I finished drawing the layers of magic into place just in time. Hinges squeaked overhead. Footsteps thudded down the stairs.

No voices reached me until the Stormhursts had come all the way to the basement floor. "You called him again?" Baron Stormhurst demanded.

"Twice," her husband said. "And sent texts. His phone is either off or he's ignoring it."

"Which amounts to the same thing." She exhaled sharply. "If he would make even a brief appearance..."

They had to be talking about Connar. I held myself as still as I could. If they were going to retaliate against him for his decision to skip the party, I could at least warn him of their intentions.

"It has raised a lot of eyebrows," Mr. Stormhurst muttered. "He had to know it would."

"Of course he knew." The baron stopped outside the

cellar door and spun on her heel to face her husband. "He obviously isn't what we need if his behavior can be warped that quickly by the arrival of one pretty girl. Maybe it's time to consider a change before this gets any more out of hand."

"Our options are pretty limited."

She shrugged and yanked open the door. "We have another heir. Bring a doctor in, announce that with an experimental magical intervention, Holden has made a miraculous recovery, and the rest won't matter. We'll just need to be completely sure we have *him* in hand before we take that step. Which is why we'd better start on that now."

Their voices faded as they stepped into the cellar. I stayed where I was, my pulse racing.

Connar's brother could be cured? His parents *knew* they could produce a "miracle"? From the things he'd said, he obviously had no idea.

I'd seen what his temper was like when anyone he cared about was threatened, and I knew his altercation with his brother still weighed on him. How awful would it be to throw this possibility at him if it turned out I'd misunderstood? I could do a little digging, see what I could confirm from medical records or lack thereof if possible—and I'd do it quickly. Because if this was true, he deserved to know as soon as I could tell him.

# CHAPTER NINE

*Rory*

I hadn't come to the blacksuits' headquarters since the first day my mother had woken up from her magically-induced healing coma. Looking up at the boxy gray building, I wasn't sure I felt any less nervous about the conversation I was hoping to have now than I had back then.

With a few discreet inquiries, I'd been able to find out that Maggie, Lillian's former assistant, was working out of an office in the building, presumably until they decided to assign her to a new blacksuit. I hadn't given any warning that I was coming. If my suspicions were wrong, then this would simply be a very short conversation.

The blacksuit at the front desk snapped to stiffer attention at my entrance. He didn't look exactly friendly, but the wariness I'd experienced right after my arrest and hearing had faded. Maybe my show of working alongside my mother had put any lingering worries they'd had about me to rest—and now they were just worried about staying on the good side of the Bloodstones.

"I don't need access to any of the higher security areas," I told him. "I'm just checking something with the administrative department."

"Not a problem. Do you need any help finding the offices?"

I shook my head. I'd rather approach Maggie alone. "Thanks, but I'm good."

He let me through the inner entrance, and I headed left down the first floor hallway to where the lower level employees who weren't quite blacksuits themselves maintained the organization's records, communications, and scheduling. There were only a few rooms devoted to their work. I spotted Maggie's spill of chocolate-brown curls when I peeked into the second. She was stationed in one of six cubicles that took up most of the space.

I cleared my throat and knocked lightly on the open door. All of the employees glanced up, but the others showed nothing but mild curiosity. At the sight of me, Maggie's jaw twitched, her posture going rigid for a second before she caught her reaction. Just like that, I knew I'd come to the right person.

"Hi," I said with a quick smile, as if this were more a social call than anything else. "I need to speak with Miss Duskland for a minute. Is there somewhere we can talk alone?"

The request shouldn't sound odd to the other employees. After all, Maggie had recently been employed by a woman with whom my mother had worked closely. There were all kinds of confidential subjects I might want to discuss with her.

Maggie hesitated for a second, but she must have decided that refusing the request wouldn't be a good look in the long run. "Sure," she said, managing one of her usual bright smiles. "One of the meeting rooms down the hall should be empty."

I stepped back to let her pass and followed her around the corner. She didn't say anything else until after she'd nudged open one of the doors and ushered me into a room not much bigger than my bedroom, with a modern rectangular table and matching chairs. A silence that felt magically charged fell over the space with the click of the door shutting.

I dragged in a breath of the chalky-smelling air, but Maggie spoke first. "What's this about, Miss Bloodstone?"

She'd positioned herself around the table from me. Her tone had been light, but her arms had crossed over her chest in a defensive stance. She had to be hoping that this visit was unconnected to our recent texts—that I still had no idea she was my mysterious harasser.

I didn't see any point in dragging the confrontation out. I propped myself against the edge of the table as if I wasn't all that tense, but my gaze didn't leave her for a second. "Well, I'd like to know why you've suddenly developed the hobby of threatening and trying to gather dirt on me. Since you weren't willing to explain much over text, I figured an in-person visit was called for."

Maggie wet her lips. "I don't know what you're—"

I cut her off with an incredulous look. "Can we please skip the bullshit? You know my specialty is Insight. I don't *enjoy* poking around in other people's heads without their permission, but I'm pretty sure I could break through your defenses to confirm it if I needed to. How about we don't let it come to that? I've got nothing against you. I just want to understand what *you've* got against me."

The other woman stiffened again. For a second, I thought she was going to make me drag the acknowledgement out of her. Then she sighed.

"I don't believe *you* can't figure that out. Why don't we cut that bullshit too? Or are you not really here to talk, just to create an excuse to knock me down like *you're* in the habit of doing?"

The accusation came out so flat and plainly stated that it rankled me even more than our comments over the phone had. "I *am* here to talk," I said. "And I really don't know. Yes, I told my mother what Lillian did to me. Why the hell would I want someone around who tried to sabotage my entire life? If anything, it was self-defense. Other than that, I can't think of anyone I've 'knocked' around. And you've been kind of weird with me since before Lillian's arrest."

Maggie sniffed, a dismissive sound. "If it was really about self-defense, then why didn't you complain to the other blacksuits about her, or even to your mother right away? Don't tell me that timing wasn't strategic."

It had been, in so much as I'd been willing to take the risk of bringing it up with my mother if it'd interrupt plans I didn't agree with. I'd been protecting myself with that caution, not waiting to hurt Lillian more. I got the sense Maggie meant something beyond that. Did she really think my position had been so simple I could have made the accusation at the drop of the hat with no consequences?

"I didn't have any direct proof," I said. "And the blacksuits had only just cleared me of a murder they'd wrongly arrested me for. I didn't think they'd take my word over Lillian's to conduct whatever kind of invasive magic it'd have taken to get the truth out of her. As for telling my mother, in case you missed the many times Lillian mentioned it, the two of them were best friends. I assumed that Lillian had explained it in some way that my mother had accepted. As soon as I realized my mother didn't know, I told her."

Maggie didn't answer for a moment, but her expression stayed wary. "That was the biggest problem, though, wasn't it?" she said finally. "You didn't really want your mom to come back and take the position you were so close to getting for yourself."

"Why would you say that?" I asked, but a chill touched my skin at the same time. I could guess. Maggie had watched the rituals the blacksuits used to locate my mother from the sidelines rather than participating directly. She could easily have noticed something they hadn't about my reactions.

She fixed me with a look sharp enough to rival Lillian's now, the cheerful kitten-y persona she normally put forward falling away completely. "You disrupted the locating spells purposefully at least once, didn't you? You were hoping they'd give up or think they were wrong that she was out there at all."

The first part, at least, was true. And I had in fact lied about it to the blacksuits afterward, pretending I didn't know what had gone wrong, which must have convinced Maggie my intentions had been malicious. The *full* truth was I'd been overwhelmed by the spell and the sense I'd gotten of how viciously angry my mother was, and I'd jerked away from her presence instinctively.

I couldn't explain that to Maggie without admitting I'd ruined the one spell, and I didn't trust her not to spin even a partial admission against me, no matter what else I said. So I stuck to other truths that contradicted her second claim.

"The last thing I'd have wanted to do is leave my mother to be locked up by our enemies for even longer than the ordeal she'd already been through. I was there helping every step of the way. If I wanted to sabotage the efforts, I was really bad at it."

"You probably realized Lillian and the others would catch on if you tried any harder," Maggie shot back.

I held up my hands. "Look, all I can tell is you're determined to see everything I've done in the worst possible light. I don't know how I can defend myself if you're going to refuse to listen no matter what I say."

Maggie raised her chin defiantly. "You've been putting yourself in that light from the moment you turned up. Do you think word didn't get around about how your first move on campus was to challenge the scions from the other families? I'm going by your actions, that's all."

Maybe I couldn't totally blame her for interpreting events through such a negative lens. Professor Viceport had seen a lot of my early actions at Blood U in the same way, filtered through her understanding of how barony families usually behaved and the history of the Bloodstones, and she'd been able to observe me firsthand. Of course, my mentor had been worried that I was following in my mother's footsteps, not that I was out to usurp her. This whole situation still didn't quite add up.

"Why are you so focused on what I'm doing and who gets to be Baron Bloodstone anyway?" I asked abruptly. "There are all kinds of conflicts going on in the other families, way more obvious than anything I've done or you think I'm doing. Unless you're a lot older than you look, you can't have been more than a kid when my mother went missing, so it's not like you could have been so close to her."

"I've heard and seen plenty through my work with Lillian," Maggie started.

"But you're not working with her anymore. Haven't you got better things to do now than make up reasons to hate me? Why is anything I've done so awful compared to the barons or the rest of the families?"

Maggie's lips pressed into a tight line. "I think I'm in a position to judge that. Deflecting isn't going to do you any good."

As I stood there, taking in the resistance in her pose, weariness washed over me. None of this talk was getting me anywhere. I could have tried to force an answer with magic, but Maggie would be focusing most of her energy on her mental defenses right now. While I could probably break through those defenses, I wasn't sure I could do it before she called a whole bunch of her colleagues down on me and accused me, rightfully, of attacking her.

I exhaled slowly. "Is there anything I could say or do that would change your judgment? Or are you going to see me as some kind of evil mastermind no matter what?"

Maggie's eyes flashed. "Unless you prove I'm right by destroying my life too, I'm just going to keep working toward what I think is right."

Fine then. I pushed myself away from the table. "Then there's no point in talking any further. I'm not interested in 'destroying' you or anyone else, so you're not going to trick some kind of evidence out of me. I hope you can find real crimes to go after people for."

"We'll see."

I left the building with my stomach in a tangle. She *wouldn't* discover any evidence of power grabs and glory-hunting if she kept poking around in my life—but she might catch on to the fact that I did have an agenda that clashed with my mother's. I had no idea what Maggie would make of my Nary sympathies. Considering how most fearmancers felt about them, it seemed likely she'd consider that just a different sort of mark against me. And one that could turn all four of the older barons against me in an instant.

I'd just have to proceed with the same caution I'd already been using. Maggie wasn't likely to pick up on much that even my mother didn't notice. I probably could have come up with a story that would get the blacksuit assistant sanctioned, but then I'd only be confirming her assumptions. That could backfire in a bad way.

And honestly, I didn't want to be any more of an underhanded schemer than I'd already had to become.

It was a simple drive back to the university, country highways with only a few turns along the way. As I came up on the town just off campus, though, I eased up on the gas.

A couple of the dark sedans the blacksuits favored were parked on the shoulder about a hundred feet from the town's first buildings, after the stretch of farmland ended. Several figures in black slacks and jackets were moving across the fields on both sides of the road. A faint tingle of magical energy brushed over my skin.

I drew up behind the sedans and stepped out beside my Lexus. A few of the blacksuits had looked over at the sight of the posh car, and at my emergence, one of them drifted toward me.

"What's going on?" I asked the woman. They weren't barricading the road, but their presence unnerved me anyway. "Is there a problem in town or on campus?"

The woman gave me a smile that was all deference. "No problems, Miss Bloodstone. Just a little scouting work. There's nothing to worry about."

The way she said that reminded me of the many times in the last few weeks when my mother had told me I had no need to worry, even though I clearly did. My body balked against getting back in the car. "Scouting for what?"

She let out a polite laugh. "Oh, ensuring the wards are

performing at full capacity and that sort of thing. We can't be too careful."

Ah, this might be in response to the attack on Jude, then. Maybe it'd even provide him with a little protection, despite his attacker's standing.

"Okay," I said. "Sorry I interrupted!"

She bobbed her head. "That's quite all right, Miss Bloodstone. Have a good day."

I drove off somewhat reassured, but when I glanced at my rearview mirror, I couldn't help noticing that the blacksuit had lingered by the side of the road where she'd spoken to me, watching until I turned out of view.

# CHAPTER TEN

*Rory*

I knew something was up outside my dorm bedroom before I even opened the door to leave. The walls were thin, and the girls who'd been using the common room had been keeping up a steady chatter for the last several minutes. All at once, their voices fell silent.

I peeked out into the larger room, still in the process of pulling on my jacket. Cressida was sitting at the dining table, and three girls I hadn't really talked with were lounging on one of the sofas. They were all studying a girl I'd never seen before, who'd come to a stop with one of the maintenance staff by my friend Shelby's former bedroom. Like Shelby, the new girl had a gold leaf pin on her shirt—she was a Nary.

"This will be your room for as long as you're with us," the staff person was saying. "You'll share the kitchen and bathroom areas with the other girls, but the bedroom is just for you."

"That sounds great." The girl glanced around at us through thick-framed glasses, her heavy black hair falling to her shoulders. She must have been eighteen, just starting college, thinking Bloodstone University was simply a quirky, exclusive one of those. "Hi," she said. "I'm Morgan."

I offered a smile back and a raise of my hand in greeting, even though my gut had clenched with trepidation. "Rory. Nice to meet you."

Cressida nodded without speaking. The other girls just kept watching her impassively. The girl's smile faltered, and she ducked into her bedroom, dragging her wheeled suitcase behind her. The maintenance woman wiped her hands together and headed off. Not quite the thorough introduction to campus life the fearmancer students appeared to get.

I shut my door behind me and murmured a few words under my breath to ward off any attempts to enter it. None of the bedrooms came with locks. Part of our training here at Blood U was learning how to protect our own space and possessions. Of course, the Naries had no protection at all.

When I turned back to the wider room, the girls on the sofa were exchanging sly smirks. One of them waved her hand toward our new dormmate's bedroom and mouthed a few words. I braced myself.

A second later, a shriek split the air, barely muffled by

the walls. Something clattered on the floor. One of the other girls spoke a casting word, and a yelp rang out, followed by a choked breath.

The door swung open, and the new girl dashed out. Her face was white, her shoulders trembling. My heart wrenched, but before I could say anything, the third of my dormmates curled her lips with a sneer.

"Welcome to Blood U," she said, and flicked her fingers with another murmur. A swarm of wasps, presumably an illusion, appeared out of thin air and descended on the Nary girl in a cloud.

"What the hell?" the girl gasped out, stumbling away from them, her arms flailing in an effort to fend the insects off. She tripped over the edge of the rug and sprawled on her ass. Another cry leapt from her throat as those illusionary stingers provoked a pain that would hurt plenty now even if it'd fade as soon as the illusion did. "What are you doing to me? Please, stop it."

The girls just giggled, their faces giddily bright with all the fear their spells had provoked for them. Assholes.

I took a step toward the girl, and she flinched, a waft of panic rushing from her into me. She was terrified that I'd give her the exact same treatment. With a shudder, she scrambled to her feet and fled out the door. A wave of laughter followed her.

Anger prickled through me in the wake of the girl's fear. I bit it back with a queasy sensation. If I told off my dormmates, how long would it take for word about that to get back to my mother? I didn't think she'd appreciate me defending my dormmate any more than she'd liked me standing up for Naries in general with my classmates before. I hadn't figured out enough to *really* protect them yet.

That didn't mean I was helpless, though. I just had to find the right angle. No way in hell was I going to stand by through that kind of torment right here where I lived.

"Very funny," I said in the same cool tone I imagined my mother would have used. "Now that you've gotten your kicks, maybe we can keep the terrorizing to outside the dorms?"

The girl who'd cast the first spell tensed in her seat. "Why should we? The Naries are all fair game now."

I shrugged. "Sure. But *I* don't want to have to listen to someone screaming and crying every time I'm in here trying to study or sleep or whatever. A little consideration for the rest of us?"

The girls hesitated, none of them obviously wanting to say they weren't interested in considering a scion's feelings. One glanced toward Cressida, who just gazed mildly back at them, not lending support to either position.

"You managed to have enough self-control not to use any magic around the Naries for years," I added. "I assume you haven't lost all of that in just a couple weeks."

The first girl looked as if she'd restrained a glower. I definitely wasn't making any friends with the attitude I was giving them, but then, with the attitude *they'd* shown the Naries, they'd never have really been on my side anyway.

"I'm sure we can handle that," one of the other girls said icily. "No need to bring all their freaking out in here."

"Exactly. I'm glad you agree." I gave her a tight smile that showed I noticed her unspoken annoyance and headed out. It wasn't much, not anywhere near as much as I'd have liked to offer, but at least I'd spared our new Nary dormmate a little torment.

I'd gotten ready early enough that even with the short delay, I made it to the fourth floor hall just as Jude was leaving his dorm.

He raised his eyebrows at me with a crooked grin. "You could have met me at the garage. I think I can manage to find my way there unescorted."

Maybe, but evening was descending outside, and I didn't totally trust that someone dangerous wouldn't find *him* on the way there. I'd rather not sting his pride by putting it like that, though. I sauntered closer and rested my hand on his chest. "I'm sure you could. But then I wouldn't get the pleasure of walking with you."

A happy gleam came into his dark green eyes. He made a humming sound and touched my waist, turning us so he could nudge me against the wall. "I can do better than simply *walking* with you."

The teasing remark and the way he kissed me afterward, heated and deliberate and without any care that our classmates might wander out and see us, was so much like his usual self that my spirits lifted. I curled my fingers into the fabric of his shirt and kissed him back hard. He'd been putting on a show of being typically carefree since the infirmary had released him, but there'd been something brittle about the performance that'd told me not to believe it. This moment felt totally genuine.

He slipped his hand around mine as we descended the stairs and ambled along the path to the garage. Technically we could have walked to town for the dinner I'd suggested—it was only about a mile down the road—but Jude loved driving us around in his Mercedes, and I'd rather not linger in an isolated stretch where I'd be his only line of defense. In town, there'd be witnesses preventing a major attack; here on campus, I could call for immediate help.

"I know what you and the guys are doing," Jude said as we came into the glow of the garage's outer lights.

I glanced at him. He was looking straight ahead rather than at me. His tone had been mild, but his mouth had a bittersweet twist to it. "What do you mean?"

"As incredibly charming as I know I am, my company has never been in *quite* this high demand before. You're making sure I'm never alone after dark, unless it's to sleep."

I couldn't tell if he was annoyed by the observation or simply putting it out there. "Jude," I said, squeezing his hand. "It's not like— We aren't trying to—"

He turned to me then, on the way through the garage doorway, his smile going softer. "You're trying to keep me alive. I'm not complaining. I—I appreciate it." He swiped his free hand over his face and into his hair. "I just wish I didn't need the protection."

"Hopefully it won't be for too long." I paused, and

then asked tentatively, "Have you noticed any improvement so far?"

"Barely. I'm still leaky as a wrecked ship. It doesn't *all* pour out, but the little magic I can hold onto at a time isn't enough to do anything all that useful."

"It's only been a few days. The doctor said it could take a while."

He dipped his head. "Or my situation might not improve much at all. It's almost fitting, in a way. My 'father' arranged for me to have a life as if I was some spectacular mage for four and a half years, and now it's like all that extra talent I pretended to have has been siphoned away from what was really mine."

"You *could* do spectacular magic," I insisted as we came up on his car. "And you will again if I have anything to say about it. He owed you a whole lot more than he ever gave you."

Jude let go of my hand but stayed close enough to brush his fingers over my cheek before he went to the driver's side. "I'm just trying to stay realistic, Rory."

I didn't know what I could say that would take away the pain that rang through those words. As long as I'd known him, Jude had struggled to believe he was enough—for me, for his friends, for this school, for his entire community. And that was while he'd been the most talented illusionary mage on campus. If his capacity for magic never came back, if he could never cast more than tiny spells ever again… I hated to think what he'd believe about himself then.

All I could do was keep showing him how much he

mattered to me no matter what his abilities were. I slid into the passenger seat beside him. "I'll still want to be with you no matter what kind of magic you can do. You know that, don't you?"

He chuckled. "I know I can't imagine you saying anything else."

"And I'm paying for this dinner, by the way."

"Hold on there." He gunned the engine and whipped out of the parking spot smooth as silk. "It's my magic that's been draining away, not my bank account."

I rolled my eyes at him. "I know you don't need me to. But I'm picking the restaurant, and I don't want any complaints about it. Anyway, *my* bank accounts are holding up just fine too, and you've paid every time we've been in New York."

"When we go to my apartment, you're my guest. It's simply what's polite."

"Like you usually care *so* much about politeness." I elbowed him lightly. "Consider yourself my guest at this place."

The restaurant I'd chosen was one I'd been to with Shelby a few times. I hadn't yet found anything on the menu that left me unsatisfied, but it wasn't fancy, which was why Jude might have turned his nose up a little if I hadn't put my foot down ahead of time. The little building held just eight tables, catered to by a husband and wife. The wife was the head chef, and the husband worked as the sole waiter. It had a homey feeling that I never quite got anywhere on campus.

The owners cared a lot about their patrons, clearly. The

husband beamed at us as we came in and made a point of mentioning the new pasta dish on the menu, probably because I'd swooned over the one I'd tried last time. His wife passed by the kitchen doorway and shot me a wave. After I'd taken the pasta suggestion and Jude had asked for a steak, my date watched with some amusement as the man hustled off.

"How often have you been here?"

"Three or four times in the past couple months. I think they try to pay attention to anyone who starts to become a regular."

Jude broke apart one of the fresh rolls from the basket on the table and inhaled the crisp doughy scent with a sigh. "They know how to bake. That's a good start." He contemplated the rest of the space with its simple décor, the exposed brick wall at the other end of the room, a tinkling of folk music drifting from speakers overhead. "I'm guessing you'd have come with your Nary friend before. Have you heard much from her?"

He had a certain investment in Shelby. One of his illusions had startled her into breaking her wrist, and he'd somehow arranged to have it magically healed despite the school rules forbidding that kind of intervention, so that she could continue her musical studies at the university. With a little help from me, she'd gotten hired on at a prestigious orchestra not long ago. Thank God I'd gotten her off campus before the full-out torture had begun.

"I got to see her first official performance last week," I said, a smile crossing my lips at the memory. She'd looked so intent in the midst of the other musicians, gripping her cello, but it'd been a joyful sort of intensity. I'd never seen her grin quite as brightly as when she'd taken her bow at the end. "She's loving the work. A lot better than still being stuck at Blood U."

"Especially the way things are now."

"Yeah." I cringed, remembering the events right before I'd gone to meet him. "They've filled her spot in my dorm with a new Nary student. Some of the other girls launched right into her. I don't know how any of them are going to survive even a month without having a nervous breakdown."

"The pricks around campus have to ease off once they've gotten their fill of flinging their power around," Jude said, but the corners of his mouth had slanted downward. He ripped the roll into a couple more pieces, but didn't move to eat any of them. After a stretch of silence, he added, "It's partly my fault, isn't it?"

"What is?"

He waved his hand in the vague direction of the university. "The fact that so many people there think it's okay to *give* the Naries nervous breakdowns. I used to hassle them all the time in the subtle ways that we had to resort to before. I talked shit about them. Most of the other kids looked up to me as a scion. I made it seem okay to think that way."

His voice had gone raw. A lump rose in my throat. I reached over to clasp his hand. "The way most fearmancers look at them, I don't think you swayed them *that* much. They'd still have had their parents and friends and whoever else saying it was okay. And now you can be a model for rising above that crap."

"If anyone's paying attention." He frowned at our joined hands. "I helped make this stupid policy happen, and that just means I'll have to help even more to tear it down. Whatever it takes."

## CHAPTER ELEVEN

*Malcolm*

Even if I hadn't thought the Naries deserved better, I'd have believed most of my peers on campus looked like a bunch of jackasses. They'd had a few days to get used to the new rush of power, and still every time I crossed the green, one idiot or another was making some over-the-top spell to harass the nonmagical students. I expected the only reason the Naries came out onto the green at all was their dorms and classrooms weren't any safer. Some of them holed up in the clubhouse Rory had arranged for them, the magical protections on which were holding, but they couldn't *live* in there.

Didn't my classmates realize how pathetic their demonstrations made them out to be? As if they couldn't find ways to generate the fear that powered their magic in any way that wasn't a total horror show? I could command enough nervous respect with just a glance and a shift in my stance to keep me well-fueled. They were probably wasting most of the magic they were collecting making their terrorizing spells so grandiose.

So much for fearmancer discipline.

When I came out of the tower to some genius splitting cracks across the whole lawn while a couple of Naries scrambled to avoid tripping, exasperation and pity collided inside me. I let them spill out in pure irritation.

"Do you *mind*?" I said to the junior who was controlling the spell, letting plenty of acid seep into my tone. "Some of us have important things to do, places to get to. If you're that magic-starved, find a better strategy—one that doesn't make you look like a clown and inconvenience the rest of us."

The junior's face paled at the sight of me. He mumbled a couple of quick words to close up the gouges in the soil and scurried away with a hastily tossed out apology. And a healthy boost of fear, which hadn't required any spell-casting at all, let alone tormenting people who didn't have a chance at defending themselves.

I hadn't heard Rory coming out of the tower behind me. She touched my arm as she came up beside me, the brush of her fingers provoking an instant flood of heat despite everything else I'd been feeling.

I wasn't sure I'd ever *not* react to the affection she offered so easily now. Not that she could offer all that much here in public view. We were still keeping the more intimate part of our relationship secret until I could be sure it wouldn't cause even more problems for her with the barons.

"That's the strategy I've been taking too," she said quietly. "Focus on how the harassment affects us rather than the Naries. It's not perfect, but it's something."

"It should be enough for them to cut it out by itself," I muttered. Didn't my father and the other older barons see how pathetic this policy made *them* look? They'd turned the school into a caricature of itself. We might as well officially rename the place Villain Academy now.

But Dad had brushed off the disparaging observations I'd passed on to him, telling me it would all come together well in time.

"They don't seem likely to back off without being forced to." Rory's other arm tucked across her stomach as if to hug herself. When I glanced at her, worry lines had formed at the corners of her mouth. She'd been holding it together incredibly well, but I couldn't imagine how much watching this catastrophe was hurting that big heart of hers. Watching and pretending she didn't hate every second of it.

"Are you doing all right?" I asked. She'd been through an awful lot in the past half a year, no small part of it at my hands. Most of the rest hadn't been anything I could really help her with. I was a Nightwood, even if my parents had forgotten what they'd always taught me that name was supposed to mean; I'd taken lead with the scions my whole life. I was going to find a way to make this right for the woman beside me or die trying.

"You know..." She shrugged with a twist of her mouth. We couldn't talk all that openly out here anyway.

"Let's go down to the lounge," I said. No one outside

the pentacle of scions would intrude on us there. I was supposed to meet up with a few of my dormmates soon, but that could wait.

Rory crossed the green with me. Inside Ashgrave Hall, we headed down the stairs to the big basement room I'd claimed for the scions' use during my first year on campus. Not everything we'd experienced down there had been pleasant, but walking into the broad space with its pale walls and leather seating, breathing in the cool air with the slightest tang of alcohol from the bar cabinet, I always felt a little more centered.

The Bloodstone scion let out a rush of breath and leaned back against the closed door. She closed her eyes for a second as if gathering herself. When she opened them again, her indigo gaze fixed on me, as intent and fond as the moment not that long ago when she'd told me she loved me.

The memory sent a giddy tremor through my chest. I hadn't expected to hear those words from her, not any time soon. I'd thought I had so much more to prove. But she'd seen me, believed in me, without needing an endless stream of groveling. Not that I'd have avoided the groveling if that'd been what it took.

My body moved of its own accord to do what I hadn't been able to outside—what I hadn't had the opportunity to do in days. I stepped up to her, slipping one hand over her cheek as I set the other on her waist, and drew her into a kiss.

Rory swayed into me as she kissed me back. Everywhere our bodies touched, mine caught fire. I tugged her even closer against me, kissing her harder, coaxing a pleased sound from her throat with the teasing of my tongue.

There wasn't much I'd rather have done than strip the clothes off her and bring her to the trembling, moaning bliss we'd shared before, but right now I didn't really want to get into *that* somewhere anyone, even my friends, might interrupt us. I was willing to share, and I appreciated what the other scions brought into Rory's life… but some moments I wanted to just be for the two of us.

Besides, Rory was already nudging me back with an amused if also hungry gleam in her eyes. "I thought you suggested we come down here so that we could *talk*."

"What can I say? I'll take my opportunities as I get them." I tucked my arm around her waist, reining my other desires in. "Have things taken a turn for the worse with your mother?"

She shook her head. "No, that's pretty much the same. It's just harder, as things get worse, to keep my mouth shut as much as I have to. What if I don't find out anything from her after all? How can we convince the barons they're wrong? And we still don't even know what they might have in the works that could be even more horrible."

"I don't like going along with them either," I said. "But—look what happened to Connar and to Jude when they pushed back openly. We're strong mages, but I'm not so reckless as to think it'd be a good idea for us to go up against four barons with decades more experience than we have. What would our end goal even be? Brainwashing *them* into submission?"

Even as frustrated as I was with my father, after seeing Connar in the grips of that kind of spell, the thought of ordering around anyone possessed like that nauseated me. Maybe the barons weren't better than that, but *I* damn well was.

"I don't know." Rory sighed. "If more families were willing to push back, there'd be a point where they'd have to listen, right?"

"I have been chatting up a lot of my classmates. There are a few I'm pretty sure are uncomfortable with the new status quo—they definitely haven't been joining in with the fearmongering. The difficult part is going to be getting them from uncomfortable to defiant. No one's going to be all that keen on talking back to the barons."

"Of course not. If we can figure out enough people who feel that way, though, it might be easier to encourage them all to stand up together."

As her brow knit, she worried her lower lip under her teeth in a way that made me want to go back to kissing her.

"I'll keep putting out feelers," I said. "There'll be more families who are on the fence or outright against the new policy. Then all we'll need is a call to action, and we'll know who to turn to."

"Right. So, I'd better get a move on figuring out what a useful action would be."

"Hey." I set my hands on her shoulders, gazing down at her. At this beautiful, determined, passionate woman

I'd somehow failed to properly appreciate when she'd first blazed into my life. "We'll get there. I know that, because I know there's no way in hell you'll give up until we do, and I've seen enough times that when Rory Bloodstone sets her mind to accomplishing something, you'd better believe she's going to make it happen."

The corners of her mouth quirked upward, and I couldn't resist leaning in again. The soft brush of her lips against mine set off such a potent combination of protectiveness, admiration, and lust that my heart literally skipped a beat.

How the fuck was I ever going to give this woman up? She was everything I could possibly have wanted in a partner, and she was the only person like that I'd ever met.

I didn't give a shit about heirs or succession or even being officially tied together. There were other Nightwoods; there'd be other generations even if I didn't provide them. The pang in my heart said it clearly as anything: I'd have happily ruled as Baron Nightwood alone and accepted whatever time I could get with Rory around that role if it meant I still had her. I wouldn't have been going along with this bizarre relationship the five of us had right now if that wasn't true.

But Rory would need heirs, and for that she needed an actual husband. What were the chances *he'd* accept her having other lovers on the side? Rory wouldn't have been Rory if she'd have been okay with sneaking around on someone she cared about.

So I didn't say any of those thoughts out loud. I just

kissed her once more and murmured, because this time I wanted to say it first, "I love you."

Rory wrapped her arms around me in a brief but tight embrace. "I love you too," she said back, the words lighting me up inside just as much as they had the first time. The fact that she could love three other guys at the same time, and show us all so much caring, was just one more incredible thing about her.

"Did the pep talk help?" I asked with a crooked smile as I eased back.

"A little." Her own smile turned mischievous. "I did manage to convince Malcolm Nightwood to see things my way, so maybe I should give myself a little more credit."

I guffawed and gave her hair a light tug. "You definitely should. Go get 'em. I've got to kick some ass on the squash court now."

Her smile and her touch and even her sweet scent lingered with me as I headed up to my dorm to change into more sport-appropriate clothing. When I made it out to the squash court next to the main gym in the Stormhurst Building, the three guys I'd arranged to play with were all waiting, their stances vaguely impatient until they saw me and snapped to attention. None of them was going to admit he was pissed off that the heir of Nightwood had taken his time coming down.

I grabbed a racket, spun it in my hand, and launched right into my real purpose for suggesting this game. Rory needed *me* to be holding up my end of the deal—and I intended to find every potential ally I could as soon as possible.

"Got held up leaving class," I said, keeping my tone casual but watching my companions' reactions carefully. "Another idiot throwing around spells at the Naries, not caring whose way he gets in. I never thought I'd say this, but I kind of miss discretion."

# CHAPTER TWELVE

*Rory*

The Uber driver dropped me off just before the looming gate of the Bloodstone residence. I pretended not to notice the curious look he shot me. After he'd driven off, I crept to the gate and opened it with a soft murmur of Bloodstone magic, easing it aside just far enough for me to slip through the gap.

I didn't want to give anyone in the house obvious warning that I was on my way. For the same reason, I'd parked my own car in the nearest town and gotten that Uber.

I'd been supposed to meet my mother at one of her offices today. She'd texted me a couple hours ago calling off our plans, saying unexpected business had come up that she needed to handle on her own. Declan was out at the Fortress of the Pentacle doing some research in their records—he'd been able to confirm she hadn't ended up there.

Either she'd be home, in which case maybe I'd be able to catch her in the middle of one of the schemes she'd been avoiding telling me about… or she wouldn't be, and I'd have a little time to poke around in her rooms while she was off on her important business. One way or another, I could hope to get something useful out of this furtive visit.

The front door to the house opened at my command too, all the locks keyed to the Bloodstone family. Eloise stepped into the front hall at the creak of the hinges. She blinked at me.

"Miss Bloodstone—I didn't realize you were coming by. I can let your mother know—"

So the baron was here. I shook my head quickly to cut her off. "There's no need to disturb her. I just needed to grab a couple things. She's upstairs?"

"I believe so. She asked that the staff be kept away, but I'm sure that wouldn't apply to you."

Good. Then no one was likely to catch me at my spying. "I think she had some important business to take care of," I said. "I won't interrupt unless it looks like she's finished."

I walked up the staircase gingerly, staying close to the polished banister to avoid any further creaking. The curve of the stairs took me out of view of Eloise and any other staff below. I paused in the upstairs hallway, considering the doors. My mother's bedroom and private bath was to my left, her study at the other end of the house to my right. If she was here for business, she'd probably be in her study, right?

I padded over with a whisper of my soft-soled shoes against the hardwood, the waxy smell of a recent polishing drifting over me. Outside the study door, I stopped and murmured a quick spell to test what magic was already cast on the room.

It had a security spell in place—a strong one that would have taken me several minutes to untangle. I'd have risked that if my mother hadn't been home to potentially catch me. I didn't sense any other magic on the space, though: no silencing spell or anything like that. Despite that, no sound seeped through the door. If she was working in there, it was very quiet work.

I waited a little while, until my skin started to creep with the worry that I'd be noticed. When the study stayed silent, I slipped back down the hall to my mother's bedroom.

That door had only a basic security spell on it, the kind you'd put up if you didn't expect to need it there all that long. My cast-out magic also brushed up against a barrier that I suspected was dampening any noise that might have come from the room.

Well, I must have found her. Now I just had to figure out what urgent business she was up to without tipping her off that I was listening in.

I eased away from the door, a few feet farther along the wall. The silencing spell wrapped around the whole room, as far as I could tell, but it was thinner away from the door. Concentrating on the thrum of magic in my chest, I slowly wore away at the barrier with one cautious casting word after another. I didn't need a large gap. If I worked this right, she'd never realize the spell had been compromised.

I felt the severing of the spell like a sagging of loosened threads. With another quick word, I urged some of my magic to bring any sounds from within more audibly to my ears. Then I leaned close to the wall, my body braced in case some member of the staff came up the stairs after all—or in case my mother abruptly emerged.

At first, like with the study, I heard nothing. Then a strange choked sound reached my ear. I frowned and leaned closer. Had that been a particularly incomprehensible casting word?

The next noise that reached me couldn't have been anything other than a stuttered breath. Then a hiss that sounded pained, and something that might have been a muffled sob. "Damn it, damn it, damn it," came a muttering in my mother's voice, broken by another wrenching sound.

The hairs on the backs of my arms rose with an eerie chill. Was she *crying*? The thought was alien after the coolly controlled poise my mother had shown even when she'd just woken up in the blacksuits' infirmary. My mind had trouble wrapping around that idea.

What could have gone so wrong that it would bring this woman to tears?

My gut twisted. I hesitated, wavering on my feet, and then moved back to the door. It didn't feel right to just stand there listening to her in this state, and I couldn't walk away. I'd helped Lillian find her and risked my freedom to help her regain hers because I cared what happened to her, even if I didn't agree with everything she'd done since then. She was still a human being. She was still my mother.

I knocked on the door. "Mom? Are you there?"

No response came at first. She wouldn't know I'd heard her. I had to assume she was composing herself—or maybe she'd pretend not to be there at all?

The lock clicked over, and my mother opened the door. At a glance, I wouldn't have known she'd been crying. Through some sorcery, her eyes weren't at all red or puffy, although they did look overly bright. Her face might be pale, but then, it was usually pretty pale in general. Her hand gripped the edge of the door tightly, and her slender frame was wrapped in a thick bathrobe.

"Persephone," she said. "What are you doing here?"

I gestured awkwardly. "I'm sorry. I was just— I came by to grab something from the house, and Eloise mentioned you were here. I thought I'd see if I could pitch in with whatever you're working on, since I'm here anyway."

"Always eager to contribute. I appreciate that. The business concerns are taken care of. You'll have to excuse my appearance—I just got out of the bath." She gestured to her robe with a self-deprecating laugh, but I noticed that her shoulders tensed with the movement as if bracing against discomfort. Her jaw tightened when she smiled at me. Was she in some kind of physical pain?

She'd been imprisoned and drained of her magic for

nearly two decades. I'd been surprised before that she didn't seem to be suffering more lingering effects from that. Maybe she had, and she'd simply hidden them incredibly well.

I didn't think she'd appreciate me pointing out the hints I'd seen. I stuck to a more general approach. "It's good that you're getting some relaxing in. I don't know how you can manage to be working so hard after everything you've been through. You deserve a little recovery time."

"That work has been put on hold for seventeen years," she said. "Better not to leave it any longer. But there's nothing wrong with a little indulgence here and there." She paused and then motioned me in. "I have a new employee coming by in half an hour or so, but we can talk while I get ready. Maybe you can advise me on my wardrobe. I'm realizing I'm about seventeen years behind in fashion respects too."

I came in cautiously and sat in a chair by the bed. "I don't know—from what I've seen, the clothes you had are pretty timeless." My own wardrobe consisted mostly of pieces the staff had picked out for me from her old outfits, since all of my previous clothing had been left behind in California. The sheath dress and thin cardigan I was wearing right now had been hers.

A wry smile crossed my mother's lips. "Perhaps you ended up with the best pieces. I won't begrudge you that."

She opened the wardrobe across from the foot of the bed, and her arm wobbled. It looked as if she caught herself, grasping the handle, just shy of losing her balance.

I was half out of my chair when she straightened herself stiffly and quickly reached toward the rows of clothes, obviously trying to hide her lapse.

"I have wondered about pieces like this." She tugged out a black dress with ruffles along the cuffs of the sleeves and the bottom hem. "It seems a little… much, in the wrong way."

I cocked my head, forcing myself to sink back down. "I think if you were looking to get attention, it'd still work. But definitely not regular business-wear these days, from what I've seen."

"There. The advice can flow both ways in this family." She hung the dress back up, and a tremor ran through her body again. She managed to lower herself into another chair beside the wardrobe as if she were simply bored of looking through the clothes, but my heart squeezed anyway.

"If you want to take a little more time to rest, there really wasn't anything I needed to talk to you about," I said.

"No, no. I'm just fine." She drew in a breath, and I thought I made out a whisper of a casting word in it. Something to push back the pain or to otherwise steady herself? Her gaze fixed on me, shifting from fond to sharp in an instant. "One of the most important pieces of *my* advice you need to remember is that a baron and her scion do not show weakness."

I couldn't quite manage to keep my mouth shut. "I don't think it's weakness to be a little tired after a terrible ordeal. You've been doing a lot almost from the moment you woke up back here. Maybe… maybe all those plans can happen a little more slowly, as you build up all the energy you lost." That would give me more time to figure out what they were and whether I should be trying to counter them too, but honestly in that moment I just didn't want to end up watching my mother collapse from agonized exhaustion.

She looked away for a moment, and an expression crossed her face that was so forlorn my throat constricted at the sight. "Oh, wouldn't it have been nice to have more time to really think it all through?" Then her head jerked back to face me, her hands splaying firmly on her lap. "But I've had plenty of time. It's been slow enough. We're working toward what I've wanted for twenty-some years. I won't get in the way of that."

But I might have to. Was it possible she'd come to see that as a good thing in the end? With that stray comment, it'd almost seemed she wasn't as happy with the direction the barons were taking our community in as I'd expected.

Even if she had been imagining these developments way back when, that didn't mean she necessarily liked the outcomes she was seeing as they came to life. How much was she determined to push on, and how much did she simply feel she had to maintain a certain resolve to present a strong front to the other barons?

"Giving yourself space to breathe while you work through it wouldn't be getting in the way," I started, but she stood up abruptly, her expression firming even more.

"Don't worry," she said in a smooth but equally firm

voice. "I know what I'm capable of, Persephone. Never doubt that."

She browsed through the other outfits in the wardrobe and pulled out a sleek forest-green dress suit without checking for my approval. "Would you look for my emerald earrings in the jewelry box there?" she said, tipping her head toward the vanity beside me. Her tone made it more a command than a question.

Whatever she'd been going through, it appeared she'd fought it off. I got up to retrieve the earrings, and when I found them and turned back around, she'd already shimmied into the skirt and blouse and was slipping on the jacket. She took the earrings from me with a queenly air and fit them into her lobes without hesitation.

"Is there anything I can help with while you're working with this new employee?" I asked, not knowing how I fit in here now. On one hand, this was my home too. On the other, I couldn't shake the feeling that I'd dropped in on someone else's domain without an invitation. I had to try to stay as involved as possible, though.

My mother gave her head a brisk shake. "It won't be anything new to you today. I'll just be bringing her up to speed on baseline expectations. It's probably good that you're here to welcome her too, though, as I expect you'll be seeing a fair bit of her as she assists with various aspects of our family's business going forward."

I guessed it was a good thing that she was taking on more hired help to remove some of the weight from her shoulders, not that I dared make that observation out loud.

The knocker on the front door rapped, the sound carrying up the stairs. The silencing spell didn't keep noise out, only in. My mother swiped her hands together and moved to the door. "That should be her now. I'd imagine you need to be getting back to school soon as it is. You can say hello on your way out."

Her dismissal couldn't have been clearer. It might even rankle her that I'd witnessed that rare moment of discomposure. "Of course," I said, and we headed down together. To my relief, her steps stayed steady the whole way down.

Eloise was just answering the front door. We reached the bottom of the stairs, and the house manager stepped back to admit… a far too familiar curvy figure, chocolate-brown curls pulled back from her heart-shaped face by a silver clip.

Maggie Duskland gave us both a cheerful smile, her gaze coming to rest on my mother. "Baron Bloodstone. I'm so glad to be here."

# CHAPTER THIRTEEN

*Rory*

The woman who let me into the Fortress of the Pentacle didn't blink at my arrival, so I supposed Declan had given her a heads up that I was coming. I'd texted him to confirm he'd still be there—and that the other barons wouldn't be—before I'd headed that way from the Bloodstone property. I didn't actually need to be back at school just yet, and after what I'd seen from my mother this afternoon, I wanted answers I wasn't sure I could find anywhere else.

I might have only visited the Fortress once before, but my mother's tour of the place was burned into my memory. I headed through the chilly halls to the records room.

The rasp of turned pages met me when I nudged open the door. Declan glanced up where he was leaning against one of the shelving units with a thick volume in his hands

—and so did Malcolm, who had a smaller text propped open against a shelf farther down. I didn't think I'd ever seen the Nightwood scion in any library before, though I guessed from his class performance he must do a fair bit of studying. I'd definitely never seen the delicate reading glasses he currently had perched on the bridge of his nose.

"I didn't know you had company," I said to Declan, shooting a smile at Malcolm to show I wasn't implying it was a problem.

The Ashgrave scion gave his friend a teasingly baleful look. "He insisted on coming along. Which is probably a good thing, since as far as I can tell he wouldn't be able to find anything in here if he couldn't ask me where to look."

"To be fair, I've only been here a couple times and you've probably spent half your life in this place," Malcolm retorted with similar good humor. He nudged at his glasses, an unusual awkwardness coloring his typical confidence. They didn't detract from his divinely good looks at all—if anything, they gave him a charmingly academic air. But obviously he didn't let people see him wearing them often.

I tipped my head toward him. "Aren't there spells to help with sight issues?"

"There are," he said with more characteristic assurance. "But the ones that work on my eyes give me a headache, and the ones you put on your reading material make it hard to skim quickly. Naries do on occasion have better solutions to practical problems than magic can come up with." He raised an eyebrow at me. "You can be sure my parents have no idea I own these."

"Well, I'm definitely not complaining about them." I let my smile stretch into a grin, but my own lightened spirits only lasted briefly. I could ignore the reason I'd come here for a little chitchat, but I couldn't make it disappear.

I turned to Declan. "Unfortunately, I'm going to have to call on your guidance here too. If I wanted to look up records of decisions my mother was a part of in the first few years she was baron, before the joymancers took her, where would I find those?"

He gave me a curious glance as he motioned to the shelf beside him. "The meeting records and the like are right here. The most recent ones before her imprisonment would be…" His fingers slid over the spines. "Here." He tugged out a thick book like the one he was holding and offered it to me. "What are you looking for in there?"

"I just…" It was hard to put the feeling that had come over me during my visit with Baron Bloodstone into words. "I talked with her at the house. She seemed a little out of sorts—I think that's why she called off the more official meeting we were supposed to have. I got the impression that maybe she's not quite as sure of the changes the barons are making as she's acted before. So I'm wondering how much her decisions have been affected by her time in captivity. Whether she pushed for different things in the past, even on a small scale. If I can remind her of those… I don't know. It's a long shot. I'd just like to see."

"That makes sense. If there's any chance she'd be open to moderating the direction they've been heading, that'd help a lot. Did anything else come up while you were talking with her?"

I grimaced. "Apparently she's taking on Maggie Duskland as an assistant."

Malcolm's forehead furrowed. "Isn't she the one you figured out has been hassling you and trying to set you up as some kind of traitor?"

"Yep. Lillian's former assistant." I sighed and sagged against the opposite shelf, clutching the book Declan had given me. "I'm not sure how exactly that came about. From their conversation before I left, it sounded like she volunteered to act as a go-between with the blacksuits and with whatever else my mother might need, and my mother thought it was a good idea since she'd know more about the business Lillian was already involved with than anyone else."

"But it's probably got at least something to do with getting at you," Declan said, frowning.

"I've got to think so. She was definitely still part of the anti-Rory brigade even after I tried to hash things out with her. I guess this is a way for her to keep an eye on how I'm interacting with my mother more directly. I'm going to have to be even more careful navigating that. At least my mother doesn't see her as a definite ally, considering what happened with Lillian. When she walked me out, she said something Maggie didn't hear about 'keeping friends close and enemies closer.'"

"I'll see if I can find out anything useful on her," Malcolm volunteered. "You said her family name is Duskland? I don't think I know any other Dusklands around here… There should be something, though." He waved the book he was holding in the air. "I'm already digging up everything I can about the families I think are more on the pro-Nary side, to see if I can confirm those impressions before we stick our necks out."

So that's what he was up to here. I was about to say I'd appreciate the help, but Declan shook his head.

"I did some investigating into her background when Lillian first started coming to see you. There aren't any Dusklands in the country other than her. She came over from the Netherlands when she was fifteen to attend Blood U, although I got the sense from the bits and pieces I dug up that she'd moved around quite a bit in Europe. Not sure why she decided to come here for school or to stay here. The Dusklands over there haven't done anything notable enough that we've got records on them."

Of course he'd already have the territory thoroughly researched. I gave him a fond if crooked smile. "Nothing startling since she arrived over here, I assume?"

"She's kept a pretty low profile. Good but not exceptional performance in her classes, never appears to have aspired to a job beyond being an assistant to the blacksuits. She started out working for a middle-management type and then a year later—about three years ago—ended up under Lillian."

She really shouldn't have any personal stake in the Bloodstone barony, then. She hadn't even been in the country while my mother or grandfather had been ruling.

"I'd bet the other barons got to her somehow." Malcolm made a face at the shelves around us. "The more people they've got seeing you as the enemy, the easier it'd be for them to push you around. She's just taking it to another level."

"Maybe." Maggie hadn't said anything about the other barons talking to her—but then, they wouldn't have wanted her to mention that, would they? "I'll just have to do my best to avoid her."

We fell into silence, each of us poised in our spots throughout the records room, focused on our own reading. No sound seeped through the narrow windows that let in streaks of dim sunlight, so there was nothing but the rustle of pages and Malcolm's occasional disgruntled muttering to himself.

The baron meeting records didn't exactly make for exciting entertainment. They were fairly dry notes on topics discussed and decisions arrived at, with only occasional mention of which specific barons had contributed what opinions. None of the rulings from the year when my mother had been taken mentioned anything to do with changes to how fearmancers interacted with Naries, at the university or anywhere else. They were mostly private concerns relating to one or another fearmancer's business dealings or family conflicts.

I sifted back through the year before that, the accounts blurring together in their repetition, until one particular case made me pause. It looked like at least once there had been some disagreement between my mother and her usual allies. This case was a family matter, a marriage between a man from a prestigious family and a woman who was obviously much worse-regarded. The husband had died, and his parents had demanded custody over their two young grandchildren, arguing they were better equipped to provide a proper future for them than the mother.

The details of the debate weren't recorded, but the vote was. The matter hadn't required unanimous agreement. Barons Nightwood and Killbrook had voted in favor of the grandparents; the earlier Baron Stormhurst, Declan's mom, and my own had sided with the mother. The children had stayed with her.

Baron Bloodstone didn't always value status over all else. She was willing to defy her strongest ally and side with the baron she'd liked least when it came to keeping a family together.

My thumb dropped to rub over the band of the ring she'd given me, the silver smooth but warm against my skin. Another feeling that had been wriggling through me since I'd first heard her crying rose up to grip my chest.

"Do you think—" I paused, my voice sounding too loud in the quiet room. Declan and Malcolm lifted their heads. I swallowed and pushed on. "Do you think I *am* kind of betraying her? I mean, she has been through an awful lot, and she's hardly had any time to recover. Maybe I jumped to seeing her as an enemy too quickly. Maybe there's a way I could get through to her instead of going behind her back."

"You tried telling her how you feel about the new policy, didn't you?" Declan said. "She hasn't budged at all. Everything she's said about it during the baron meetings has been enthusiastic. Even if she's had some doubts, I don't think she's willing to act on them."

"Because everyone expects her to be a certain way, to be all powerful and authoritative." But I didn't have a clue how to convince her that she could open up more candidly with me, if there was even much she'd have wanted to say beyond what she'd revealed this afternoon. She'd still said these were plans she'd wanted. That didn't dislodge the lump of guilt in my stomach, though. "I don't like it, that's all."

"Of course you don't. That's why you're you." Malcolm set his current book aside. He flicked the glasses off his face and into his shirt pocket in a motion so smooth it was hard to believe he'd been wearing them a second before. I suspected he'd perfected the move just in case he was ever in danger of being interrupted by someone he'd rather not see them.

He sauntered over to me and slipped his fingers around my forearm with a gentle grasp. His head bent low, the nearness of him and the sharply aquatic scent of his cologne making my heart thump. I still wasn't totally used to the fact that this guy and I had shifted from wary opponents to devoted lovers, and every demonstration he made of that devotion came with a little thrill.

Maybe it did for Malcolm too. His voice dropped, languidly smooth. "If there's something worthy of your loyalty in your mother, you'll find it and bring it out. If you could manage that with me, no one else could possibly stand a chance. But until you know for sure it's there, you've got to look after yourself and the people you know can't defend themselves. And if you don't like going behind her back, you can blame it on me for telling you to."

I had to roll my eyes at him. "Right. Because I'd definitely have no choice but to follow your orders."

He chuckled. "I didn't say you had to *believe* I'm to blame." His hand shifted, tipping so the backs of his fingers rested against my skin. He trailed them up my arm. "But really, how much time have *you* been able to take to recover from the shit you've been put through in the last six months? Why the hell would your mother deserve more consideration and compassion than you do? You just never think about yourself and what you'd want." He glanced over at Declan. "Does she?"

Declan had been watching us, his bright hazel eyes intent. He shut his book. "No," he said. "She really doesn't."

"You're one to talk," I pointed out.

He shrugged, an amused smile curving his lips. "It takes one to know one."

Malcolm's fingers had traveled all the way up to the side of my neck. He unfurled them, teasing them into my hair and over my scalp. "So, clearly it's up to us to make sure you're looked after."

He closed the last short distance between us and claimed my mouth. I'd been affected by the Nightwood scion's kiss even when I'd wanted nothing to do with him in any other way, and it was only better now that we were on the same side. A tingle shot through me from head to toe. Malcolm eased closer, aligning his body with mine with a press of perfect, solid heat.

Declan cleared his throat. "I'm not sure this is the best place for that kind of 'looking after.' There are a couple of staff around."

Malcolm kissed me again, stretching out the moment, and then looked over his shoulder at the Ashgrave scion. "They're not allowed in every part of this building, are they? You've got your office."

Declan's gaze slid from him to me, an eager longing sparking inside it. There was a question in it too—whether this was what I wanted. But I hadn't found anything useful about my mother, and damn it, I could use this incredibly potent reminder of how much some people in the world were willing to offer me. And the thought of hooking up here in the building that belonged to my fiercest enemies without them ever knowing made me a little giddy.

I tipped my head slightly in acknowledgement. Malcolm grinned. Declan shoved his book onto the shelf without any further prompting needed and motioned for us to follow him.

Malcolm let go of me as we stepped into the hall, but he stayed close enough that I could feel his presence behind me with rising anticipation. Declan pushed open his office door and ushered us inside. As he spoke the casting words to ensure the room's security, I had a few moments to take in the space, which he'd made his own: practical but tasteful wooden furniture, books and pages of notes stacked on the desk. Then his voice fell away with a quiver of magic snapping into place, and Malcolm pulled me into another kiss.

His mouth devoured mine, his hands roaming down my sides, and Declan came up behind me, a more measured though no less passionate presence. The Ashgrave scion touched the small of my back with a subtle caress and lowered his mouth to my shoulder, just above the collar of my dress. A shaky breath escaped me.

Declan slid the zipper of my dress down, and Malcolm tugged the sleeves right off my shoulders. I reached for his shirt, fumbling with the buttons as he stroked my breasts. He sank down to capture one in his mouth and then the other, the flick of his tongue making me gasp with the jolts of pleasure.

Declan turned my head toward him and leaned over to capture my mouth for himself. His tongue tangled around mine as Malcolm's drew my nipples to even stiffer peaks. Declan's hands came to rest on my waist, my ass flush against his thighs, the solid length of his erection unmistakable even through the layers of fabric between us.

I couldn't resist squirming against it until he groaned. His grip on my body tightened, his fingers working to ease up the skirt of the dress. With each whisper of the fabric up over my thighs, the desire pooling between my legs pulsed hotter.

Malcolm hummed approvingly. He raised his head and dropped his hand at the same time, cupping my sex just as Declan tugged my dress up to the level of my panties. I clutched the open sides of his shirt as bliss rushed up from my core. Malcolm gave me that familiar cocky grin and swiveled the heel of his hand against my clit until I trembled.

"Let's see just how well we *can* look after our heir of Bloodstone," he said, catching Declan's eyes and then mine. "So many possibilities when there are two of us to join forces."

A breathless laugh tumbled out of me. "You make it sound like warfare."

"Not a battle. Only a challenge." His eyebrows arched, and then he was dropping to his knees in front of me, but not at all like the one other time he'd knelt for me. My chest hitched at the heated flow of his breath down the front of my dress. He came to a stop at my bared panties and kissed me through them. Oh, God.

"Worth the wait," he murmured, and yanked my panties down. As he brought his mouth to my clit, Declan teased a finger between my legs from behind. The tip traced over my slit. Two streams of pleasure collided with a resonance that made me moan.

"That's right," Malcolm said under his breath between kisses and skillful swipes of his tongue. "The best we can give you inside and out. But I want to be the one who prepares you. You shouldn't have to worry about a thing, Glinda."

With the fond nickname, his hand was already dipping to follow Declan's. He spoke a casting word of his own invention, but the meaning was obvious in an instant. A shiver of energy flowed up into my channel, protecting me—but also tingling through my sex with a pleasure all its own. He'd added his own flourish on the usual spell.

He withdrew his fingers at the rasp of Declan's zipper. I edged my feet farther apart instinctively as Malcolm returned his full attention to massaging every shred of pleasure he could from my mound with his mouth. A teasing brush of his teeth brought a gasp to my lips, and then Declan was aligning his cock with my slick entrance.

I dug my fingers into Malcolm's shoulders, leaning forward, and Declan plunged into me. The heady friction of him filling me brought a fresh wave of magical stimulation alongside the physical. The tingles radiated all through me.

He peppered kisses across my shoulder blades as he found his pace. The rhythm of his thrusts rocked me against Malcolm's mouth. The Nightwood scion ate me up, the Ashgrave scion filled me to the hilt, and between the two of them I couldn't have felt more adored. Ecstasy swelled and swelled inside me until I felt as if I'd be swept beneath it, drowned in the undertow. But what a way to go.

"Please," I mumbled, not totally sure what I was pleading for, but Declan gave it to me all the same. He bucked into me faster, deeper, and propelled me over the edge. I tumbled into bliss with a shudder and a cry, and his breath stuttered as he followed me.

Malcolm urged my pleasure higher with the swirl of his tongue until Declan withdrew. Then the Nightwood scion was standing, spinning us around together. He set me on the desk with a thud of toppled books, yanking his slacks open at the same time. His mouth crashed into mine as his cock rammed into me, my own musky flavor unexpected but not unpleasant on his lips.

I kissed him back hard, arcing into him, chasing the second release I could already sense on the horizon. Malcolm tugged me tight against him. Each thrust came with an aftershock of pleasure that radiated through me, building and building until my eyes rolled back with the final wave of it. Malcolm groaned with a jerk of his hips, and I knew he'd joined me.

He stayed bent over me for a few moments longer. His next kisses were tender, charting a path from my mouth along my jaw. Then he glanced down at the desk.

"Sorry," he said to Declan. "I made a bit of a mess of your office."

Declan laughed, slipping in beside me so he could steal another kiss for himself. "A minor sacrifice to see her looking this satisfied."

I grasped the front of his shirt, pulling him closer as I leaned my head against Malcolm's arm, wanting to include both of them in my embrace. I *was* satisfied... and yet somehow beneath the lingering ripples of bliss, a pang was echoing through me. Wanting more than I knew how to ask for.

# CHAPTER FOURTEEN

*Connar*

I was just coming out of class when the prickling of a magical alert shot over my skin. I froze at the top of the stairs and found just enough wherewithal to move to the side, out of the way of my classmates.

Days ago, after my fellow scions had snapped me out of the spell my parents had placed on me, I'd cast a spell of my own at the far end of the road into the university to detect my mother's presence. She had a habit of turning up on campus without warning, and I didn't want to risk her catching me unaware. I'd known it would only be a matter of time before she came to check on me in person —and I'd been dreading the moment.

She was on her way to see me now. It'd been easy enough to avoid her when all I was faced with were texts and phone calls. Face-to-face…

I was still a scion. I had enough dignity not to run and

hide, which would put my friends in the line of fire too. It was my job to deal with her. But that wasn't likely to happen without a fight, and one I wasn't sure I could win. Scion or not, she had just as much power as I did and decades more experience at using it.

Assuming she was driving, it wouldn't take her long to make it to campus. I propelled myself into motion, hurrying down the stairs. As I went, I grabbed my phone from my pocket and sent a quick text to Rory. If this confrontation didn't go well, I wanted her to at least be prepared for the outcome.

*My mother's on her way to see me. I'm going to do everything I can to make her back off.*

Her reply was almost instant. *Where are you meeting her? I'll be there for backup.*

My heart wrenched, both with affection for how quickly she'd offered her help and fear of what might happen if she gave it. My thumbs darted over the keypad.

*No need. I'm the one who should handle it. I just wanted you to have some forewarning.*

*I'm not going to need forewarning for anything,* she wrote back, so firmly I could practically hear her determined tone as I read the words. *I'm not letting her mess with your head again. I'll stay out of the way and simply be ready in case you need extra magical support. She'll never know I was involved.*

I hesitated, my fingers tightening around the phone as I came out into the cool autumn air on the green. I didn't want Rory taking that risk, even if she could tip the balance in my favor.

In my silence, she sent another message. *If you DON'T tell me where you're meeting her, I'll just have to race around campus until I find you, and I definitely won't be able to stay out of sight that way.*

Damn it. My lips twitched between a smile and a frown. Rory obviously wasn't willing to accept any arguments.

*I'm going over to the parking lot at the front of the school,* I wrote back. *That seems like a good place to make a stand. But whatever happens, please don't make yourself a target. It'll be easier for her to get to me if she can threaten you.*

*I understand. I won't give her a chance to hurt me OR you.*

My chest constricted as I strode around Killbrook Hall. My mother's car was just emerging from the shadows of the trees where the road passed through the woods. I came to a halt on the grass in between the lot and the front steps of the hall. A series of hasty casting words tumbled from my mouth.

If we were going to face off, it might as well be here. We'd be in view of the junior dorms and the staff offices on this side of the building, and that might moderate my mother's actions somewhat. She wouldn't want to grapple with me too openly. And I had multiple avenues to retreat if I needed to. I tried not to think about where Rory might position herself and how well she'd actually stay concealed.

My mother parked to the side of the lot, in front of me. I spoke another casting word under my breath, testing and bolstering the protective walls I'd drawn up around me—to deflect any magic she threw at me, to prevent her from coming physically closer than I'd prefer. After the way she'd possessed my mind so completely last time, I wasn't taking any chances.

She came around the car and stopped by the hood, studying me with her chilly eyes. If she'd bothered to check, she'd be able to sense the protections I'd cast. Her mouth set in a thin line of displeasure. The sinewy muscles in her arms flexed as she set her hands on her hips.

"You seem to be expecting me," she said.

I shrugged, much more casually than matched the tension churning inside me. "I had a hunch. What did you want?"

She looked a little taken aback at having her usual bluntness thrown back at her. Her jaw worked. "We clearly have a lot to discuss about your future and our family's goals. Why don't we find somewhere private to talk? None of this needs to be aired in public."

*She* didn't want it aired in public, she meant. That was my one point of leverage.

"No," I said. "If there's something you need to say to me, you can say it right here."

I didn't need to tell her why I wasn't interested in going anywhere with her. She'd remember what had happened the last time I'd gotten into her car just as well as I did.

My mother let out a sigh. "Don't be ridiculous, Connar. You're wasting both of our time."

"I'm just making sure I don't lose even more of my time than before."

"So, that's your current stance? You're simply detaching yourself from the family?"

I folded my arms over my chest. "I'm still just as much a Stormhurst as you are. I'm also old enough to make my own choices—and to decide that when it comes to personal matters, I'm not going to let anyone else control me. What good would I be as a scion if I wasn't willing to defend myself?"

Her gaze turned into a glower, but she didn't have a quick retort to that point. She *didn't* want a weak heir, as much as she'd also have wanted me to fall in line with her intentions. I sure as hell wouldn't have been worthy of becoming baron if I were willing to let anyone, even my parents, turn me into a virtual zombie.

"All I want to do is talk," she said, in a tone I didn't believe at all. For good reason, because an instant later, her lips moved with a subtle casting.

Subtle but not soft. It hit the barriers I'd cast around me with enough impact for the magic to fray and a jitter of energy to lash against me. I spoke the walls more solid as quickly as I could, but she was already casting again—

And a tickle of other magic brushed past me from behind, flowing into the shields and layering them twice as strong. I imagined I caught a hint of Rory's sweetness in it.

Her support wasn't blatant enough for my mother to catch on. The next spell the baron cast rattled the walls a little but didn't come close to breaking them. My mother's brow knit. She started to walk toward me instead, and I summoned even more of my magic into my casting.

"That's close enough," I said in warning. Much farther and she'd bump against the invisible but solid first line of defense. Another stream of what I assumed was Rory's magic wafted past me to contribute—and another on top of that, from a slightly different direction. She must have called on additional reinforcements.

My mother spat out a few quick casting words, but even a baron couldn't shatter the combined efforts of three scions. She scanned the area around me before returning her attention to me with a frown, obviously puzzled by the strength I was showing but uncertain of its source. She might have been able to guess I had help, but she couldn't point to it.

"If you don't stop this idiocy now, our next conversation is going to go much worse—for you," she said.

"I'm willing to take that chance."

And she wasn't willing to risk embarrassing herself with any more failure. Her gaze flicked to the windows looking over the parking lot, and her jaw clenched tighter. With an icy flash of her eyes, she spun on her heel and stalked back to her car.

I stayed where I was, my heart thumping heavy in my chest, until well after her car had pulled out of sight. When I was sure she wasn't going to return, I brought down the barriers around me and headed back to the green.

Rory came out one of the back doors of Killbrook

Hall just as I walked around the corner of the building. Declan was right behind her. She hurried straight to me and threw her arms around me without a word.

I hugged her back, choking up at the tremor that ran through her shoulders. "Hey," I said. "I'm okay. We held her off."

"She *tried* to force you," Rory said against my shirt. "Lord only knows what she was planning on doing if she'd managed to drag you out of view."

"She didn't manage, though. If she tries again, I'll make sure she doesn't." I kissed the top of her head. "Thank you."

"Of course." She looked up at me, her eyes gone watery, and raised one of her hands to touch the side of my face. Her voice dipped low enough that only I and maybe Declan could have heard her. "I love you. I don't want to lose you again."

The emotion in my throat swelled. It took me a second to answer her. "I love you too."

I kissed her on the lips then, gently but without hesitation, because I could. Because there wasn't any reason to hide how I felt about this woman. If I could have kept kissing her for the rest of my life…

Thinking along that line didn't do me any good. I was just more grateful than I could say that I'd get to spend the rest of my life ruling beside her in our own pentacle.

Beside her and the guy standing a little awkwardly off to the side. I eased back from Rory to give Declan his fair acknowledgement. "Thank you too. You could have gotten in a lot of trouble with the barons if she'd realized you were helping me."

Declan waved that comment off. "I was careful. It was more important to make sure she didn't manipulate you again."

"I would have called everyone to lend a hand in case we needed it," Rory said, "but Malcolm's off dealing with some family business of his own, and Jude..." Her mouth slanted downward.

Jude didn't need any more reminders of what he was lacking right now. I nodded. "The three of us together was more than enough."

"If she comes back, let us know right away. We're all in this with you." She bobbed up on her toes to give me one last peck. "Now I'd better get back to my assignment for this afternoon."

As she left, Declan caught my eyes. "There's something I think we should talk about," he said. "Do you have a few minutes—or better, more?"

Something about his tone made my body tense. "Sure. I don't have my next class for a few hours. What's up?"

He gestured for me to follow him. Rather than going into the scion lounge, he made for the Stormhurst Building. My stomach sank as we ducked into the stairwell that led to the boiler room. We'd only used this space before to talk during extremely dire and sensitive circumstances. Whatever Declan had to say, it was big—and potentially dangerous.

And he hadn't looped Rory in on the conversation, so

it wasn't scion business but something specifically to do with me.

In the dim, warm space, Declan swiped his hand over his already slicked-back hair. The pipes around us hummed.

"Maybe I should have brought this to you as soon as it came up," he said with a regretful twist of his mouth. "I was hoping I could find some kind of confirmation, to be sure of what I heard, but I'm pretty sure even as it is. And I think it's important that you know now that your mother is starting to escalate her attempts to bring you in line."

"You heard what?"

He looked at the floor and then back at me. "During the gala the other night at the Stormhurst residence—I was able to overhear your parents talking when they thought they were alone. They weren't happy about your absence, and your mother indicated that if you continued to resist their influence… they could heal your brother and have him replace you as scion."

*What?* I stared at him for several seconds before I found my voice. "That's impossible. After… after the way I hurt him, the doctors said there was no way he'd be able to recover enough to do any significant casting."

"Did you see those doctors? Were you part of that conversation?"

I sucked in a breath and paused. I hadn't, had I? The goading session our parents had put us through, ending with me attacking Holden, had left me so drained and ill that I'd been pretty out of it for days afterward. It was only when I was steady on my feet again that my mother had told me, with an edge of malicious glee, that I'd taken Holden completely out of the running as scion.

I'd just assumed—the idea that they wouldn't even have *tried* to help him heal seemed so inconceivable—

A wrenching sensation tore through my chest. Fucking hell. All this time, he might have been walking again, talking properly again. Why had I ever trusted them on that when they'd proven the ruthless lengths they were willing to go to in order to get their way, over and over?

"No," I said quietly. "They told me after the fact."

"Then I think there's a good chance they didn't make much, if any attempt, at the time," Declan said. "You could have your brother back. But I suspect your parents would find some way to put *you* out of commission if they decide that's necessary."

They'd destroy me before they saved him. Yeah, that sounded about right. A rough laugh escaped me. "Only if they can get to me."

But how could I stand back and let my brother continue to live with the horrific injuries I'd dealt him if he could be healed? I owed him—so much. And now I finally had the chance to make up for my weakness back then.

# CHAPTER FIFTEEN

*Rory*

As I stood alone in front of my wardrobe's mirror, I was hit by a fresh pang of loss. My mother had called me yesterday telling me there was an official function she was going to pick me up to attend, and that I should dress to reflect my status. Now I was second-guessing every outfit I tried on.

A month ago, I could have asked my familiar's opinion, or my Nary friend and dormmate's. Now both Deborah and Shelby were out of reach. Not that either of them had been experts on fearmancer fashion standards, but I'd still have welcomed some sort of friendly outside input.

Shelby, at least, was only distant rather than gone completely. I could have sent her a barrage of selfies asking for her thoughts, but that seemed obnoxious, especially when she was probably busy rehearsing her prestigious orchestra pieces. If she could figure out how to play to their standard, I should be able to figure out the standards for a Bloodstone scion.

Finally, I settled on a knee-length silk dress with a subtle diamond pattern and a trim cardigan to make sure I didn't completely freeze my ass off. The October day outside was sunny but crisp, my windowpane cold to my touch.

I slung my purse over my shoulder, took one last look at myself with a furtive pat of my hair, and headed out of the dorm. I had no idea what this "function" was even about—or for that matter, where it was happening. My mother had been very short on the details. The other scions hadn't known anything about it, so apparently it wasn't official in an entire pentacle sort of way.

That fact didn't stop my pulse from kicking up a notch as I set off for the parking lot where I was supposed to meet her. I held my head high and touched my glass dragon charm on its chain where I'd tucked it under the neckline of my dress. The necklace might not contain any more magic after I'd used up the illusion-detecting spell on it to help break Connar out of his parents' brainwashing, but it still offered a little comfort. Whatever happened with my birth mother, I'd still had a Mom and Dad who'd given their all to do right by me.

I reached the lot just as my mother's gold Lexus was pulling to a stop in one of the spots. Maggie leapt out of the back seat to open the front passenger door for me, and my grip on my purse strap tightened instinctively. I managed to give her a tight smile and slipped in next to my mother.

Baron Bloodstone looked over my outfit and nodded with apparent approval. “I appreciate you joining me for this, Persephone,” she said as she swung the car around. “I think it’s especially important for people to see our solidarity today.”

“I want to be involved in the business as much as I can.” I peered out the window. “Where exactly are we going?”

“Just into town. A shift like this needs to be carried out step by step.”

Something in her tone made my skin prickle. “A shift?” I didn’t think she was talking about a physical transformation like Connar into his dragon form.

“Better if you see it as we move forward.”

More vagueness. I tamped down on the urge to squirm in my seat. “You didn’t need to pick me up, then. I could have walked it.”

“Not much solidarity in that,” Maggie piped up from behind me, making me want to strangle her.

My mother’s lips curled upward. “Yes. I think it’s best for us to arrive together. Especially since preparations may be a bit… chaotic.”

That didn’t sound ominous at all. I clasped my hands together in my lap, paying even closer attention to our surroundings now.

The forest that stretched along the road between campus and town tapered off. A couple of blacksuits were standing by the road at the edge of town, with a nod to our car as we passed them. Was this connected to the group of them I'd seen puttering around the outskirts before? The woman I'd talked to had only mentioned checking wards. That didn't seem to warrant any kind of special appearance by the barons.

I'd expected that we'd park outside one of the fearmancer-owned establishments where most of the students came on their spare time. Instead, my mother pulled over to the curb just before the main square with its ring of benches and aged statue of the place's first mayor.

A crowd was already gathering in the open space there, focused on a low stage that had been set up opposite the statue. I didn't recognize most of them, but I spotted a few families from the gala the barons had hosted in the swarm. From their bearing and clothes, I suspected a lot of the others were fearmancers too. What the hell was going on?

A few blacksuits were standing on the stage. We got out of the car, and my mother motioned for me to walk next to her up to it. Maggie trailed behind us.

As we eased around the crowd, I spotted figures coming over to see what the commotion was about who definitely weren't fearmancers. There was the couple who ran the restaurant I'd eaten at with Jude the other day, and a woman from the ice cream place Imogen, Shelby, and I had frequented during the summer, and a guy who was often on cash at the grocery store. They hung back at the fringes, craning their necks to see what the fuss was about.

It appeared to be about us. The low chatter carrying

through the crowd faded as my mother and I climbed onto the stage. Baron Nightwood was just stepping up at the other end. Within a couple minutes, Barons Stormhurst and Killbrook had joined us too, the blacksuits flanking us.

No sign of Declan. They'd completely left him out of whatever this was. The other barons hadn't brought their scions, but I guessed when it came to Connar and Jude, that wasn't at all surprising. Maybe my mother had only asked me to come to make some sort of point about my loyalty to her or her control over me.

My stomach started to churn. Baron Bloodstone squeezed my shoulder and left me in the middle of the stage to step up to the microphone up front. Baron Nightwood moved to join her.

"It's wonderful to see so many of you here to celebrate what I'd like to see as the dawning of a new era," my mother said into the microphone, her voice pealing out clear and vibrant, no sign of the hesitation or the discomfort I'd seen in her just days ago. "What we're about to do here today will allow us to step out of the shadows and take the role we deserve in this world."

She stepped to the side to let Nightwood have a turn. He offered the audience a slow smile. "No longer are we going to hide from the feeble beings that surround us. We will own our magic. We will show them that we can take whatever we want. And today we take this town. From now on, we make the rules here. Anyone who challenges those rules will face the consequences." He snapped his fingers with a quick casting word, and flames shot up over his extended hand.

Applause burst out among the fearmancers with a few cries of support. It nearly drowned out the gasp of someone standing on the sidelines. A "What the hell are they talking about?" reached my ears.

My stomach had outright lurched with the announcement. Now it felt as if it'd plummeted right through the bottom of the stage. They'd just publicly acknowledged their magic to all the Naries who'd come over to watch—they were announcing it to the whole town. They were turning this place into a larger version of the horror my classmates were already enacting on campus.

As if to put proof to that thought, one of the fearmancers near the edge of the gathering turned to face a Nary man who was pushing toward the stage. "No one approved this event," the guy was saying. "You need to—"

The fearmancer's lips moved, and the man's legs jerked out from under him. He fell flat on his ass. When he tried to speak again, a conjured toad leapt into his mouth. He shuddered.

"And so it begins," my mother said, clapping her hands. A fresh wave of applause broke out. My legs locked in place.

I wanted to shout out a protest, to defend the townspeople from whatever else the mages were going to unleash on them now. But I didn't have a hope in hell of stopping the developing chaos on my own. And if I embarrassed my mother in front of all these people, I could kiss any progress I'd made with her good-bye.

My teeth gritted. I *had* to see this through, as painful as it was. It didn't do any good charging into a fight you couldn't win yet. I'd be failing the people around me if I did that.

I just wished I could tell them that I'd fight for them as soon as I had the means to ensure victory.

My mother turned, beckoning me up to join her. I forced my feet to move. Nausea clutched me from throat to gut as I took my place beside her, the other two barons coming up to join their colleagues too. It took everything I had in me to push my mouth into a smile. The hollers of encouragement hit me like thrown knives.

What if I never found a way to win? What if this just kept getting worse and worse? They couldn't really hope to extend their power over the whole *world*, could they? I didn't even know how they'd manage to control just this one small town.

I clung to that idea when we eased back on the stage. The moment my mother stepped away from the other barons, I touched her arm.

"How are we going to stop them from spreading the word to people outside the town? We're not ready to take on a whole police force of Naries."

My mother gave me a smile that looked amused. "We're getting there. But for now, while we flex our strength, we're simply cutting them off from anyone they'd have wanted to call in against us. The blacksuits have set up wards all around the town. They won't be able to communicate with anyone outside those boundaries or cross them to escape."

So, they were stuck just as much as the Nary students on campus were. I held back a wince. As well as I could, I kept my tone conversational. "I'm surprised Declan wasn't part of this announcement. He is practically baron. He never mentioned to me that this was in the works."

My mother's chuckle came out dry and dark. Her voice came out lower. "Mr. Ashgrave has a ways to go before he can stand up with the rest of us. And an Ashgrave's opinion isn't worth much in general." She looked at me, her gaze abruptly intense. "His mother is the one who called the joymancers in on us all those years ago, you know."

I blinked. "What? But—they killed her."

"Yes. It wasn't a very smart move, was it? As if they'd ever see any of us as an ally. But she got off easy. It's because of her we both lost seventeen years of the life we should have had."

# CHAPTER SIXTEEN

*Rory*

In theory, I was eating tortellini in rosé sauce for dinner. In actuality, I was mostly pushing the noodles around on my plate while my stomach contorted into various unpleasant configurations. I hadn't managed to eat lunch right after the big announcement in town either, but I knew I should get some kind of sustenance into me. I wasn't going to help anyone if I died of starvation.

Of course, it wasn't like I'd managed to help many people in the last few weeks since the fearmancer world had started going even more to hell in the first place.

I finally convinced my throat to swallow a few mouthfuls, and then I had to stop or I might have puked it all back up again. As I scraped the remainder into the garbage, Cressida came into the dorm. She paused when she saw me and then walked over, stopping by the dining table. I rinsed my plate and set it in the sink with the other dishes the maintenance staff would handle. I wasn't in the mood to chat, not that Cressida was anyone I'd normally have chatted with anyway.

It appeared she was in the mood to chat me up, though. When I turned, she tipped her head with an awkward smile, twisting the end of her white-blond French braid between her fingers where she'd tugged it over her shoulder. The pink and purple streaks were starting to fade.

"Can we talk?" she asked, speaking in an undertone even though no one else was in the common room. "I… I think I'm ready to claim my side of our deal."

Our deal. When Lillian and the barons had set me up for Imogen's murder, I'd only convinced Cressida to provide her witness testimony on my behalf by engaging in a magical pact with her. I owed her a favor of her choice, as long as it was legal and within my power.

I hadn't expected her to call in that favor so soon, before I was even baron and could offer a heck of a lot more. What did she think I could do for her right now?

I didn't have much choice other than to find out. "In that case, of course," I said. "Let's use my room."

Cressida stepped into the space gingerly as if she wasn't sure it was quite safe. I managed to restrain myself from rolling my eyes. She and her friends had done a lot worse to me than I'd ever offered in retaliation. She didn't seem inclined to sit down, so I propped myself against my desk.

"We might as well get straight to the point," I said. "What do you need?"

She crossed her arms over her chest, keeping them rigid as if holding them back from outright hugging herself. She obviously didn't enjoy asking for this favor. For a few seconds, I thought she might say, "Never mind," and walk back out.

"You were there for the announcement in town," she said finally. "You know what's going on."

I nodded, doing my best to keep my expression impassive. I could vent to my fellow scions about my true feelings, but I wasn't going to trust Cressida with them.

"Well, I..." She shifted her weight. "The blacksuits are recruiting students from the university to help with the policing—to keep an eye out for any Naries in town who try to push back against fearmancer authority. I guess because we're so close by and we've got fewer commitments than the older mages. They're promising extra credit to people who participate, and it'll look good with the barons, so my parents want me to be a part of the program."

It took me a moment to decipher the unspoken problem. "But you don't want to."

Cressida ducked her head as if my comment had included any judgment. "I just don't like the idea. It feels... risky, being that public with our magic—not something I could ever take back if things go wrong. And I don't really want to be fighting with people, having to face off against them if they get combative."

"Can't you tell your parents that?"

She gave me a narrow look. "Can you tell *your* mother what you really think about the whole thing? They've already put my name in without asking me. If I pull out without a good reason, it'll look bad."

Maybe I hadn't spelled out my feelings, but my Nary sympathies hadn't exactly been a secret around campus. I could take her point. Her parents might not be barons, but that didn't mean they wouldn't crack down hard if they felt she was embarrassing the family.

"You need a good reason, then." I rubbed my mouth, my gaze sliding away from her as I considered. What reason could I give her that the blacksuits would see as valid rather than wishy-washy—that she couldn't simply come up with on her own? It wasn't as if we had any pre-existing friendship or professional partnership I could point to the way Malcolm often used "scion business" as an excuse.

"I just want you to get me out of it, one way or another. Without making me or my family look any less loyal. Can you handle that? I did get *you* out of a murder charge."

I couldn't stop myself from glowering at her then. "A murder I hadn't actually committed anyway. Give me some time to think about it. I don't want to promise anything if I can't come up with a good strategy. When I have an idea I think will work, I'll let you know, and you can decide if it's worth completing the deal for."

"That's fair." She bobbed her head a little awkwardly and slipped out of the room.

Leaving me with yet another conundrum to work out.

I flopped down on my bed and grimaced at the ceiling. If I *could* take care of the favor I owed Cressida this way, it'd be to my benefit. Get it over with so it wasn't hanging over me any longer. We weren't currently connected, but the request didn't have to come from me. Maybe I could arrange for one of the teachers to say they needed her for some special project? Although I didn't love the idea of having to rely on another party to see the deal through.

Malcolm's "scion business" tactic worked because people accepted that anything we were working on as a pentacle automatically trumped just about any other responsibility. What could trump serving the blacksuits—and by extension the barons—in their new program of intimidation and dominance? They hadn't specifically asked for Cressida, so the alternate responsibility didn't need to be *that* overwhelmingly larger…

An idea tickled up through my mind. Here at school, being a scion did trump just about anything else. So should anything that worked to our benefit. Cressida might not have any direct association with us now, but considering the chaos the campus had been thrown into lately, we could create new connections without anyone seeing them as resistance—even though the people we brought together might become part of a resistance down the road.

If this worked, I'd be making progress on two of my biggest problems in one.

A jolt of eager energy propelled me off the bed. Before I set down anything definite, I'd need to get permission from a higher authority, but the school authorities would serve just fine. And to bolster my case, I really should bring along another scion.

I grabbed my phone, my head spinning with the threads of the plan quickly snapping into place.

* * *

Jude let out a light huff as we reached the staff wing of Killbrook Hall. "So, this is my new lot in life," he said in a self-deprecating tone. "Poster boy for patheticness."

I nudged him with my elbow. "You're not pathetic. You just happen to have direct experience with the dangers we can face as scions. Experience that's public knowledge, unlike the crap the rest of us have dealt with."

"Hmm. Well, if this plan of yours lets us stick it to the barons, that'll make it worthwhile."

His demeanor was easy-going enough, but I didn't sense the playful energy that was so typical of him. He was still struggling with his casting, so much that he hadn't returned to any of his magical classes yet. Even if he didn't want to talk about it other than to joke, I could tell the loss was weighing on him more as time passed.

I took his hand and squeezed it, and he returned the gesture with a fond smile. "Just to be clear, I don't mind pitching in when you call on me," he said. "At least I'm doing something useful, one way or another."

"Just to be clear too, how much I want to spend time with you has nothing to do with how 'useful' you are."

"I know, Fire Queen." He swung our joined hands between us. "That's why you're my favorite."

I didn't think any of the other scions cared all that much about Jude's usefulness either, but maybe he was simply mocking himself again. I didn't have time to press the subject when we were just coming up to the headmistress's door.

Ms. Grimsworth answered a few seconds after my knock, but her face was clearly weary, a few stray strands drifting loose from her usually neat coil of hair. "Miss Bloodstone, Mr. Killbrook," she said with a nod, gesturing us in.

"I'm glad you could see us so quickly," I said. "What with, well, everything that's been going on here and around campus, I feel like the step we'd like to take is fairly urgent."

She eyed us as she took her seat behind her expansive desk. I settled into one of the firm armchairs across from her, Jude doing the same.

"What exactly is this step?" the headmistress asked.

I had to choose my words carefully here. I motioned between Jude and me with a broad enough sweep to encompass the scions who weren't with us as well. "The five of us feel that in light of the recent attack and the increased hostile magical activity in the area in general, it'd make sense for us to recruit some of our classmates as a sort of protective force. The Scions' Guard. To give us increased security on campus."

"I definitely wouldn't want any of my fellow scions to find themselves in as precarious a position as I did," Jude put in. "And I'd *really* prefer not to find myself facing anything similar."

Ms. Grimsworth hummed to herself, tapping a pen against the edge of her desk. "And what exactly do you envision this 'Guard' doing? How many students would be involved? How large a responsibility would it be?"

"Nothing that should interfere with their studies," I said quickly. "A lot of the time they wouldn't even need to be directly with us. We'd each pick four or five people we trust to have our best interests at heart, and expect them to keep an extra watch for any activity on campus that could affect us, to be prepared to help defend us if any dangerous situations arise in classes we share, and we'd call on one or a few of them to join us if we were venturing somewhere we felt we needed extra protectors."

Jude leaned back in his seat, stretching out his legs. "It'd be to their benefit too. They'd get the prestige of being chosen by a scion and proving their worth to us and our families. It'd help us decide who we might want to continue working with in future."

The headmistress's gaze stayed contemplative. "Is this your initiative or your parents' idea?"

"Our parents don't even know we're thinking about this," I said. "There's no need to involve them when they're so busy handling this huge transition. I'm sure they'll appreciate us making our own preparations. We just wanted to get official approval from you before we got started, since we'll be organizing the Guard on campus."

"Much appreciated," Ms. Grimsworth said, her cool voice turning wry. She glanced toward the window, knitting her brow for a moment before returning her attention to us. "Well, I can't see any reason why it should be a problem for you to go ahead with this 'Guard' of yours. I expect you'll have many takers. I assume you'll be looking for students whose values align with your own, as well as having strong abilities."

Something about the question set my nerves on alert, but I didn't get a hostile vibe from her. No, it made me remember seeing her on the first day when the new group of Nary students had arrived, frowning as she led them through their tour.

She'd never expressed any definite feelings about the Naries one way or the other, but she knew perfectly well from watching my actions here at the university what *my* values had always been.

"That would make the most sense, I think," I said tentatively, watching her expression.

Her lips formed a thin smile. "Then I expect they should be a very welcome addition to student life. Certainly, if the need arises for you to have allies on your side for any reason, I'll be glad to see you so prepared."

"As will we," Jude said with a grin, getting up. He gave Ms. Grimsworth a half-hearted salute.

I rose too, still wondering if I was imagining the implications I thought I was picking up in her words.

"Thank you," I said.

Ms. Grimsworth held out her hand to shake mine. As she gripped my fingers, she held my gaze with a glint in hers. "I look forward to seeing a call for order at a time like this, however small it starts out."

That comment and the intentness of her gaze

convinced me. I walked out of her office with a tickle of nervous elation running through me.

The headmistress wasn't just okay with us recruiting students to support us. If I was right, she'd be perfectly happy to see us use those allies to push back against the barons' plans when we had the chance.

# CHAPTER SEVENTEEN

*Rory*

I did already have a few allies on campus, even if they weren't ones I could draw into our Scions' Guard. When Professor Razeden had a break in between Desensitization sessions, I went down to the basement of Nightwood Tower to consult with him.

"I can see why you'd make this move," he said, knowing but discreet, after I'd explained about the group we were assembling. "Is there some way you feel I can help?"

"That's why I'm here. I was hoping…" I looked down at my hands, clasped together in my lap where I was sitting on the bench across from him. "I realize there are certain expectations of confidentiality, so I wouldn't ask you to tell me exactly what you've seen from any specific student. But it would be really helpful if you can think of anyone whose sessions have shown signs of distrusting the barons or the new policies. And I'd like to give you a list of people we're considering, so you can tell me if you've seen anything that would make you think any of them might be hostile toward the scions or particularly happy about how things have been going."

Razeden considered me. "You're looking not just to find guards but people who might campaign on your side."

That was a polite way of putting it. I gave him a tight smile. "Something like that. I'm sure you can understand why. No one wants to stand up to the barons when they think they're alone. If we can get a bunch of people who recognize how harmful these steps could be for not just the Naries but the fearmancers too, maybe we can get my mother and the other barons to listen."

I thought the professor's expression turned skeptical, but he didn't voice any of those doubts. *I* doubted whether the barons would really listen too. But we had to start there, and if speaking up as a group didn't work, then we'd see what we could do with whatever leverage we had by then.

"I'll need to go over my notes, but I can come up with a list of my recommendations based on what I've seen in the sessions," he said. "And I can check over your list for any reasons to be concerned. If I have them for you tomorrow morning, would that be a reasonable timeframe?"

"That would be amazing," I said, getting up. After the meeting with Ms. Grimsworth yesterday, the other scions and I had gotten started organizing our Guard right away, but we hadn't wanted to rush when it came to deciding who to trust. We only had a few people officially on board so far.

I handed Razeden the list I'd written of our candidates, and he tucked it into his pocket. "Come by around nine, and we'll have time to discuss it."

I headed back to Ashgrave Hall with raised spirits. The sight of a couple of juniors harassing a Nary student who was scurrying to her dorm made my stomach twist, but maybe things wouldn't have to stay like that for very much longer. There was strength in numbers, and we were building those numbers now.

Just inside the door, I headed down a flight of stairs of the main basement. Malcolm had managed to talk maintenance into giving us scions another room down below, and we'd spent a good part of yesterday evening redistributing the supply boxes that had been stacked there into the other rooms along the dim hall. The room was still pretty bare, but it held a couple sofas and several armchairs at one end and a large mat I suspected Connar had "borrowed" from the fitness center at the other. One side for talking, one side for action. This was going to be the Scions' Guard headquarters for the time being.

Even though we were just getting started, it was already filling up. Victory and Cressida were sitting on one of the sofas kitty-corner from the Stormhurst scion, talking through something with him with intent tones. They glanced over at my entrance, Victory tipping her head in acknowledgement and Cressida offering me an actual if small smile.

My first two choices for the Guard probably would have looked strange to anyone who knew our history. But I owed Cressida this—and while she might not have held a lot of respect for Naries, she obviously didn't see torturing them as fun either. Victory I'd asked because she'd trusted me enough to tip me off to the new Nary policy when it'd still been a partial secret, and because her family didn't seem to be caught up in supporting the barons' current moves. Whether she liked me or not, she knew I could get things done and that those things aligned with her goals better than anything the barons were up to right now.

They were both strong mages. Maybe more importantly, if I suggested anything they thought would turn the majority of fearmancers against any cause we stood up for, they wouldn't hesitate to let me know in blatant terms.

If either of them thought it was odd that I hadn't included the third member of their usual trio, they hadn't mentioned it. I'd considered Sinclair, but only for a matter of seconds. She'd been in on the secret during its earliest stages and hadn't shown any signs of unease about how she was bolstering her power. Malcolm had spotted her parents at the gala, fawning over ours.

Malcolm himself was standing at the edge of the mat with the one guy he'd picked out for his contingent so far, motioning with his hands as if demonstrating a casting. And Declan was in the corner in hushed conversation with a teenage boy who looked like a younger, slightly stockier version of himself—his brother Noah.

"I don't think it's a good idea," the Ashgrave scion was saying when I came over.

His brother pulled a face and then looked hopefully toward me. "Maybe we need a second opinion. Do you think juniors should be excluded from the Guard?"

I glanced between the two of them. Declan's stern expression told me exactly where he stood on the subject. "Shouldn't you be one of the people being guarded?" I hedged. "You're practically a scion yourself."

"That's what I've been trying to explain to him," Declan said.

Noah rolled his eyes. "It doesn't make any sense. I'm *not* the scion, and unless something happens to you, I never will be. And since I'm not a conniving jackass, I'd like to make sure nothing happens to you. I've been near the top of my classes since I started my official schooling. I've got three strengths just like you do. And I probably picked up at least a few techniques in Paris that they don't focus on here. Who better to have on your Guard?"

He might have been more brash than I could imagine Declan ever having been, but he shared his older brother's ability to make a determined appeal to logic.

"Okay," I said, meeting Declan's eyes. "I think he's making a solid case."

Declan let out an exasperated breath. "The barons have already targeted him once to get to me. He should be staying out of the way as much as possible, not going *out* of his way to put himself between me and them."

"I haven't fallen for any tricks since then, have I?" Noah

pointed out. "And believe me, it's not because no one's tried to one-up me. I've stayed off on the sidelines for too long while you've had to do all the work. I'm practically an adult now. I can handle taking some of the blows so you don't have to."

"Noah… You don't know just how bad things can get."

My heart ached for Declan, knowing how hard he'd worked to protect his brother. But at the same time I could understand where the younger guy was coming from.

"Why don't you take him on and see how it goes at first?" I suggested before the argument could go on. "Noah is obviously picking up on the political situation fast, and you're not going to find anyone more loyal. We're still deciding what the Guard does and who we ask to take on what tasks. It's not like you're sending him into battle or something. You might even be able to keep a closer eye on him."

Noah flashed me a grin. "There! Thank you! Not that I need to be watched over."

Declan sighed. He looked as if he might have been about to raise another complaint, but then he cuffed his brother lightly on the shoulder instead. "Let me think about it. I'm starting to wish stubbornness didn't run in the family. Didn't you have a class to get to?"

Noah checked the time on his phone and winced. "I can make it. I'll be back later." He shook his finger at Declan warningly and hightailed it out of the Guard room.

“Sorry,” I said to Declan. “I know that’s probably not what you’d have wanted me to say.”

“No, I’d have wanted you to say what you really think. Maybe I should give him a chance. It’s just hard not to feel like then I’m tossing away all the work I’ve done keeping him out of the politics and the rest.”

“Well, if he doesn’t *want* to be kept out… there’s only so much you’re going to be able to do. He’s his own person.”

Declan chuckled. “That he is.”

Just like Declan was his own person, separate from whatever legacy his family had left him, good or bad.

I wavered, but my mother’s revelation yesterday morning had been weighing on me ever since. I doubted the Ashgrave scion would enjoy hearing it any more than he’d liked me supporting Noah’s bid to join the Guard, but he needed to know what the other barons at least believed about his mother.

I motioned for him to follow me out of the room, away from the others. In the hall, I cast a quick spell to confirm no staff were in the supply rooms. Declan watched me with a frown.

“What’s wrong, Rory?”

I found I couldn’t jump straight into it. “The announcement in town yesterday—did you call out the other barons for going behind your back?”

His frown deepened. “They gave me the same bullshit answer about how this was all part of the original plan my aunt approved, so permission had already been given from the Ashgraves, and a bunch of other excuses.

Unfortunately, now that your mother's back, they feel even more secure in jerking me around, knowing I can't easily push back when it's four against one."

"But if they're breaking the rules of the pentacle..."

"If I can prove they've purposefully done that, you can be sure I'll bring them to task. Although with the way things are going, I'm not sure they even care about official sanctions—they might bluster right through them."

The speed with which the barons were moving forward with their plans was unsettling. And so were the other reasons they might be using to justify leaving Declan out.

I paused, grappling with the words, but there really was no pleasant way of saying it. "I thought you should know— My mother mentioned something yesterday after the announcement in town. According to her, the joymancer attack where they killed my father and your mother and those other fearmancers, and captured her and me... Your mother told them we'd be there."

Declan's gaze turned into a stare. "Why the hell would she have done that?"

I spread my hands. "I don't know. My mother seems to think it was to get back at her and my father for something or other—that your mother thought they'd attack them and not her. I don't even know if it's true. But if my mother believes it enough to be telling me, there's a pretty good chance the other barons think it's at least possible."

"I know my mother didn't agree with a lot of their attitudes, but to give the joymancers an opening to launch an assault—to outright betray the pentacle…" Declan rubbed his forehead. "I don't want to think she could have done that. But it's not as if I even remember her all that well. I'll have to—I'll have to talk to my dad and see if he knows anything about it."

"I'm sorry. I wish I hadn't needed to tell you."

"But you did need to, just like you needed to be honest about Noah." He touched my arm. "It's okay, Rory. If that's what they're saying, I have to know so I can find out what's true."

As we went back into the room, Victory and Cressida were just leaving. "Let us know when you've got anything for us to take on," Cressida said to me.

Connar had ambled over to see them out. "Your brother took off?" he said to Declan. "He seemed pretty keen."

"He is," Declan said. "He's only gone temporarily. We'll see how the rest goes." His gaze traveled through the room, but I got the impression he wasn't really seeing much of it. His attention was still on the revelation I'd just shared with him. "I think I'd better get going too. If any of you need anything, you know how to reach me."

He ducked out without another word.

"Is he all right?" Connar asked.

I hoped so. I wasn't going to spread around the story about the former Baron Ashgrave any farther. It was up to Declan when and what he told the other scions. "He's just got a lot on his mind, I think."

"Funny how much the same he and his brother are,

isn't it? Both of them working their asses off to try to protect the other."

Connar smiled, but his tone was bittersweet. I studied him, remembering the other topic I'd meant to bring up with my guys.

"I'm sure you and Holden would have been the same way if your parents hadn't forced you to fight."

Connar's face fell. "I'd like to think so."

I dropped my voice even lower to make sure Malcolm's friend wouldn't overhear. "I've been thinking about what you told me—about what Declan found out about him. I know getting enough access to your brother without your parents knowing is a big part of the problem, and I'm not sure how to help with that, but for finding a doctor who might be able to do the work—I could ask Professor Viceport if she knows any Physicality specialists who went into the medical side. She's said more than once that I should go to her if there's something she can contribute."

Connar brightened so eagerly I wished I'd thought to suggest the tactic when he'd first shared the news with me. "Do you think she'd come through?"

"I don't know. It'd be a big ask, to go against a baron's wishes for her own son, even if Viceport still feels really guilty about how she treated me… but it's worth a try, right? She isn't too fond of the barons anyway, so she's probably got friends who aren't either, who might be willing to pull one over on them."

"See what she says, and let me know. I'm not sure when or how we'd be able to arrange the treatment, but just having someone ready to carry it out would make a big difference."

I might have gone to call on my mentor right then, except my phone chimed. The last name I expected to see with the text was Baron Nightwood's. My body had gone rigid before I'd read any farther.

*Miss Bloodstone, your presence is requested at a meeting of barons in half an hour. To save you the trouble of coming out to the Fortress, we'll convene near the university.*

He sent a set of coordinates that showed a vacant area about a half a mile outside of town. A prickle ran down my back as I processed the message. He couldn't mean all of the barons—if Declan had gotten the same call, I'd have been hearing from him about it already. What the hell was this about?

A half an hour didn't give me much time to dawdle before heading over there. I bobbed up to give Connar a quick kiss and slipped out. On my way up the stairs, rather than replying to Malcolm's dad, I sent a quick message to my mother. If there was a meeting, the weirdest thing was him telling me about it rather than her.

*What's this meeting about?* I typed. *Are you okay?*

*I'm perfectly fine*, she wrote back. *But what meeting are you talking about?*

My gut knotted. *She* didn't know about it? What was Baron Nightwood playing at?

I gave her the gist of his summons. *I don't know what he wants. I thought you'd be part of it.*

*I will be. Send me those coordinates. Tell him you're*

*coming, and drive nearby, but don't arrive until I let you know I'm almost there.*

I didn't know whether to be relieved that she was coming or worried about what it meant that Baron Nightwood had tried to call me out behind her back. Both reactions seemed reasonable. The whole situation was unnerving.

Following her instructions, I drove most of the way to what appeared to be a stretch of abandoned farmland and parked by a rusted silo. Her next text came five minutes later. *Go ahead. I'll be right there.*

With a stutter of my pulse, I drove the last short distance to a grassy laneway that ended by a partly collapsed wooden fence. The Barons Nightwood, Stormhurst, and Killbrook were waiting by their cars there. Nightwood straightened up as I got out, but before he could even start speaking, my mother's Lexus rumbled over to join us. Nightwood's jaw twitched.

My mother sprang out and crossed the grass to us in a few brisk strides. The cool wind tugged at her hair. She must have jumped in the car without worrying about the weather, because she had no jacket on over her sleeveless dress, but her glare gave no sign that she was fazed by the chill.

"A meeting of the barons involving my daughter, and I wasn't looped in? Don't tell me my invitation got lost in the mail."

The vehemence in her voice surprised me. Yes, the whole set-up was weird, but these were her friends, her allies—and she sounded as if she were speaking to enemies.

It hadn't been that hard to switch the way she thought about Lillian, though. The paranoia that had wormed through her thoughts since her rescue had made her suspicious of just about everyone. Maybe she'd had her anxieties about even the other barons.

"Althea," Nightwood said in a cajoling voice. "We'd have spoken about this in just a little while. It simply seemed like a conflict of interest to address a concern that affects all of us when of course you'll be inclined to take your daughter's side."

My mother folded her arms over her chest. "I won't be if she's wrong. I should have some say in that too. What's the concern?"

"This 'Scions' Guard' she's spearheading," Baron Stormhurst spat out. The look she gave me was just shy of a glower. "It's above and beyond acceptable limits for the pentacle of scions to be arranging themselves a small army."

Maybe my underlying intentions hadn't been quite so hidden. Not that I was going to admit she was on the right track. "It's not an *army*," I said, with as much disdain for the idea as I could muster. "We're ensuring our own security. I'm surprised it hasn't been done before."

"It was never necessary," Baron Killbrook said with a hint of a sneer that I'd have liked to punch off his face, considering he was probably mostly worried about how he'd take another stab at Jude's *life* while he was under extra guard. My hands clenched, but my mother spoke before I had to.

"You seem awfully blasé about your own heir's safety when the menace that attacked him is still unaccounted for," she said, giving Killbrook a sharp look. Her gaze snapped to Stormhurst. "And if our heirs decided they needed an army for their own purposes, what exactly would be the problem with that? They're gathering formal support and establishing loyalty. Do you have some reason to think yours would use that loyalty toward ends you wouldn't approve of?"

Stormhurst's lips pursed as if she'd tasted something horribly sour. "Do you have a reason to think yours *wouldn't*?"

"Marguerite," Nightwood said, sounding taken aback, even though he'd probably been thinking along similar lines. He was just smart enough not to say it that baldly. "Surely there's no need—"

"My daughter," Baron Bloodstone cut in, "is the *only* scion who's stood by us through everything we've done these past two weeks. If she causes a problem, I will deal with it—when that actually happens. I don't appreciate your insinuations when your own heir couldn't even make an appearance for a party at his home."

A lump rose in my throat. She was so angry and insistent in my defense… and she was wrong. The other barons were right to distrust me, and they knew it after everything they'd seen of my behavior before she'd returned.

But when it came to them or me, she was putting her trust in me, whether I deserved it or not.

"Maybe the Guard isn't a problem in itself," Killbrook started. "If we could have a say in exactly how it's carried out—"

"No." My mother set her hand on my shoulder. "This meeting is over. Persephone came up with a sensible idea that should serve her and the other scions well, and she shouldn't be interrogated over it just because you want to distract from how your heirs might be going astray. Don't you dare summon her again without my knowledge."

Her grip on my shoulder tightened just for a second, with a quiver I didn't think anyone could see. Then she nudged me toward my car, her voice softening. "Go on back to school where you belong."

I could hardly tell her I deserved an interrogation. I nodded to her and sank into the driver's seat, with a sensation rippling through me as if my chest were slowly being torn in two.

# CHAPTER EIGHTEEN

*Declan*

Over the years, I'd gotten very good at concealing my feelings and intentions from just about everyone around me, but my father had been my sole parent since I was four. If anyone knew me, it was him. When I got to the house, I found him just finishing brewing coffee for both of us. He carried the mugs into the sitting room off the foyer where we'd had most of our serious talks, obviously having anticipated that I wasn't making a simple social call.

No one got the brew quite as right as he did. I sipped the hot liquid, letting the rich flavor and the tingle of caffeine wash through me, wishing the words I needed to say didn't taste even more bitter.

Dad leaned back in his favorite chair, holding his mug by his chest. He studied me with his light green eyes, a small crooked smile crossing his lips.

"What's on your mind, Declan?"

The Ashgraves, at least in recent generations, hadn't gone in for the same scheming and dissembling that the other baronies tended toward, and my mother had chosen her partner to those tastes. Dad was the type to cut to the chase. I supposed I was best off doing the same, even on this subject.

"I need to ask you a few things about Mom," I said. "At least one of the other barons is making claims about her—I have to know how true they are."

Dad's smile tightened, but he nodded. He'd never shied away from talking about my mother, even though her loss was obviously the most painful thing that had ever happened to him. I didn't believe that he'd even dated in the seventeen years since her death, let alone considered remarrying. He'd dedicated everything to raising Noah and me the way she'd have wanted and to preserving her legacy.

But maybe some parts of that legacy weren't the sort you'd want to preserve.

"Of course," he said. "Go ahead."

I took another gulp of coffee to fortify myself. "The confrontation where she died—the building she was looking at with the Bloodstones and some staff, where the joymancers found them—did she do or say anything beforehand that would make you think she might have expected a fight? Or even that she tipped the joymancers off, *hoping* for them to make an attack?"

I wanted him to laugh at the thought as if it couldn't

possibly be true. Instead he sighed, his forehead furrowing. "That's quite a claim."

"It is. You can see why I couldn't just let it rest."

"I can." He contemplated his mug for a moment and then looked at me again. "Your mother didn't share with me every decision she made on the political side of things. I offered a sounding board in certain situations, and I supported her as well as I could, but some things… she felt she had to carry those burdens herself. As I'm sure you can understand. I've seen you doing the same as you've grown into the role."

"Yeah." My throat tightened a little at the thought of how much I might resemble the woman I only remembered fragments of—of how different my life might have been if I'd had her to guide my growth on the way to becoming baron. "I suppose treason wouldn't be the sort of thing she'd have wanted to discuss with you, especially when then you could be implicated."

"Yes. If she had done something like that, I can't say I'd have known. The blacksuits interviewed me after the attack—they didn't ask anything that specific, just gathering information—and I told the truth when I said as far as I knew there'd been no indications of danger ahead of time. But…" His hands tensed around his mug. "I can't say it'd completely surprise me if it were true. It's possible. And they never could explain how the joymancers knew where to strike."

"You really think she'd have betrayed her own community like that?"

"I think she might have seen it as *saving* her community," Dad said. "You've seen the changes the barons are implementing now... From things she said back then, I suspect they were moving toward a similar outcome back then. And she was the only one of the five who objected. They needed her agreement, but you know that the barons will turn to questionable methods when it comes to getting their way... She was afraid for you and your brother. She was under a lot of pressure, being the lone hold-out. I could imagine that she might have thought an attack from the joymancers would redirect the pentacle's focus for at least a little while."

My stomach clenched. "Or cut them off at the knees completely, if it took one of the other barons out of the picture." Which had actually happened, if not permanently.

"It could be." A sadness came over my father's expression like a falling shadow. "All I know for sure is she faced more and more stress the longer she was working among them, and she was trying her best to do what she thought would benefit the entire community, not just the most prominent families' greed. Desperation can push people to making choices they wouldn't have found palatable before."

I sat in silence as his words sank in. If Dad didn't know for sure, then Baron Bloodstone was probably only speculating. If there'd been clear evidence of my mother committing treason, the barons wouldn't have hesitated to air it to diminish my own standing, back then or now. Which meant... I'd probably never know for sure whether

Mom had brought about those deaths and Rory and her mother's capture.

Was it even worse that I couldn't say she'd definitely been wrong even if she *had* called in the attack? Who would Rory be now if she'd been raised by her fearmancer parents instead of by the joymancers who'd clearly cared about her and given her more strength than maybe they'd realized she'd ever need? What would my world look like if the barons had managed to bully my mother into agreeing with their plans and they'd started their campaign of openly terrorizing Naries back then?

I couldn't say she'd made the right choice, but I could believe she hadn't had any good ones.

"I'm sorry I can't enlighten you any more than that," Dad said.

I shook my head. "You know what you know. Thanks for being honest with me."

"I try my best." He raised his mug to his lips. "Now do I get to keep you long enough to have a meal with you?"

* * *

I'd just pulled into the university garage after a hasty but satisfying dinner when a text from Jude popped up on my phone.

*Hey, Almost-Baron. If you're around, it looks like your little bro is setting himself up for some kind of scrap. They headed over to the west field. Should I call in the cavalry?*

What the hell had Noah gotten himself into now? I

loped out of the garage, tapping out a response as I went. *Thanks for the heads up. I should be able to handle it.* Bad enough if it turned out his big brother needed to swoop in to save him—even worse if the entire pentacle of scions made an appearance. Noah would never live that down.

Only a few traces of daylight lingered in the darkening sky, and the October breeze had turned nearly frigid. I hunched the collar of my wool jacket up to my ears as I hurried across campus. The green seemed quiet enough, maybe even unusually so after the bedlam of the last few days, but I caught terse voices as I reached Nightwood Tower. I stopped there to take in the situation before intervening.

Noah was standing some thirty feet away across the field, his stance tensed, facing three other juniors I vaguely recognized in the dim light. It didn't look as if they were doing anything other than talking so far. I stayed where I was with a murmur of a spell to carry their voices to me more clearly.

"What fucking business was it of yours anyway?" the guy in the middle of the trio was saying. "We're allowed to do whatever we want to them. That's what the rules say now. You can't just make up your own, even if you're an Ashgrave." He gave the name a slight sneer.

"She'd had enough," Noah said. "It wasn't like you could scare her any more than you already had. It doesn't help any of us to keep flinging crap at them when they're already a sobbing mess."

"You don't get to decide when I'm done."

"I get to decide whether I think you've messed enough

with people I've got to share the school with. They *are* people, you know."

It wasn't hard to decipher what had gone down. The guy had been tormenting a Nary student, and Noah had stopped him. A glow of pride lit inside me even as my shoulders stiffened, waiting to see how the confrontation would play out.

"Barely," the other guy spat out. "Maybe you just don't like the idea that someone could build up enough power that they'd put yours to shame. Since you're obviously too good to draw on those 'people' yourself."

Noah scoffed. "I'm not worried about taking you on. Some of us remember how to keep our energy up without being totally lazy about it."

"Maybe we should test that out. I'm all juiced up. You really want to try me?" The other guy took a menacing step forward, his shoulders flexing.

Noah raised his chin, his hands balling and then opening at his sides. "If that's what it'll take for you to feel better, give it your best shot."

My body shifted instinctively, itching to stride over and interrupt the developing fight. With a clench of my jaw, I held myself in check. I had to let Noah handle his own battles unless he absolutely needed bailing out.

His opponent muttered an abrupt casting word that must have launched some sort of spell Noah's way. My brother countered it instantly, his hand swiping through the air. The magic he sent after his defense knocked the other guy off his feet to sprawl on his ass in the grass.

The guy wasn't deterred. If anything, he looked twice

as furious as before. I braced myself, bringing a shielding spell onto my tongue, as he shoved himself upright. He whipped out his arm with a snapped word, and whatever he cast slammed into the shield Noah had conjured for himself hard enough to slice through it. Noah stumbled backward with a pained hiss of breath.

I might have jumped in then—I took a step before I'd even realized it—but Noah didn't need me. A couple of words tumbled from his lips, and a small but brilliant light seared through the space between them. It flared in the other guy's eyes. He clapped a hand to his face.

"I can't fucking see. You asshole."

He tossed another spell Noah's way, but Noah was already circling him, and the guy had no way of aiming.

"It's temporary," my brother said, his tone more flat than haughty. "But you might want to get your friends to help you back to your dorm room. And maybe you should consider focusing more on honing your skills rather than sucking up all kinds of energy you can't do much with."

The guy swore at him a few more times and mumbled some words I suspected were attempts to bring his vision back. When they didn't work, he waved to his friends with a jerky motion, and they stalked off toward Killbrook Hall. Noah hung back, presumably preferring to let them get a good head start so he didn't have to deal with them any more than he already had.

When the three were out of hearing, I crossed the field to join him. Noah's eyebrows shot up at the sight of me, and his shoulders stiffened defensively.

"I didn't know you were there," he said.

"I got a heads up that you might be getting into trouble." I hesitated, looking him over. He'd actually handled himself pretty well—not revealing just how deep his sympathies for the Naries ran, holding his own but avoiding dealing more harm than was necessary to end the fight. With how gung-ho he'd been about defending *me*, I hadn't been sure of his temper. Apparently he could moderate it better than I'd given him credit for.

"It looked like he got a jab in," I added.

"A little burn." Noah rubbed his forearm. "Not even bad enough to bother with the infirmary. I'm fine."

He was still watching me warily, probably waiting for me to berate him for getting into the fight in the first place. The protective part of me wanted to—wanted to tell him this was exactly what I needed to keep him out of.

But I couldn't, could I? Not if he was going to stay true to the principles that drove me too. This fight hadn't had anything to do with me, and it'd happened anyway. And he *had* been fine.

Maybe I'd been looking at the situation wrong. He might have technically been safer when he'd been off in Paris, but he'd also in some ways been alone. Like our mother had been.

He was stronger with me here to turn to, to guide him. And if I gave him the chance, it could be that I'd find I was stronger with him by my side too.

"Come on," I said, turning with a beckoning motion.

"Let's get out of the cold and discuss exactly how you'll fit into the Guard."

# CHAPTER NINETEEN

*Rory*

Whatever I might have thought in the past about Malcolm's posturing as high lord of Blood U, he did have a way of commanding a room. The eyes of the fourteen classmates we'd assembled for the Scions' Guard stayed trained on him as he strode from one side of the training mat to the other.

"Obviously you want to stay alert for any direct threats to whichever of us you're supposed to be supporting," he said, his voice as smooth and assured as always. "But we all feel it's equally important to reduce threatening behavior across campus in general. Aggressive magic has become a lot more common since the change in policy regarding the Naries, but any of us can be caught in the crossfire when people are getting careless—and anyone who wants to target us can use the general commotion as cover to launch an attack."

The rest of us scions were standing around the edges of the room, since Malcolm had asked to take the lead. We nodded along with that point to show we did all agree. The more support these students could see they had in pushing back against the hostility toward the Naries, the more confident they'd feel in doing it. And Malcolm clearly knew exactly the right way to present the idea so it sounded like it was for our benefit and not an attempt to undermine the barons' plans.

"I don't think people are going to be all that happy about us telling them to cool off," said the guy Jude had brought in. "They're getting off on the power."

Malcolm made a dismissive gesture. "We're not telling them they can't provoke fear here and there. They'll still be able to soak up plenty more than they used to. You'll just be reminding them of things like… 'Hey, a couple of the scions are nearby, and they'd appreciate being able to use the green in peace.' Or tell them we're watching to see who's able to adapt to the change while still showing they've got self-control. You'll have your Scions' Guard badge to give you extra authority."

Declan spoke up from the other side of the room with his air of calm authority. "People have understandably been excited about testing their limits since the change. We're not saying they're doing anything wrong, just encouraging them to settle into a more measured approach."

"Exactly." Malcolm rubbed his hands together. "You're all here because we figured you could handle that. I don't know about you, but I've been more embarrassed than impressed, seeing the way people have been throwing magic around and chasing after the Naries. Anyone who can't build up their magic without acting like a lunatic doesn't deserve it." He paused and winked at his audience. "But you don't need to repeat *that* to them if you're afraid they'll turn lunatic on you."

The quiet laughter that followed sounded a little anxious, but for the most part our forming Guard looked relieved, even my former nemesis, Victory. We *had* chosen everyone here for a reason, and part of that reason was we didn't think they'd been comfortable watching the chaos playing out on campus. Now the Nightwood scion had given them permission to feel that way. Some of them were already standing straighter, their chins raised, eager to take up the cause.

Inspiring our Guard wouldn't stop the Naries from being harassed, but if we even halved the torment they were facing right now, that'd be a huge step in the right direction. And all under the guise of supporting the baronies.

Malcolm answered a few more questions as the meeting wound down. "You've got your schedules," he reminded the group when it was time to wrap up. "We'll expect to see you around." He added a personal comment here and there with the several classmates he'd recruited, a couple of them for himself and others to support the rest of us, with a clap on one shoulder and a chuckle at someone's comment.

Getting to take charge and make things happen lit him up too. It was hard to look away from him while he was in regal mode. The energy stayed with him even after everyone except the five of us had left.

"I've got a few more ideas for people we can bring in," he said, and pointed at Jude. "You especially need your ass covered. Your dad can forget it if he thinks he's going to take another shot at you."

Jude grimaced at him, but he didn't argue. "If it pisses him off, I'm on board."

"If you let me know the names, I'll run them by Professor Razeden to make sure he hasn't seen any reasons to be wary of them," I said.

"I think I've got a pretty good read on them, but it can't hurt to double check when we're skirting this close to potential treason." He gave me a wry smile and motioned for me to get out my phone so I could take the names down.

"It seems like you know just about everyone on campus pretty well," I remarked as I typed them into a note. He'd greeted everyone who'd arrived by name and with a brief mention of some interest or history they shared.

"Hard to rule if you don't know who you're ruling over." He arched his eyebrows at me. "I know you think I'm too hard on people sometimes, but I'm always paying attention. I put the pressure on where it's needed and ease off when it's deserved."

"Like you did with me?" I couldn't help saying, with a pinching of guilt at the way his face fell.

"You *know* I realize now that I went about that totally wrong," he started, his voice dropping low and rough.

I grasped his shirt to tug him closer. "I do. You've proven that. I'm just never going to completely forget it, you know."

"Believe me, neither will I."

His regret came through so clearly that I had to change the course of the conversation. I peeked up at him through my eyelashes. "I have to say that when you're *not* caught up in some grudge, I do enjoy watching you take charge."

His smile came back, a hint of a smolder lighting in his dark brown eyes. He stepped even closer, his head bowing toward mine. "Any time you want to do more than watch, I'm all yours."

I tipped my head to meet his kiss, firm but not demanding. I remembered very well what it was like to let Malcolm take charge of *me* for a little while. But seeing him today had brought an ache into my chest that was a lot more than just lust.

Regardless of the things I hated about his father, growing up with the Nightwoods had taught Malcolm some things that were useful. It'd prepared him for life as baron better than maybe any of the rest of us were. He was meant for that role—it was made for him. He would enjoy directing the fearmancer community as much as he'd enjoyed leading this meeting, and he'd be good at it too.

All of those facts made me love him more, and they also made it all the more certain that our time together came with an end date. Even if he'd offered to give up the future he'd worked toward for so long, I couldn't imagine letting him.

Even if, in moments like this, the thought of letting him go, watching him form a life with another woman, sent a dagger straight through my heart.

I pushed down that pain and kissed him again before easing back. "I'm supposed to meet my mother in town soon," I said with a grimace. "Some kind of tour, she said."

"That sounds delightful," Jude said with open sarcasm, and swooped in to give me a quick hug and a peck on the cheek.

Connar glanced over with a frown. "Do you want any of us there nearby, just in case? With that new assistant hanging around trying to screw you over..."

I waved off his concern. "I'll be okay. I've managed to survive this long. And my mother is still keeping Maggie at a bit of a distance because of what happened with Lillian. I'm not too worried about that." Yet.

Despite the nonchalance I'd tried to convey, my stomach tied itself in knots as I went to grab my car. My mother had said more about the tour than I'd conveyed to the guys. Apparently some of the prominent families were joining us so we could show off the benefits of having the Nary population under our thumbs.

I hadn't gone into town since the announcement, worried that what I'd see there might be too much for me to keep my mouth shut. Maybe if the Scions' Guard strategy worked out here at the university, we could adapt it to reduce any terrorizing that was going on in town too. In the meantime, I wasn't sure what I could do without proving the other barons right and losing whatever trust I'd built with my mother before I had any way to really change her mind.

On the surface, the town's streets looked more peaceful than usual in the muted sunlight, but there was an eeriness to the quiet. Normally in the middle of the day, I'd have seen locals ambling along the streets, doing some shopping or heading to lunch or just stretching their legs. Today I only passed a couple pedestrians, and both of them froze and watched my car rumble along with widened eyes. One of them dashed into the nearest store as soon as I'd driven by.

There *were* other people out and about. A blacksuit and a few seniors I recognized from campus were standing at the edge of the square when I parked nearby. One of the patrols the barons had called for, I guessed—the responsibility I'd gotten Cressida out of by insisting I needed her as part of the Scions' Guard.

The sky was clouded, and as I got out of the car, the breeze smacked my face with a waft of dampness. The one troop marched off through the streets, but when I came into the square, a couple other blacksuits and two more student patrollers were standing off to the side of my mother and the cluster of fearmancers gathering around her.

"You can see how subdued they all are already," Baron Bloodstone was saying as I reached them, with a sly little smile that made my skin creep. "It didn't take them long to see how outmatched they are. Just a few demonstrations, and now we call all the shots."

"Were they *all* so quick to surrender?" one of the men asked.

"None resisted for very long—that much you can be sure of. When the other families arrive, we'll take a stroll around town and you'll see our authority is recognized everywhere." She beckoned me over. "My daughter can assist with the tour, since she's become familiar with the place over the months she's been at the university."

I not only had to join in this demonstration but narrate our supposed triumph as well? My stomach flipped right over. I managed a smile and a nod, hoping I was concealing my discomfort well enough for it to go unnoticed.

My uneasiness only increased a minute later when Maggie came trotting over with three other couples in tow. Her gaze skimmed right over me, and she bobbed her head to my mother. "I believe this is everyone."

"Then we can get started." My mother patted my arm. "Where would you normally have gone on your trips into town, Persephone, and what would the atmosphere have been like before?"

"Yes," Maggie chirped helpfully. "Let's hear your take."

What was *she* expecting from me here? I swallowed thickly.

"Well," I said, keeping my tone as even as I could, "normally I'd have seen more people out taking care of… whatever they needed to take care of. If I had to buy groceries, the store I'd usually go to is just down this street."

I stepped forward, and the others followed me. I realized belatedly that mentioning I bought my own groceries was probably a little odd for any high-ranking fearmancer, let alone the daughter of a baron—some of our group exchanged glances that might have been puzzled or amused. No one commented on it, though, so it might not have been that large a faux pas. They all knew my history and could chalk some strangeness up to that.

As we meandered through the familiar streets, my queasiness only bubbled higher. The one Nary woman who was shopping in the grocery store abandoned her cart and fled for the back door at the sight of us; the cashier stood stiff as a board behind the counter. My mother blatantly lifted an apple from a stand right in his view and started eating it on her way out, without the slightest gesture toward paying for it or acknowledgment that she should have.

The fearmancer-run bar we went by had a decent bunch of students patronizing it; the other restaurants where I'd gone more often stood empty other than a waiter or waitress eyeing us warily from the back of the room when we peered through the front windows. My new favorite café had a CLOSED sign hanging on the door, the windows outright shuttered. I glanced up at the second floor where I assumed the couple lived, wondering what they were going to do now that their business had been interrupted.

"Isn't this wonderful?" Maggie said to me, loud

enough for the group to overhear. "Your mother and the other barons have accomplished so much, so quickly."

By sheer force of will, I kept my gaze mild when I looked back at her, as much as I'd have liked to shoot her a death glare. "It is amazing how much they've accomplished." Was she trying to get me to admit that I wasn't happy with those accomplishments? What did she think I'd have wanted instead? She'd accused me of being power-hungry—it could be she simply figured I wished I'd been the one getting the "glory" for this progress.

"This is, of course, the initial stage of transition," my mother said as we turned down a residential street. "They're retreating as they come to terms with their new reality. Once they've adjusted, they'll continue living their lives and doing their work much the same way they did before—other than having the rules we impose to follow, and giving us due respect and preference when we have need of it."

"How long do you think that transitional period will take?" asked a woman beside her.

"Well, we don't have any similar examples to go by, so we can only speculate based on—"

A wordless bark of a voice cut her off. A half a dozen kids—preteens and young teenagers by the look of them—burst from one of the driveways, all of them glowering at us. One of them raised a butcher's knife he must have grabbed from his parents' kitchen.

"We don't want you here," he shouted. "And we're not scared of you."

# CHAPTER TWENTY

*Rory*

My mother blinked at the squad of Nary kids for a moment before a laugh spilled from her lips. The wry sound carried down the gloomy town street with its line of white- or cream-faced houses. A few of the kids cringed, but the one holding the knife kept it raised, his knuckles pale.

"What are you going to do with that?" the baron said. "Do you really think you could hurt us with something so mundane?"

She spoke a casting word, snapping her fingers for effect, and the blade shimmered. In less than a second, it'd transformed into a flayed silver ribbon that sagged across the boy's hand.

He let out a cry of dismay and flung it on the ground. My mother no doubt expected them to run away after that display. She turned to continue down the street—and the boy hollered, "Come on!"

Faster than any of us were prepared for, the kids hurled rocks they'd been hiding at our group. As soon as they'd let their projectiles fly, most were groping on the ground to dig up handfuls of dirt and pebbles that they threw too. Their faces were sallow with terror, and quivers of that emotion raced into my chest as it must have the fearmancers around me, but that didn't stop the determination that burned in the kids' eyes.

The rocks weren't all that big. The mages closest to them muttered with disgust and waved a quick barrier into place that deflected most of the barrage that followed, but I didn't see any of them so much as wince. My mother spun back around with a blaze of fury in her expression, though.

"Rein them in," she demanded to the blacksuits who were already striding forward. "Let's make sure they remember never to badger us again."

At the sight of the blacksuits and their student helpers descending on them, the kids scrambled backward—but only to the front of the house. The boy who'd held the knife snatched up a larger, sharp-edged stone that bordered the garden, inspiring the others to do the same, and lunged at the officers before anyone had a chance to transform that makeshift weapon too. The other kids sprang in with a volley of ragged yells.

I cringed inwardly, but I expected the blacksuits and their helpers to push the assault back with about as much force as the other fearmancers had before. These were *kids* after all. I didn't think the oldest could have been more than thirteen. But our protectors were all calling out spells at once, sending the stones flinging away from the attackers' hands, pushing them back—and one of the students shoved out his hands with a force so brutal it whipped through my hair even behind him.

The wind he'd conjured blasted into all of the kids and hurled them up the driveway. Some of them tumbled with pained yelps and the crack of broken bones on the concrete between the two houses. Three bodies rammed straight into the brick side of the neighbor's wall with a sickening crunch.

Bile rose up my throat as those three kids crumpled at the base of the wall. Blood streaks marked the bricks; more of the scarlet liquid pooled beneath their heads. The guy, who I doubted was more than eighteen himself, dropped his hands, a tremor running through him. He'd *killed* them.

And not just the ones who'd been charging at us. "Sammy!" one of the girls who'd fallen in the driveway cried out. She stumbled to her feet and hurried over with a lurching limp before collapsing beside the bodies with a sob. When she reached toward the boy in the middle, I registered how much smaller he was compared to the others. He looked more like a kindergartener.

I hadn't seen anyone that young in the onslaught. He must have been a younger sibling, tagging along to see what the big kids were up to and hanging back behind the pack... where he'd been caught up in our rush to defend ourselves.

The girl touched his little blood-flecked face and rocked as she wept. I had to clench my teeth and will back the urge to vomit. They'd attacked us like monsters—because we were acting like monsters.

One of the blacksuits spun on the guy who'd cast the final spell. "What did we say about control?" he rasped, keeping his voice low. "You only exert the amount of force needed to offset the threat."

"There were so many of them," the guy said with a vague motion of his hand, but the color had drained from his face. "I was just trying to stop them—to protect everyone."

"They should have known better," a woman near me said in a clipped voice. "They looked as if they'd have liked to kill us. Everyone here has to learn the consequences."

A few heads nodded, but I thought several of the others we'd brought on our tour were taken aback, their eyes averted or startled. I guessed I should be glad they weren't all celebrating, but it was hard to feel much of anything beyond the mash of guilt and horror swelling inside me.

My mother sliced her hand through the air in the direction of the blacksuits. "Your people need to deal with this. Clear the area, see that they end up where they belong."

Her voice was cool and steady, but her lips pressed tight when she was done speaking. Her gaze fixed on the little boy. A shudder ran down her back, so small I wasn't sure anyone else would have noticed it or thought much of it.

I knew how hard she had to be shaken for even that little lapse to show through. She shifted her weight, but she couldn't seem to wrench her attention away from the bloody bodies.

She was horrified too. A quiver of hope penetrated my nausea. Was she horrified enough to reconsider the path she'd set us off on? I had to try—for her, for every Nary in this town who might have to face the blacksuits and their accomplices in the future.

I couldn't say anything to her in front of all these spectators, though. Her pride would take over before I could get through.

"Well," I said, smoothing the ragged edge from my voice as well as I could, "clearly the Naries don't stand a chance against the powers we can wield. And now you've all had a very thorough tour." I stepped closer to my mother and tucked a hand around her elbow. "It's just about time for the business matters we needed to attend to. We don't want to leave them waiting."

My mother managed to tear her gaze away to look at me. She had the wherewithal not to show her confusion with more than a brief blink. She might not know what I was after, but she could tell I was angling for something between the two of us. And she trusted me enough to nod.

"That's right. We were just about to wrap up as it is." She glanced around at the other fearmancers. "Thank you for joining us for this demonstration. As you can see, we can dominate the Naries with no trouble at all."

I turned away from the scene in the driveway, my jaw

clenching. A few more blacksuits had just arrived—alerted by their colleagues, I assumed. One of them started directing the tour group back toward the square where most of them must have parked while the other officers gathered around the dead or injured kids.

My mother and I drifted to the back of the crowd. Maggie stuck close by us, her eyes narrowing when I looked at her, but the other families were too busy talking amongst themselves to pay us much mind. At our first opportunity, I tugged the baron toward a side-street, and she followed me. She moved with brisk strides, but her arm trembled in my grasp. When we'd passed out of sight of most of the others, she rubbed her forehead like she had when I'd found her in her bedroom the other day.

Maggie pulled out her phone. I tried to ignore her as I led my mother toward the outskirts of town where we could talk without even the locals overhearing, but she obviously wasn't satisfied with supervising us on her own. As we reached the sparse forest across the quiet highway from the town's first buildings, two cars pulled up with five blacksuits between them.

Great. We still had an audience. At least it was a smaller one, and made up of people whose opinion I didn't think my mother cared about quite as much as the families from the tour. I'd still have to handle the situation delicately.

Hell, I'd have needed to take a delicate approach even if it'd been the two of us on our own.

I stopped amid the trees and turned to my mother. Whatever Maggie had said to the blacksuits, they hung back, in easy reach but not intervening. This shouldn't look like anything other than a baron speaking with her scion to them.

"What's this about, Persephone?" my mother said, peering at me. "I think you'd better explain quickly."

How could I put it in a way that she'd accept and not get defensive? The last thing she'd want was for me to point out her own regrets—her weakness—in front of anyone.

"I think you'd better—" Maggie started to say in a cutting tone, and understanding struck me.

I wouldn't make it about my mother's weakness. I'd make it mine. *I* didn't give a shit what the people around us thought of my supposed strength or lack thereof. And the fact that I was saying it in front of them would give her witnesses to prove she'd acted for me rather than because of fears of her own.

"I'm sorry," I said, cutting Maggie off and grasping my mother's hand. It didn't take any effort at all for my voice to come out choked. "I didn't want to say anything in front of the other families. I just—what happened to those kids—what *our* people *did* to those kids—I don't think I can take it if this is how things are going to be now."

Let her comfort me. Let her be the strong one while being compassionate at the same time. I was giving her an opening to change her mind without having to look fickle.

She drew herself up with a cock of her head. "What do you mean, Persephone?"

I waved toward the town. "I know you want us all to be more free. I think that would be amazing. But is it really going to change our community for the better if that's the kind of magic it's going to bring out of us? We're going to be so busy policing and punishing Naries that we have no time to look after anything we used to do. We're supposed to be mages, not jailors." *Not murderers.* At least not if I had anything to say about it.

"I'm sure things will settle down given time," my mother said, but her gaze wavered with uncertainty. She was listening.

"I don't know. People don't give up easily. They'll just get smarter in how they rebel, and we'll have to keep fighting with them…" I hugged myself. "Honestly, I wish we could just wipe everyone's memories of the whole thing and go back to the way we used to live. I know that's probably not what you want to hear, and I really am sorry—I want to do other things with my magic, that's all. This doesn't feel like freedom."

I let my voice break on the last few words. Then silence fell between us. I didn't dare glance Maggie's way, but I could see her at the edge of my vision, rigidly still. She didn't interject any critical commentary. Lord only knew how she'd interpret this as part of her assumptions about me.

She could think whatever she wanted. The blacksuits could know the Bloodstone scion had an aversion to blood. All that mattered was whether my mother would take the opening I'd just given her.

They *could* wipe the townspeople's memories and roll

back the changes. She could blame it all on me and wanting to make sure the heirs weren't saddled with responsibilities beyond what we could have expected or something like that. Please, let her give in to that horrified pang she must have felt staring at the little boy, a kid as magicless as I'd been at that age, when for all she'd known I'd been dead too.

The baron's hand clenched around mine. Her expression twitched. She closed her eyes for a second, and a fresh flicker of hope rose up inside me.

Then one of the blacksuits watching us stirred with a rustle of the grass, and my mother's gaze snapped to them. To the figures standing around us, waiting for her response as much as I was. I read my loss in the stiffening of her posture.

Her attention came back to me, her eyes going hard. "This is what we've always been meant for, Persephone," she said. "We can give our people everything they deserve. No more hiding, no more tiptoeing around the feebs. You need to focus on that and not sympathies they don't deserve. It'll be difficult, but it'll be worth it. We *have* to do this for ourselves. No one else is going to stick up for the fearmancers. We're in this alone. Now come along."

My stomach had sunk farther with each word she said. Her tone was so unyielding I knew there was no point to making another attempt. That would take this confrontation from a momentary lapse to outright disobedience.

But as she nudged me with her back toward our cars,

one thing she'd said dug a little deeper inside me with a resonance I couldn't ignore.

We weren't *really* alone in this world—not as a barony, and especially not as mages. Maybe it was time I stopped thinking as if we were.

Because there was no way I could stand back and let this awfulness continue after the blood I'd watched spill today.

# CHAPTER TWENTY-ONE

*Rory*

I felt a little silly parked at the edge of the fallow field beyond town, like a kid playing secret agent. But if the barons felt spots like this made for ideal clandestine meetings, then I figured this once I should take a page from their book.

I leaned against the hood of the Lexus, my arms crossed against the damp breeze. The clouds overhead had only gotten thicker and darker since yesterday afternoon. No sound reached the meeting place I'd picked except the rustle of the autumn leaves on the nearby saplings and the occasional drone of passing traffic—rising to a growl when it was one of my fellow scions arriving to join me.

When I'd texted the guys about this meeting, I'd suggested we leave campus at different times and take different routes so it wouldn't be obvious to any blacksuits who spotted us in town that we were getting together.

Even with all that subterfuge, as soon as the last car—Jude's Mercedes—pulled onto the uneven grass to finish our rough circle, I cast a spell around us to deflect any attempts at listening in.

The guys had all gotten out, matching my pose against their own cars. Declan was the only one who looked apprehensive rather than puzzled. He must have experienced meetings like this with the barons before, and I'd imagine most of those hadn't been any more cheerful than my recent confrontation with them.

"You have an idea for pushing back against the barons," he said before I could figure out how to start.

I guessed it wasn't hard to guess what this gathering might be about considering the circumstances. My hands braced against the cool metal. "Yeah. It's probably going to sound really extreme. You all might think I'm crazy. But… after what happened yesterday, I think we have to do *something* before even more people die over this."

An image of the fallen kids, of the little boy and the blood, flashed through my mind. My stomach lurched with it. I closed my eyes for a second, though that hadn't helped keep the memories back all the other times they'd risen up.

"The barons don't see any problem with how the incident went down," Malcolm said in a derisive tone. "I talked to my dad about something else last night, and he didn't even bother mentioning it. Just another day's work."

I shivered. "Exactly. I know it upset my mother in the moment, but even then, nothing I said to her got through. I don't think we're going to be able to shift their opinions just talking about it. We have to force their hand, make the price of continuing with this too much even for them. Show all the families supporting them how easily even an experiment on this small a scale can fall apart."

"I'm in if there's a way we can make that work." Connar adjusted his position with a flex of his brawny shoulders. "And I can't imagine that any plan you'd come up with would be horrible, Rory. What's your idea?"

"First, I wanted to check…" I motioned in the direction of the town. "The blacksuits put up wards to make sure no Naries can enter or leave town, and that no one in there can communicate with the outside world. The wards around the university have made it totally impossible for even other mages to find the location if they haven't been granted access. But the school ones are a lot older with more layers and built-up strength, right? The ones around town wouldn't be anywhere near as potent?"

Jude raised his eyebrows. "Are you thinking of smashing the wall and letting the Naries run loose? If they go blabbing what's been going on to anyone who'll listen, the barons might bash up a lot more skulls."

I shook my head. "That's not— I just want to be sure that they could be broken… and that someone right here who'd broken through those still wouldn't be able to find the school."

Declan's expression had become even more pensive as I'd spoken. Maybe he could guess where I was going with this too. After all, he was the only one of the guys who knew my most direct inspiration.

"Someone who hasn't been granted permission could be standing right at the barrier around the university, and I don't think any amount of magic would penetrate it or even confirm for them that what they're looking for is there," he said. "I've looked at the records of the castings. There's layer upon layer of wards with different functions and approaches. You can't crack over a hundred years of spells laid by the top mages around very easily. What they've got around town will be much weaker. They only needed it to hold off the Naries anyway."

"Okay." I dragged in a breath. "That solves one part of the problem. I'd hate to end up causing even more destruction than if we didn't intervene."

"Where exactly are you going with this, Rory?" Malcolm said, his tone more gentle than impatient. "Connar's right—if this is *your* idea, it's obviously not going to be a bloodbath. You're going to have to tell us eventually."

I was. I grimaced at the grass, resisting the urge to hunch my shoulders defensively. Then I forced myself to raise my head so I could look them all in the eyes in turn.

"It could be a bloodbath if it goes wrong. So we'll have to figure out how to control the situation so it doesn't. But… I think we should tip off the joymancers."

For the first few seconds, the only response I got from the guys was disbelieving stares. Then Malcolm let out a sputter of a laugh. "Very funny. You *are* kidding, right?"

I swallowed hard. "No. I'm not saying that we *trust*

them or tell them anything more than we need to… But they have the power to make this experiment way more trouble than it's worth. They won't be held back by worrying about how the barons could retaliate, the way we and the other families who aren't happy with the situation have to be. And they'll definitely want to intervene if they find out this is happening."

"And once they know, they'll be even more on guard against the fearmancers taking steps like that again," Jude said slowly. "You know, I'm hardly a joymancer fanboy, but I think she has a point. As long as everyone at the school will still be safe…"

"What about the people in town?" Malcolm demanded with a swing of his arm. "We know what the joymancers are like. *You* know how they treated you even when you were trying to make peace with them, Rory. They'll blast apart every fearmancer they can catch, and probably a heck of a lot of Naries if any get in their way. Our classmates are out there helping the blacksuits patrol, and not all of them even want to be there."

Like Cressida hadn't. "I know," I said. "That's why we're talking about it and not racing straight ahead. I don't want to give the joymancers the details unless we can make some kind of deal with them, magically-enforced, that they won't resort to lethal spells unless they have to in self-defense—and then only to the extent that they need to defend themselves. I *don't* want a bloodbath. But we *have* to step in somehow. What happened yesterday…" My voice caught. I paused to steady myself. "I was hoping the four of you might have some ideas for how to put that deal in place."

Declan had stayed silent so far. When he did speak, there was a carefulness to his even tone beyond what I was used to. "It *is* possible to magically enforce an agreement through a combination of persuasion and physicality. We cover it in the junior years—any of us could cast it alongside the joymancers, and you'd be able to pick up the technique quickly. But the parties need to be in close proximity."

"If you go to negotiate with them, they could grab you all over again," Connar said. "Or maybe kill you this time. You can't take that risk, Rory."

"It wouldn't have to be her," Jude put in.

"It shouldn't be any of us," I said. "It's too big a risk. But there's got to be a way we can make it work without putting ourselves or anyone else in that much danger. We do have some leverage. It'd be more important to them to tackle a whole bunch of fearmancers than to take one into custody."

"If they even see that as the choice." Malcolm frowned. "They do have plenty of power of their own. If they get their hands on any fearmancer who knows what's going on, they could pull the information they want out of them through magic given enough time."

I held up my hands. "We're supposed to be the most powerful fearmancers in the country other than our parents. Surely we can figure something out to make this plan viable if we take a little time to think on it. I just can't see any other way we're going to turn this disaster around if we don't bring in outside pressure. If any of you can think of something, I'd love to hear it."

Malcolm opened his mouth and closed it again with a deeper frown. Jude just winced. Maybe I shouldn't have made that comment about how powerful we were all supposed to be.

Declan bowed his head. I was waiting on his reaction more than anyone else's. He'd had to hear that his mother might have betrayed the fearmancers in a similar way—he knew what that decision, if it had been hers, had cost her and his family.

If he said he didn't think we should go through with my plan, I didn't think I could argue with him.

"I've been trying to come up with a viable counter-strategy since we first found out about the policy," he said after a minute. "I've scoured the records for precedents, looked at the probable allies we could bring to our side, and I still don't have anything definite. The assault on the Naries is only getting worse. I don't think we should invite the joymancers to our doorstep without plenty of precautions in place, but if we can restrict how much violence they can deal out… It could work."

When he looked at me, my throat closed up. "Are you sure?" I couldn't help asking.

He gave me a crooked smile, his gaze so fond it sent a pang through my chest. "I trust your judgment. I know you wouldn't have suggested it if you hadn't given it a ton of thought already. It's a desperate measure… but this situation has gotten pretty desperate."

His vote of confidence filled me with not just relief

but a rush of love. Declan didn't hand over authority or bend the rules easily, but he had that much faith in me. He was putting his future in my hands all over again.

I'd better make sure I deserved that faith.

"We agree, then?" Connar asked. "Even if we don't *like* the plan, it's our only real option?"

"Seems that way," Jude said.

Malcolm sighed, but he gave his acceptance with a jerk of his hand. "I guess it's back to the books to see how we can work around the sanctimonious assholes."

"I don't want to hold off any longer than we have to," I said. "I thought I could contact their headquarters and let them know something's happening in New York state, that if they'll send a force to New York City, we can give them more details then. It'll take them a little while to get organized… and hopefully by the time they're in place to strike, we'll know how we're going to handle the rest."

If one more kid—or anyone else—died because we'd wasted a day being overcautious, I didn't know if I'd be able to forgive myself.

"That's reasonably vague and keeps them at a good distance," Declan said. "Do you know how to contact them?"

"There's a phone number registered to the building where I talked to them before," I said. "I haven't tried it yet for obvious reasons, but I'm hoping it'll work. If it doesn't, then we'll have even more time while I figure that out. I guess I could find out now."

"It'll be safer doing that here than making the call on campus," Jude said.

I pulled out my phone. I'd already added the number to a note when I'd looked it up yesterday as I'd mulled over the idea. My thumb hesitated before I tapped in the digits. A chill raced down my back at the ring on the other end, even though I hadn't actually set anything in motion yet.

These were the people who'd dragged off my mother and me, held her prisoner for years, and treated me like a criminal when I'd come to them only wanting to negotiate before. The people who'd killed my familiar, even if that'd been an accident. But they also held themselves up as the defenders of regular society from the fearmancers' machinations. Please, let them do the right thing by us.

I was just starting to get nervous that the number would lead nowhere when a click sounded on the other end as someone picked up. "Hello?" a woman said. The one who'd interrogated me last month? I wasn't sure I remembered her voice well enough to recognize it.

"Hi," I said, quick but clear, willing my voice to stay steady. "I wanted to notify the joymancers about a destructive plan the fearmancers are carrying out."

The woman's voice snapped to sharp alertness. "What plan? Who is this?"

I'd obviously reached the right people. "I can't tell you everything right now. We have to be sure you're really prepared to stop them. You'll need a lot of people. If you can assemble them in New York City, we'll reach out again with more information."

"Wait a minute. What—"

"I can't talk any more right now," I said. "Please get there quickly."

I hung up, my hand trembling. A sweat had broken out on my back. The guys were watching me intently.

"Do you think they'll come?" Connar asked.

"I'm not sure. But… I didn't ask for much. It's not as if we could easily ambush them when they've got all of NYC to work with." I wet my lips. "I think they'll decide it's worth the risk."

* * *

Malcolm hadn't been kidding that we needed to go back to the books. The next morning found me holed up in the library bright and early, looking up techniques for magically confirming deals and trying to determine if any of them could be done at a safe distance.

I wasn't surprised to see Declan coming down the aisle to join me. His worried expression made me pause.

"Did something else happen?" I asked, my gut twisting at the thought of just how awful any "something else" could be.

"I don't know. Did Jude say anything to you about leaving campus today?"

My heart outright stopped. "No. Why? Is he gone?" If Baron Killbrook had managed to get to him somehow despite our efforts… My hands clenched. "Did you check with his part of the Guard?"

"That's why I'm asking. One of them saw him heading for the garage a couple hours ago. He called after Jude, but Jude either didn't hear him… or pretended not to. He took off quickly. So it sounds as if he left of his own accord, but he isn't back yet, and if he didn't say anything to any of us, not even you, that seems concerning." He raked his hand back through his hair, his eyebrows drawing together.

"I don't think he totally liked us being so protective of him," I said. "Maybe he just wanted a little time to himself." But that didn't mean taking that time was a smart move. "I assume you've tried calling him."

"And texting. He answered saying that he's fine, but when I asked him what he's doing, he just told me not to worry about it. He wouldn't pick up when I tried to actually talk to him."

That wasn't great, but it also didn't make for an emergency. "Can we—" I started, and Declan's phone pinged.

He checked the screen, and the furrow in his brow deepened. "That's Connar. He was in the scion lounge, and a note just appeared out of nowhere on the coffee table. He didn't want to open it on his own, but he says it looks like Jude's handwriting."

What the hell was Jude up to? I left the stack of books I'd been paging through. "Let's find out what he had to say, then."

We hurried down to the basement, reaching it just a few seconds ahead of Malcolm, who Connar must have contacted too. The Stormhurst scion was standing in front of the couch eyeing the folded piece of paper sitting innocently enough in the middle of the coffee table. The scrawl on the outside, which did look like Jude's, said only, *To the scions.*

Not "the other scions" or "my fellow scions." He'd cringed at including himself in that term from the moment he'd admitted his true parentage to me.

"It's not like it's going to explode," Malcolm said, and snatched the paper up. His gaze darted over the words written on the other side, and his jaw tensed. He passed the note to me. I held it so Declan could read it too.

*You all have done a hell of a lot more for me than I've ever been able to do for you. This one problem, I can fix. Make sure you give the barons hell.*

"This one problem?" I repeated, but even as I said the words, understanding was sinking in. Jude's voice yesterday in the field rang through my memory, from when we'd been talking about setting conditions with the joymancers—about someone needing to meet up with them.

*It wouldn't have to be her.*

"He's gone to New York to make the deal with the joymancers," I said with a lurch of my stomach. Had he decided he was going to take that duty on the moment I'd mentioned it? But—out of all of us he had the least ability to defend himself from them right now—

Oh. My next words fell leaden from my mouth. "And he isn't expecting to make it back."

# CHAPTER TWENTY-TWO

*Jude*

I *should* have been sitting in the comfort of my Manhattan apartment. The problem was that the apartment was linked to my name, and it didn't seem wise to leave a trail showing I'd been here in the city at the same time as the joymancer force had arrived. So I'd lowered myself to a dumpy little hotel that accepted cash—charging me double since I'd arrived well before check-in. I'd coughed up the dough even though I wasn't sure I was going to spend the night. For all I knew, I'd be long gone by then.

In the meantime, I'd settled into the stiff chair by the desk with its worn varnish, shifting every few minutes as if I might find a more enjoyable pose, while I waited for an alert on the prepaid phone I'd picked up. That device couldn't be traced to me either. As soon as I'd gotten it, I'd dialed up the number I'd been able to glean from Rory's phone and informed the joymancer at the other end that her people could text me when they were ready to arrange a meet.

She hadn't confirmed they were on their way, but she hadn't said they weren't either, so I didn't figure it would be too long. The sooner I could get out of this room with its stale-bread smell, the better.

And then… Then whatever happened would happen. If I hadn't come, Rory would have decided on some strategy that put *her* neck on the line, because that was how she was. Risking herself wouldn't have made any sense, though.

I didn't belong with her and the others anyway. The clock had been ticking on the time I had left from the moment I'd been born, only faster since Mom's new pregnancy. Better I ended up in some joymancer jail or dead from one of their spells than let Baron Killbrook get the satisfaction of ending my life. And I'd be foiling his awful plans at the same time. Win-win.

As long as I kept reminding myself that, I'd be fine.

A ringtone jangled, but not from the prepaid phone. It was my regular one that I still had in my pocket. I pulled it out with a grimace, already knowing I wasn't going to answer it.

Rory's number had appeared on the screen. No doubt Mr. Almost-Baron Ashgrave had told her I'd dodged his calls and his questions. My gut clenched at the thought of worrying her, but I wasn't sure I trusted myself to lie convincingly if one of these insight experts got me talking long enough.

The call went through to voice mail. I was about to shove the phone away when a text popped up, also from Rory.

*I know what you're doing. We found your note. Don't go through with this without talking to me, please.*

The *please* jabbed me right through the heart. I could hear Rory saying it, see the plea in her dark blue eyes, as if she were right in front of me.

Fucking mangled magic. I'd managed to contain enough to cast a disguising illusion on the note so it'd stay hidden, but the spell had been supposed to last until tonight, by which time the deed should have already been done. Obviously I hadn't managed to give it anywhere near enough oomph.

My hand wavered over the phone. I couldn't just ignore her. Hell, if I did, chances were she'd come storming down to New York City as fast as that Lexus could carry her, and then all my intentions for keeping her out of danger wouldn't mean shit.

*I'm clearly the best man for the job*, I wrote back. *Don't worry about it. Maybe they'll enjoy my company so much we'll part ways great friends.*

Her reply was almost instant. *I think you know I'm not going to just drop this. I need to TALK to you.*

I'd barely finished reading when the phone started jangling again. I scowled at the screen, but a lump rose in my throat at the same time.

The worst part about how I'd had to go about this was not getting to say good-bye to her. I wasn't sure if I deserved that luxury anyway, but *she* deserved better from me. Especially now that the cat was out of the bag anyway.

I brought the phone to my ear. "I'm not changing my mind," I said.

"This whole thing was my idea," Rory retorted, unfazed by the abrupt start to the conversation. "You shouldn't go off and decide how to handle it without me getting any say."

Her voice was so tight with emotion that my fingers clenched around the phone. I closed my eyes. "I know what you need done. I can take in enough power to make the deal—and that kind of spell sustains as long as it's cast properly, even if you couldn't put a ton of power into it."

"That's not the point."

"No. The point is that, like I said, I'm the best person to do it. I'm the only person who can face the danger without risking the pentacle or anyone really important. This might be the only really important thing *I* ever do. I'm just taking the opportunity that presented itself."

Rory was quiet for a moment. I almost thought I'd managed to convince her when she cleared her throat, and the hitching rasp of the sound told me she was on the verge of tears if not already crying. A shamed heat flooded me from my chest up to my face.

"You're important to *me*," she said, her voice watery but determined. "I'm sorry if I haven't shown you that enough. And you're important to Declan and Connar and Malcolm too. You didn't even give us a chance to figure out another option. And you have no idea what might happen, what other things you might be able to contribute in the future…"

My free hand balled against my chest, against the hollow where I'd used to sense that constant current of magic, which now held nothing more than a faint tickle. "It isn't getting any better, Rory. I'm not getting back even the power I used to have."

"Is that all that matters? People make a difference without magic a gazillion times a day." She paused. "I know it has to be horrible. I'll do whatever I can to help you get what you can back, or adjust, or whatever. Can you at least give me that chance?"

"Will you still feel that way if I hang back and the rest of you can't find a better solution, and the jackasses in town kill more people while we're waffling over it?"

"Yes. Because the whole *point* of making the deal is to make sure no one at all dies if they don't have to." There was a rustling that might have been her swiping at her eyes. "I love you. So much. You know that, don't you?"

As if I could somehow have failed to realize after all the compassion—and passion—she'd shown me. She'd been willing to tie her life to mine permanently if it meant saving mine. I drew in a ragged breath, a tearing sensation rending through my heart. "I know. I love you too. And this is the best thing I can offer you."

"No, it's not. The best thing you can offer is being *here*, with me, fighting our battles together. That's what I want."

That was what I wanted too. It was just hard to imagine I could ever really have it. But her voice and her words were working their way into my mind and my soul, and even if I doubted myself, I believed in her.

"Just wait," she said into my silence. "That's all I'm asking. Don't run in there knowing you can't possibly make it out. Wait and give us time to find a better way. Trust me. Please."

How could I say no to her? But how could I sit here uselessly while our chance might totally pass us by? I pressed my hand to my forehead.

"I'll try," I said. "If there's a way I can make it work so that I get to come back to you, I promise you that's what I'll do."

She must have been able to tell she wasn't going to get a more definite answer out of me. "Will you at least let me know before you make any move?" she asked.

That would only make it harder, but I probably owed her that. "I will."

When I'd ended the call, I sagged back in the chair, feeling drained but restless at the same time. I had about five minutes to recover before my other phone dinged.

*We've arrived*, the text from an unfamiliar number said. *Willing to make arrangements to meet.*

The joymancers. I sat up straight with a stutter of my pulse.

I could put them off. Did it really make sense to throw myself on their mercy? I'd had a plan for making sure they committed to the deal, but after that, I knew I wouldn't have a hope in hell of getting away from them if they wanted to detain me or worse.

But Rory wanted me alive. Rory wanted me with her.

She also wanted to stop the wretched plan against the Naries that had been tormenting her almost as much as it had them.

How could I come up with anything better than the basic approach I'd decided on? I could barely cast any magic of my own. No matter how you sliced it, *someone* had to go out there and talk to them. It wasn't as if this were some kind of movie where you could just—

Some kind of movie. For a second, I lost my breath. Then I was scrambling out of the chair toward the door with a brilliant spark of hope chasing at my heels.

* * *

"It's done," Mr. Oakgrime said, handing me the silver cufflinks he'd embedded the spell in. I'd asked for something small enough to easily fit in my pocket and distinctive enough that I couldn't mistake it. "This one will activate when you squeeze the clip and run your thumb over the face of the other one at the same time, and it'll have a range of about a mile. You should get a half hour or so out of the spell."

The mage studio owner gave me a curious look, but I'd just funded a full year's worth of movie productions, sparing him the need to keep scraping together the cash. It'd cost me more than half my accumulated savings, but it was worth it for this token and his discretion. He wasn't going to risk irritating me by prying any more than he already had.

It was too bad that with my magic stripped away, I'd

never get to work for the guy after all. He really was all right.

I squashed down the pang of loss and gave him a playful salute. "Sounds perfect. I look forward to seeing your next films."

"After this, you can claim a seat at the premiere screenings."

If I was around for that. This trick would go a long way toward keeping me out of danger, but tangling with the joymancers was never going to be *safe*.

He waved to me as I headed out. I flagged a taxi and hopped into the back seat, already tapping out a text to my mysterious contact.

*I'm ready. I'm here alone, but you can pick the spot if you want that security. I just need to speak to someone who has authority over your whole group. If I can't get that, I can't give you the rest of the info.*

The response came back so quickly I suspected they'd been discussing where they'd want to arrange our meet-up while they waited on me. *Central Park, just north of the Bow Bridge. We can meet your terms—but we'll be watching to make sure you've been true to your word.*

Of course they would. "Central Park," I told the driver. "West side." Hopefully I could get there fast enough to take a decent lay of the land before the others arrived.

To make that more likely, I delayed my reply while texting Rory instead. *I promised I'd let you know before I made a move. I've found the solution for you. If all goes well, I'll be back there before dinner.*

*What are you planning?* she wrote back.

*I'll tell you when it works. Save me some embarrassment if it doesn't. But they shouldn't even see me, let alone lay a hand or a spell on me.* I paused before sending and added, *Trust me?*

I didn't realize how worried I was that she wouldn't until her next message popped up. *I will. That doesn't mean I'm not going to be worrying, though. Let me know you're okay as soon as it's over.*

*That I can do.*

I confirmed the Central Park meeting with my joymancer contact, saying I could be there in an hour. It was actually only fifteen minutes before the cab reached the sprawl of trees. I directed the driver a little farther north and then handed him a few twenties as I leapt out. "Keep the change!"

His startled "Thank you!" followed me down the path.

Plenty of regular people were strolling through the park, enjoying the fall colors. I would let the joymancers decide how to handle the Naries here. I jogged around the lake beneath the blazes of red and yellow leaves to the pale gray arch of the bridge. The clouds that had clotted the sky back by the university had drawn back; the birds that hadn't flown south yet chirped gleefully overhead. I'd have enjoyed the atmosphere more if I hadn't been so wired.

When I reached the bridge, I slowed and ambled over it as if I were simply passing by. There was no sign of any mages staking the place out yet. I chose a tree not far from the north end of the bridge, dug a little hole in the dirt by its roots with a stick, dropped one cufflink in, and covered it over. Perfect.

Now I just needed a place to keep myself unnoticed and out of the way. The castle wasn't too far from here.

I picked up my pace again as I left the bridge behind. When I reached the stone walls of the modern-day castle, I circled it and sat myself on the grass nearby, taking a cross-legged pose. Anyone who looked this way could think I was meditating.

Oakgrime had said the spell would work most smoothly if I was relaxed. Ha. I did my best to actually meditate, breathing slowly in and out, relaxing into the cheerful park sounds and the streaks of warm sunlight that split the fall chill. About fifty minutes into the hour I'd told the joymancers I'd need, I reached into my pocket for the other cufflink and squeezed and swiped to activate the spell.

Immediately, most of my awareness jerked across the grounds to a view of the end of the bridge. I could still make out a faint afterimage of the area around the castle, enough that I'd realize if anyone approached me, but the clearest sensations came from the spot where I'd planted the first cufflink.

For all intents and purposes, I *was* there. Oakgrime had conjured me an illusionary self. I'd asked him to make it a man in his early twenties that didn't look particularly like me, because there was no need to incriminate myself if I didn't have to, but otherwise I wasn't sure who "I" was right now. But when I thought to step forward, the illusionary body my consciousness had slipped into moved toward the path. I let out a soft laugh and felt it tickle through my illusionary chest. To anyone around me, I'd look perfectly solid and real.

Perfect. The joymancers would have a hard time taking me into custody like this. But along with my awareness, the small pool of magic I was holding behind my collarbone could flow through this conjured body too. I might have thought of using this technique earlier if I'd still had the skills to pull it off myself.

I didn't have time to dwell on that. A middle-aged man, maybe forty with plenty of salt in his peppery hair, came striding across the bridge with a purposeful air. A quiver of magic brushed over me. Either he or unseen allies he'd brought with him were scanning the area around the bridge with magic—making sure *I* hadn't brought unseen allies.

Not a problem. I'd barely brought myself.

As he reached the end of the bridge, his gaze fell on me. I raised my hand at a jaunty angle. "Just me, as promised."

His eyes sharpened as he took me in, maybe sensing something wasn't quite natural about the figure he was faced with. But obviously Oakgrime had put every skill he used in his movie effects to work on this spell. The joymancer didn't say anything, only stalked closer until he was about five feet away. With a murmur and a wave of his hand, he cast a spell into the air around us—to ensure our privacy, I guessed.

"You're one of them, I assume," he said in a disdainful tone.

"Funny thing—turns out we're all individuals even if we work magic the same way," I said. "And I don't happen to agree with a whole lot of 'them' right now."

He made a skeptical sound, but he gestured for me to go on. "What did you have to tell us, then?"

I crossed my arms over my chest, which at the moment felt more substantial than my real body back behind the castle. "First things first. Do you have the authority to speak for all of the joymancers who came with you? Because I'll only deal with someone who does, and the deal will catch you out if you're lying."

"I can," the joymancer said. "But I'm not inclined to make any deals."

"Oh, I think you should be. You want to know that I'm giving you true information and not leaving out any details that could get you killed, right? Well, I'd like to know that you all aren't going to barge into the situation slaughtering indiscriminately. I mean, you shouldn't want to do that anyway, seeing as you're the 'good guys' and all. So you agree to keep the violence within reason, and I'll agree to tell the whole truth and nothing but the truth, and we'll both be happy."

The guy shifted his weight from one foot to the other, considering. From what Rory had told us about her interrogation in California, the joymancers had trouble believing *anything* a fearmancer said. They hadn't even trusted that an insight spell couldn't be warped. But a deal like this, offered voluntarily while the joymancer cast part of the magic, couldn't be tampered with if spoken right. And my request was perfectly reasonable.

"What *exactly* would you be asking us to commit to?" he said.

"You'll need to confirm that your commitment extends to all the people you'll bring with you, and agree that you won't inflict lethal or likely-to-become-lethal damage on any person you encounter at the location I'll tell you, except when your life is directly under threat—and then only enough to fend off that threat. You've got to defend yourself. I recognize that. But no one should die unless it's either you or them. Doesn't that fit with your joymancer principles?"

I knew it did, even if the joymancers sometimes bent those principles when it came to fighting with us. The man pursed his lips. "And you… will commit to telling us everything you know about this dire new problem you say the fearmancers are creating, including any dangers we'll face going up against it?"

"I'll commit to telling you everything I know about what's happening at this specific location, and any dangers at all you could run into in tackling that." I didn't want to risk them digging out information about the university at the same time.

"Hold on." The man stepped back and raised a phone to his ear. Of course a joymancer would need to hash out a decision with his colleagues even if he was technically in charge.

He'd better not take very long. I didn't think more than ten minutes had passed since I'd activated the spell, and Oakgrime had probably been conservative in his estimate of how long it'd last, but this gambit wasn't going to work if I faded away in front of the guy.

I maintained a casual stance as he finished his talk. My gaze skimmed over the trees around us, but if he'd brought company, they were keeping themselves well-hidden. I couldn't afford to waste my limited magic reserves to check. There wasn't any reason for them to go poking around as far as the castle.

After a few long minutes, the joymancer came back to me. "All right," he said. "We'll proceed, with the wording as already stated. Beyond that, we owe you nothing."

I didn't love that turn of phrase, but I wasn't going to argue with it, not with time slipping away. "And I owe you nothing either. Let's do this then."

I watched carefully as the man cast his part of the deal, braced for a jitter of rejection that would tell me he couldn't make this commitment for all of his colleagues here after all. But it didn't come. Carefully, I twined my small stash of magic into the words of my promise.

By the time the spell had solidified, the space behind my sternum was aching with emptiness, and my real body had broken out in a sweat. But it was done. Even the joymancer looked satisfied.

He crossed his arms over his chest. "All right. Let's hear what we're up against."

"There's a town upstate, a small one, where the fearmancers are running a sort of experiment," I said. A tug of magic encouraged the words from my throat, but I didn't need that to keep going. "They've revealed their magic to the locals and are terrorizing them into submission."

Just that statement was enough to make the man's face harden and his shoulders go rigid. "What town?" he demanded. "What sort of defenses do the fearmancers have in place? How long has this been going on?"

Apparently he'd never heard of the concept of "one thing at a time." I refrained from reminding him of that, telling him the details I was aware of, which honestly weren't a great deal beyond my own observations. It wasn't as if I'd consulted with my supposed father for an inside take. I couldn't even say what exactly the barons had been hoping to gain from the scheme.

"That's all?" the joymancer prodded when I finished, but the tug of magic had faded. Our deal knew I'd kept my end.

"I've told you everything I know about it," I said. The illusionary nerves in this body were starting to twitch. I didn't think it was going to hold much longer. "And now I think I'd better get going."

The man's tone turned dark. "We didn't make any agreements about *that*."

Clearly on cue, several figures shimmered into view around the trees. I couldn't help laughing. "And you call us the villains. Nice to see just how much we can trust you when you don't have any magic compelling you to keep your word."

The man in front of me didn't bother to answer. He snapped out a spell no doubt aimed to hold me in place as other voices pealed out around us—and I threw myself free of the illusion. My awareness jolted fully into my real body with a gasp of breath. My vision cleared, taking in the joymancer-free view ahead of me.

I shoved myself to my feet and trotted off toward the road where I could catch another cab, a smirk crossing my lips at the thought of the confusion I must have left behind with my abrupt disappearance. I'd better make sure they didn't catch me *now*, because those joymancers were sure to be pissed off.

# CHAPTER TWENTY-THREE

*Rory*

As lovely as the view from my bedroom window was, with the sprawl of forest on either side and the lake glinting straight ahead, at this particular moment I couldn't help wishing it pointed in the other direction toward the garage. Jude had texted us about an hour ago to say he'd carried out the deal with the joymancers and gotten away from them unscathed, and then a little while later to report that he was officially on the road back to campus, but I didn't think I'd feel totally at ease until I saw his red Mercedes coming up the road.

No, I wasn't going to feel completely better until I could wrap my arms around him and hug him with everything I had in me. The choked sensation that had come over me when I'd talked to him on the phone rose up again.

If we hadn't found his note soon enough, if we hadn't

realized where he'd gone… He could have been dead right now. Or at best locked away in joymancer custody, possibly for the rest of his life. It'd been bad enough seeing him attacked right in front of me, but at least I'd been with him, we'd had doctors right here to help him. Imagining him struck down all those miles away from anyone who cared about him—it brought a teary heat back into my eyes.

Somehow, I had to convince him that he wasn't a burden. That he made my life brighter. And I wouldn't get into how much I'd have liked to punch his false father in the face for not only trying to murder the "son" he'd brought into this world but also for making him feel like that was the best future he could have.

It was way too early for Jude to be back even at the speed he liked to drive, but I couldn't contain my restlessness any longer. I grabbed one of my classroom texts to keep me somewhat occupied while I waited and headed out.

I'd only made it halfway down the first flight of stairs when I caught sight of a head of chocolate-brown curls coming around the landing below.

I froze in place, my arm tensing around my book. Maggie caught sight of me and halted too. We eyed each other for a moment.

"What are you doing here?" I said, at the same time as she said, "Rory, I think we—"

At the clash of voices, she shut her mouth and then started again. "I was hoping we could talk. Properly. I know… when you came to see me before, I didn't really listen. So this time I came to you. I think I made a mistake, a big one, and I'd like to fix that if I can."

I studied her expression. Was this a new trick to try to get me to admit something she could use against me? Had she caught on that I had a plan in the works with the other scions? If she realized what we'd arranged—if she told my mother or any of the barons…

I'd better find out where she was going with this, at least.

"All right," I said. "Maybe not in the stairwell, though?"

The corners of her lips twitched with a hint of a smile. "Not the best conversation spot, I agree. Since I'm the one imposing on you, why don't you pick wherever you'd feel most comfortable?"

I didn't like the idea of inviting her into my dorm, and I didn't want her in the private space of the scion lounge. I debated for a moment and then said, "Let's go down to the lake."

With the cooling weather, no one was really hanging around by the water these days. The rough path that led past the Stormhurst Building down to the dock was completely deserted. The wind whipped through my hair, colder right off the water than it was on the green, but the chill would help keep me alert. I tucked my hands into my pockets, my book still wedged under my arm, and turned to face Maggie as we reached the rocky shoreline.

My back tensed instinctively when she spoke a few casting words, my thumb moving to the curve of my new ring, but her gesture and the tickle of energy over my skin suggested she was only making doubly sure we wouldn't be interrupted or overheard. She tugged her hair back behind her ears to try to keep it out of the wind's reach. The dock creaked with the rocking of the waves.

"The way you talked to your mother after the incident in town—you really meant all that, didn't you?" she said, giving me an unusually pensive look. "You don't actually like the way the barons have been changing things."

Did she think I could have made up my horror at the deaths of those kids as some kind of strategic move? I made a face at her. "Strangely enough, I'm not really inclined to discuss my opinions on politics with you at the moment. You've been accusing me of wanting to screw up my mother's plans for ages now. I've already said everything I can to defend myself."

"That's not what I meant. Before—I thought you just wanted to be the one making the calls yourself, not that you had any problem with her decisions."

I wasn't sure how me wanting to go against my mother was any better than me wishing I could be making the same decisions in her place. Actually, in most fearmancers' eyes, it was probably worse.

"I'm still not seeing how this conversation is going to lead anywhere good," I said.

Maggie let out an exasperated sound. "Well, it doesn't work if you can't meet me halfway."

I had to laugh. "Meet you halfway? You're pushing me to say something that'll look like I'm a traitor. How exactly are you sticking your neck out at all? And even if you were, at this point it'd have to be a lot more than halfway. You've gone out of your way to try to screw me over more than once, and I've never done anything at all to you. If I'm going to trust you, you'd better show a whole lot more trust in me than you have so far."

Maggie opened her mouth with a flash of her eyes and then closed it again. After a moment, she grimaced. "All right. That's fair. I wasn't really— You know what people here are like. I've gotten used to keeping my opinions totally private."

What opinions? I had to admit, she'd gotten me a little curious. Nonetheless… "It's going to take more than just saying a bunch of things. I'll need to be sure you're not lying."

"Okay." She hesitated and seemed to brace herself. "What did you have in mind?"

If this could go down any way I wanted? My first instinct was to turn to my specialty, Insight, but for finding out specific information, those spells weren't totally reliable. Maybe someone as practiced at manipulation as Maggie appeared to be could make sure her mind didn't reveal the warning signs. In this particular case, I agreed with my mother on the most useful type of spell. Persuasion got straight to the point. It had worked well against the guy Maggie had compelled to speak to me before.

"If you want to have a real conversation, first I'd like to ask a few questions, with a persuasive spell to make sure you answer them honestly," I said. "I know that's a big ask, but… I can't see us getting anywhere without that. If you don't trust me that much, it's okay. We can put whatever it is you're trying to get at on hold until you do."

Maggie was silent for a long moment. The wind warbled around us, and the water hissed against the shore. Finally, she said, "Okay. I'll give you that. Because your mother would never have said it that way."

I didn't know what to make of that last comment, but it didn't matter when I was getting what I'd asked for. I considered my questions carefully. "Ready?"

She nodded.

"*You will answer my questions truthfully until I end this spell*," I said, propelled by my magic. I didn't fling the spell hard, and I didn't need to, because Maggie had lowered her defenses as agreed. A quiver raced through me as the spell hit its mark and lodged itself in her mind.

"Why did you come to talk to me today?" I asked.

"Because I realized that we might actually have similar goals," Maggie replied without hesitation. "I thought we wanted opposite outcomes, but if that's not the case, we should be working together. I had to find out where you really stand."

"What goals are you talking about? What do you want to see happen with the barons?"

She winced, but she didn't resist. "I want to see the Bloodstones led by someone who'll be evenhanded and compassionate, not ruthlessly vicious. And I'd like to see the torturing of the Naries stopped."

I blinked at her, startled silent. She had to be telling the truth—I'd compelled her to—but it never for an instant would have occurred to me that her interests would line up so much with mine.

"Why were you so sure I was on the ruthlessly vicious side?"

Her gaze dropped to the ground. "I've heard a lot of stories about the Bloodstones. Not good ones. And when you came back, from the bits and pieces I overheard of your behavior on campus, it sounded as if you were already trying to bend everyone to your will. I'm guessing those stories were warped by the people telling them—or maybe they didn't have the full story themselves. After the way you interrupted the spell to find your mother, and how you took Lillian out of the picture when you saw how much she was supporting her… that seemed to confirm what I'd believed. I'm sorry."

Forcing her answers was making me increasingly uncomfortable. If we *were* on the same side, I shouldn't pay her back by treating her like an enemy the way she'd treated me before. I ended the spell with a murmured word and a flick of my fingers. Maggie's shoulders sank with relief.

"So…" she said, her stance tensing all over again as she waited for my response.

I managed half a smile. "I'd say our goals are pretty much the same, and it's too bad you didn't figure that out sooner, because I could have used a hand a heck of a lot of times in the last few months."

She let out a halting chuckle and swiped her hand over her hair. "Thank God."

"Just so we're clear," I added, "I don't want to hurt my

mother. I don't want to take the barony away from her. I just want *her* to stop hurting other people."

"You realize you might not be able to get that as long as she is still baron."

"Yeah." That understanding had been weighing on me more and more since my plea at the edge of town. "But if there's a way I can get through to her, I'll take that over forcing the issue any day."

Maggie smiled too, her expression wry. "Which is exactly the kind of attitude I wish I saw more of here."

It was still hard to wrap my head around everything she'd told me. I sat down on one of the larger rocks near the empty fire pit.

"I looked up your background after you made all those accusations," I said, deciding it was better to leave Declan's involvement unmentioned for now. "I know you didn't even live here until you came over from Europe to attend Blood U. If you're so bothered by the way things are here, why haven't you spoken up? Or gone back to however they are where you're from? Why is it specifically the Bloodstones you want to see be different? It's not like most of the barony families are any better."

"Ah." Maggie ducked her head, a renewed reluctance coming over her even after everything I'd just acknowledged. She bit her lip. "How much do you know about your family's history?"

Oh, dear Lord, had my mother or someone before her managed to clash even with people on the other side of the ocean? What crimes had they committed over there?

"Not a lot," I admitted. "I'm still finding out things

about my mother's rule. I know her father was baron before her… and that's about all I've got when it comes to anyone in the previous generations."

"Okay, well… Before I explain, I want to remind you that I meant what I said about us working together. I was compelled to tell the truth when I told you that. I'm not looking to oust you now."

To *oust* me? I frowned. "What do you—"

She held up her hand. "Let me get this out. I've managed not to let anything slip for a whole decade—it's not easy switching gears." She inhaled sharply. "Your grandfather had a brother. He moved to Portugal nearly fifty years ago, when he was in his twenties, and then he quickly fell out of touch with the family here. As far as I can tell, at this point everyone assumes he died not long after that. But he didn't. He only passed a few months before I came over here." She met my gaze with an almost defiant expression. "He was *my* grandfather."

I stared back at her as the full implications sank in. My jaw went slack. "Then… you're a Bloodstone."

"Yeah." She scuffed her shoe against the ground, sending a pebble rattling away. "But there wasn't any honor in the name for him. He left here and let himself drop out of touch because it horrified him the way everyone within the family was so busy jockeying for power, the way they treated anyone who disagreed with them. The stories he told me… He changed his last name not long after he came over, and that's the one he passed on to my father and me. He never wanted any of us to have anything to do with the family here."

"But you came back."

"My father died when I was twelve—a cancer that was too aggressive for even magic to stop. For some reason, while I was grieving I got curious about the relatives I had over here. I did some digging and found out that the Bloodstone barony was essentially vacant. And once the idea got in my head, I couldn't shake it. I could come back and fix all the things that had driven Grandpa away. He would have tried to talk me out of it, but after he passed on too… I don't think my mother totally understands why I moved, but she didn't argue with me. They never told her much about that part of our history."

She was my second cousin. I studied her face more intently than I ever had before. Her complexion and hair color was similar to mine and my mother's; her face was rounder, but the shape of her nose and jaw might have hinted at the family resemblance too. Two generations removed had been enough to disguise her heritage from anyone who didn't have reason to suspect it.

"You didn't take the barony, though," I said. "You'd have had a stronger claim than my grandfather did while he was acting baron after they thought my mother had died, since he was past retirement age."

"I couldn't have been full baron until *I* was of age anyway," Maggie said. "And it seemed smartest to get to know the politics here and understand the situation as much as possible before I stepped in and painted a target on my back. I thought it would be easy. Everyone assumed you were still alive because the heart of the barony hadn't passed on—I figured it hadn't because of me, and I'd just present myself, and the mystery would be solved."

Her lips quirked up. "But just a couple months before I was due to graduate, you came into your magic, and even if *you* didn't know it, it set off some kind of reaction that confirmed you were alive. Suddenly the blacksuits were running around like crazy, determined to finally track you down, and I knew I didn't stand a chance at making a claim against the daughter of the rightful baron who'd been denied her proper place for so long already."

"So you waited some more," I filled in. "Is that why you went to work for the blacksuits—for Lillian?"

She nodded. "I wanted to know as much as possible about you from the get-go. It was just bad luck that Lillian ended up assigned to an urgent case that had us out of the way right when you got back. Maybe if I'd been here to see more for myself how those first months went down… I don't know. It just seemed like you were headed down the same path as all the awful Bloodstones my grandfather had told me about. I figured if I could expose you for something your mother and the other barons would recognize as a major crime, I'd have a chance to step in as an alternate scion."

"Wow." I leaned back on the stone, bracing myself with one hand against the rough surface. "I guess, from what I do know about the Bloodstones and the other baronies, I can't blame you for coming at it that way. Even if I wish you'd given me more of a chance."

"Better late than never?" Maggie exhaled in a rush. "This mess with the Naries—we've got to stop the barons from going any further with it. It's bad enough when fearmancers are screwing each other over left and right without giving them the entire world full of nonmagical people to push around on top of that. Maybe if we tackle the problem together and pool our resources, we can come up with a feasible approach. I don't care how stuck in their ways the baronies are—we should have a say too."

A laugh spilled out of me, even though none of this was exactly funny. Maybe I could cross one worry out of the many dogging me off my list.

"You know, I've actually already set something in motion that I'm hoping will get us back on the right track," I said. "Whether you'll agree with my approach is another thing altogether. But we could certainly use someone helping with damage control on the blacksuit side of things, if you're game."

# CHAPTER TWENTY-FOUR

*Rory*

Jude texted us as soon as he'd parked in the garage. I'd already been heading over after finishing up my talk with Maggie, and I got there just as he emerged from the building. He walked up to me with his mouth set at an awkward angle but his eyes gleaming, looking sheepish and remorseful and proud all at once.

I grabbed him in a hug and buried my face in the crook of his neck, absorbing the firmness of his lean chest through his sweater and the sharp smell of his skin as if I needed all that to convince myself he was really here. He hugged me back just as tightly. For a minute we just stood there without talking, locked in the embrace. It took me that long to be sure I wasn't going to start crying all over again.

"I'm sorry," he said finally, his voice rough. "I was

trying to do something *for* you. I didn't mean to hurt you."

I let out a huff. "Well, keep in mind for the future that I only want you doing things for me if *you* come back when you're finished. You don't have to prove anything to me. You don't owe me anything. I just want you."

"Okay." He dipped his head close to mine, sounding a little choked up himself. Then I felt his lips curl with a smile against my cheek. "I did manage to pull it off *and* come back. I get some credit for that, right?"

I had to swat him. "It's very impressive. I just wish you hadn't given me a heart attack along the way. Now I want to hear all about how you pulled it off." When I glanced around, the other scions were crossing the field toward us. "Maybe we should take this conversation to the scion lounge?"

We all headed back to Ashgrave Hall. Before Jude said anything else, the other guys did a thorough sweep of the room both physically and magically, checking for any sign of outside monitoring. Malcolm and Connar worked together to weave a spell to completely seal the space.

"The staff might start to wonder what we're up to if we take these extreme measures too often," Malcolm said when they'd finished, swiping his forearm across his brow. "But we can't go driving off to random fields every time we need to talk."

"And the 'random fields' around here might not be the safest right now." I sank onto the sofa with Jude, my hand twined with his. "You told the joymancers everything they'd need to know? Did it sound like they're going to intervene?"

"Oh, they were definitely horrified by the information. I don't know how long it'll take them to scope out the situation in town and decide how to tackle it, especially since I did get their guarantee they'll go easy on the deadly force, but I'd guess they won't leave it too long. If not later today, then tomorrow." He ran his hand through his hair, looking briefly uneasy at the thought. He had just called down mages he'd generally considered enemies on his own people.

I squeezed his hand. "It's the best thing we could have done. The barons have to see they can't expect to take steps like this without some backlash. And we'll have some extra help in mitigating the damage. I'll tell you all about that after you explain how you handled the deal."

Jude told the story of going to one of his fearmancer movie studio contacts, his voice and gestures becoming more animated as he played out his conversation with the joymancers. Whatever worries he might have about the events he'd set in motion there—or the role he was going to take in our society in general—it obviously hadn't mattered to him that much that he'd been relying on someone else's magic. The fact that he'd come up with the plan was enough to satisfy his ego.

When he'd finished, Declan leaned forward in the armchair he'd taken. "You threw a lot of money at that studio to get the guy's help."

"He had no idea what I needed the spell for," Jude said quickly.

Declan gave him a soft smile. "That's not what I was getting at. Of course you were careful. But you can't count on accessing any more of the Killbrook funds at this point. I just wanted to say that we can all pitch in to cover our portion of the costs. You did this for all of us—and you took on all the risk. You shouldn't have to give up your savings too."

"Oh." Jude's cheeks turned faintly pink. "I didn't expect—it was my money, my decision to take that approach."

"Declan's right," I said. "It was a better idea than anything we'd come up with, and it made sense to go to an expert to pull it off." Jude might have been able to conjure an illusion that strong if he'd had his usual magical capacity, but I doubted any of the rest of us could have. To use that strategy, we'd have needed outside assistance one way or another, and to give them something to convince them to pitch in.

"Why don't we wait and make sure everything pans out the way we're hoping before you start repaying me?" Jude said with a chuckle that didn't totally hide his discomfort. He clearly liked that he'd taken care of everything himself, so maybe it was better not to push the issue just yet. He turned to me. "What's this extra help you were talking about?"

I leaned back into the firm cushions of the sofa. "That… is a long and kind of crazy story."

I repeated most of what Maggie had told me, watching the guys' expressions grow increasingly shocked with each added detail. "Holy fuck," Malcolm said when I'd finished from where he was sitting in the other armchair.

Connar, who'd sat down at the other side of the sofa, reached to grasp my free hand. "Are you sure she's willing to support you and not still looking to make a bid for the barony herself?"

"I didn't get the impression she ever really *wanted* to be baron," I said. "She just didn't want to see the Bloodstone barons continuing down the same path they'd been on, and if the only way she could do that was to take the reins herself, then she was willing to try. She seemed relieved that we could work together rather than fighting."

"And what did she make of the joymancer plan?" Declan asked with a cock of his head.

"I don't think the fearmancer community overseas has the same tensions with the joymancers there as we do here. She obviously understood why they'd be willing to step in, but she didn't see it as the same kind of betrayal most people from here would. She actually complimented me on being willing to accept their help." Which wasn't exactly the way I'd have phrased what we'd arranged with the joymancers, but I hadn't been going to correct her.

"So, now we wait." Malcolm's hands clenched where they were resting on his thighs. Standing back while others took on the brunt of the work didn't come naturally to the Nightwood scion. I wasn't looking forward to pretending everything was normal while we braced for the attack either.

A twinge of empathy ran through me, seeing his response, and then bloomed into something deeper and sharper in my chest. I let my gaze travel to all four of the guys sitting around me. For a few seconds, my throat locked up around my voice. But I couldn't deny what I'd been feeling more and more over recent days. If they thought I was ridiculous, they could just say so.

But maybe they wouldn't. Maybe we actually had a chance. *We should have a say too*, Maggie had pointed out, and that applied to a whole lot more than just the barons' policies about the Naries.

And if, despite the care we'd taken, our plans went totally wrong, I might not get another chance to say this later. They should know how much they meant to me now, before I faced losing any of them again.

"Is there something else, Rory?" Connar asked, studying my face. I mustn't have hidden my emotions very well.

I looked down at my lap, at my hands joined with Jude's on one side and Connar's on the other, and then back up. "The past few weeks," I said, "with all of us together, working toward the same things, looking out for each other… and everything else—it's made me realize some things."

Jude's fingers tightened around mine, but to my surprise it was Malcolm whose stance tensed the most. What did he think I was going to say? I hurried onward, hoping he wasn't afraid of what I actually meant to get at.

"I care so much about all of you. I don't know how I'd have made it through my time here if it wasn't for the bits of happiness I've gotten with you—and I think part of that happiness is from it being *all* of us, in harmony, caring about each other. Like a family, like you've always said, in every possible way. And I… I don't want to give that up."

Malcolm's shoulders had come down, but his mouth opened and closed as if he didn't know how to respond.

"Rory," Declan said, and trailed off uncertainly.

I barreled onward, my chest constricting. "I know it probably sounds selfish. I know I've got less to lose than most of the rest of you, and I don't want you to have to give up any of the things you've worked toward. I want to see you standing around the table of the pentacle with me too. I just had to put that out there, so you know, in case that's something you'd want to try to have too. If the barons now can change policies as huge as keeping our magic secret from Naries, then there've got to be options for adjusting the rules around the baronies and inheritance and all that. There's got to be a balance we can find between ruling and being together. If we decide to give it a shot. I won't be upset with you if you'd rather not."

I shut my mouth, my throat hoarse as if I'd been talking for hours. An anxious heat trickled over my skin.

"It wouldn't be easy for you either," Declan said quietly into the silence that had fallen. "There'll be people who don't understand, people who'll use it as an excuse to discredit you and your position."

I met his eyes, my jaw tightening. "I don't give a shit. Let them try. The only people whose opinion really matters to me are right here in this room. But if it'd be too much after everything you've already had to deal with—"

The slow smile that spread across his face stopped me, his hazel eyes gleaming brighter than I'd ever seen them before. "No. I think you're right—I think there could be a way to make it work. And if there is… I want to find it, because I've never wanted to give this up either."

Connar lowered his head to press his lips to my shoulder, his arm tucking right around mine. "If I can keep you in my life the way things are now and not screw up the rest of it—hell yes. Whatever it takes."

I turned to Jude, realizing I might need to add a little extra for his benefit. "Everything I said goes for you too, no matter what ends up happening with the Killbrook barony, or your magic, or—or anything. You belong with us. You belong with *me*."

Jude beamed at me, his expression joyful if maybe a little terrified at the same time. "Yes, I do, Fire Queen." He touched the edge of my chin and drew me into a kiss so determined it left my head spinning.

When he eased back, my gaze moved to Malcolm. The Nightwood scion hadn't said anything yet. He was watching the rest of us without any hint of what he was feeling on his face. Then he swallowed audibly, and that sound spoke of all the emotion he was tamping down.

"You're sure?" he said. "We only just— You haven't had that much time with me—not that was good, anyway. Lord knows there's no one else I've ever wanted half as much as I want you, but I wouldn't expect—"

"I know," I said, cutting him off before he had to

express all his doubts. "I know *you.* I don't need any more time to be sure."

He laughed. "Well then, what the fuck is there to decide? All I want to know is how long we've got to wait until our asshole parents step out of the way so we can christen that table the way no pentacle before has."

A giddy quiver ran through me at the thought. The temperature in the room seemed to have risen by at least a few degrees, with a thrum of energy that definitely wasn't just magic. I wet my lips. "Seeing as that might take a while… I don't think we've even properly 'christened' our lounge."

Jude teased his fingers over my hair with an arch of his eyebrows. "Just to make the agreement official and all?"

A giggle slipped out of me. "Yes. That's definitely the only reason."

I gave him a quick kiss to follow the one we'd already shared and then turned to tug Connar's mouth to mine. When our lips parted, Declan and Malcolm had gotten up from their chairs. Declan moved to me first, bending over to cup my cheek and claim my lips with his careful intensity. He drew to the side to leave room for the Nightwood scion to lean in. Malcolm's kiss was all commanding passion.

By the time I'd kissed them all, an eager trembling had spread through my body. I wanted all of them, but I didn't know quite what to do with myself to make that happen. Maybe, like the rest of this complex and yet instinctive relationship we'd fallen into together, it was a matter of figuring things out as we went.

Jude was stroking my thigh. Connar traced the curve of my breasts through my blouse and swept his thumb over one nipple. As pleasure rippled through me, Malcolm grasped the hem of the blouse and tugged it upward. It slid off my skin and whispered to the floor in a silky puddle.

Malcolm knelt to plant kisses up the side of my knee. Jude eased my skirt higher, Connar undid the clasp of my bra and sank lower to suck the peak of my breast into his mouth, and Declan bowed over me, tipping my chin up with one teasing finger so he could capture my mouth again. My hands roamed over all of them, slipping down Jude's chest, caressing Declan's cheek, digging into Connar's short-cropped hair. Wave after wave of bliss rose through me.

As Malcolm's kisses trailed higher, Jude stroked his fingers right between my legs. I arched into his touch at the pulse of pleasure when he found the spot where I was neediest. Connar swiveled his tongue over my nipple, and I moaned into Declan's mouth.

Jude caught the hem of my panties and yanked them out from under my skirt. Malcolm helped pull them the rest of the way down. Connar raised his head and Declan shifted to the side, just in time for Jude to guide me over to straddle the Stormhurst scion.

Mmm, yes. I gazed down at Connar as I reached for his fly, and the stark hunger in his eyes told me he was just as eager for this as I was. As I freed him, his hands trailed down my sides. Declan's skimmed over my breasts, and

Malcolm gave my ass a teasing squeeze. Every nerve in my body hummed with gleeful anticipation.

I had just enough wherewithal left to murmur the protective spell over my core. I pumped my hand up and down Connar's cock, grinning at the precum already slicking the delicate skin, and sank down onto him with a gasp of delight.

Connar kissed my sternum. "You always feel perfect," he mumbled against my chest.

I let out a shaky breath as his solid length stretched me in the most delicious way. But this wasn't anywhere near enough. I wanted us all together in this act, the way we should be, the way I hoped we always would be.

Jude had shown me how that could be possible. As I lifted myself and sank even more deeply over Connar, I pulled the other guy closer, catching his eyes.

"Like before," I said. "You take me too."

A sharper desire flashed in his eyes. "Ask and ye shall receive," he said in a teasing tone.

Connar spread his legs to make room for Jude to approach me from behind. Jude massaged my ass, letting his thumb dip between my cheeks. With the murmur of a spell, the muscles there warmed and relaxed even more than they already had been. When he curved his thumb right into me, I bucked harder over Connar with a whimper.

Malcolm had settled onto the sofa beside us where he could fondle my breasts as I rocked with the other guys. I grasped his shirt and tugged him higher. He followed my motion with a hint of confusion in his eyes. They darkened when I jerked at the zipper on his slacks.

"You're a fucking marvel, Glinda," he muttered, all heated affection.

I peered at him through my eyelashes, which fluttered of their own accord as Jude tested me with a second finger. My voice came out with a hitch of a swallowed moan. "Right now I'm just aiming for marvelous fucking."

His chuckle turned into a groan when I bent my head to swirl my tongue around the head of his cock. His fingers raked into my hair, holding on but not propelling me, letting me take the lead even as they tightened with his pleasure. I sucked him deeper into my mouth, high on the pleasure already racing through me and the musky flavor on my tongue.

Declan was still with us too. I reached out toward him, and he met my hand with his. My squeeze of his fingers appeared to tell him exactly what I wanted. He knelt on the other side of the sofa and guided my hand to the bulge in his pants. Oh, yes. I could take all four of them—and I would.

With his help, I delved farther. His breath hitched as my fingers closed around his cock. Jude teased my opening one last time and then eased himself in with another murmur that turned the motion slick, the burn only enjoyable.

They were all mine, these brilliant, devoted men setting off flames everywhere we touched.

I had to keep the rhythm of my rocking slow so that I

could focus on all of them amid the pleasure whirling through me from every end, but all the same, that pleasure seared hotter with every movement. Declan stroked my back, and Connar cupped my breasts; Malcolm traced desperate patterns on my scalp with his fingertips. Jude kneaded my ass and thighs as if to work the sensations even deeper into me. We were a maelstrom of bliss, colliding and swaying together toward our breaking points.

Connar came first with a ragged sound, his hips jerking up as he plunged farther into me. He stayed inside me in the aftermath, one hand dipping down to toy with my clit. Another moan quivered out of me as I licked along the underside of Malcolm's cock, and he gripped my head tighter with a curse and a hot spurt of release.

As soon as he'd pulled out, he was kissing me, our tongues tangling together so tightly he must have been able to taste himself in my mouth. Connar pressed on my clit harder, Jude thrust into me at just the right angle in the same moment, and I cried out with the final surge of ecstasy.

My grip on Declan tightened, the pump of my hand speeding up. I pulled my lips from Malcolm's to add my mouth to my efforts on the Ashgrave scion. As I shuddered through the echoes of my orgasm, he and Jude reached their peak at almost the same moment.

We tumbled together into the sofa, a mass of torsos and limbs. I sprawled across Connar's lap with my head on Declan's thigh and Malcolm cradling my legs, Jude half sitting, half cuddling against me. No longer a maelstrom but a mass of love. It radiated through me so strongly my throat closed up.

Maybe we were only dreaming. Maybe in the end, no matter what we did, we'd find ourselves pairing off apart from each other to fulfill the demands of family and politics. But right now the possibilities ahead of us were endless. I might not know where we'd end up, but we couldn't have been more united in the face of our future.

# CHAPTER TWENTY-FIVE

*Malcolm*

My parents' rigidity about my sister's and my activities had irritated me plenty of times, but just this once, I was thankful for it. My sister had been attending this yoga and active meditation class for years, just changing the date as she aged up from one level to the next. I'd attended the same one before I'd come into my magic. A lot of the families felt the techniques left you better prepared to handle your power.

I parked across the street from the unassuming building that held the studio and ambled over through the thickening darkness. A streetlamp cast a pool of yellow light on the sidewalk by the door, giving off a faint hum. I stopped at the far edge of it, staying in the shadows.

Other young teen fearmancers headed up the stairs to the doors. After a few minutes, I spotted one of the Nightwood cars down the street, dropping Agnes off. The chauffeur would drop off the car and go home for the night now. Agnes pretty much always stayed over at one of her friends' houses on yoga nights.

Which meant, conveniently for my purposes, she was carrying an overnight bag. It bounced against her back as she trotted up the stairs, her pale hair gleaming in the stark light. I waited until the car had driven away around the corner and then hustled after her, catching her just inside the door.

Agnes startled when I caught her arm. Her expression shifted from nervous to concerned when she saw me.

"Malcolm?" she said in a low voice. "What are you doing here?"

"Getting you," I said just as quietly. "I'll explain in the car. You're skipping class. Go along with it, okay?"

Maybe I hadn't been there to provide as much big brotherly support as I'd have liked since I'd started at Blood U, but she trusted me enough to nod, thank God. I walked with her to the second floor, skipping the large room where the students were warming up for the instructor's office next door.

The head instructor was just on her way out. She blinked at the sight of me. "Mr. Nightwood. Feeling nostalgic and decided to rejoin us?"

I chuckled and shook my head. "Unfortunately, no. I actually have to call Agnes back home early. A family matter. Sorry to interrupt her practice."

"No, no, if something urgent has come up, that has to take priority. Don't let me keep you."

Easy enough. But then, I'd always known that would

be the easiest part of this whole scheme. At least I wouldn't have to worry about her calling my parents to inquire about Agnes's absence.

"See you next week!" Agnes said, and we hurried back down the stairs. She had enough discretion to keep her mouth shut until we were in the car. She tossed her overnight bag in the back seat and peered at me. "What's going on? Are we in some kind of trouble?"

"Not exactly. Not yet." My hands flexed as I gripped the steering wheel. I revved the engine and cruised down the street, feeling more secure as soon as the fearmancer assembly place was behind us.

I drove out of the city and parked on the side of a country lane I'd picked out ahead of time. There, I turned to face my sister. Agnes frowned at me in the dim light, her hands balled on her lap. She knew how things worked in our family well enough to realize I wouldn't have gone to these measures if I'd had *good* news.

"It's your choice what we do now," I said. "There *is* going to be trouble either way. I'm just trying to get you away from the worst of it. But it's going to be coming because of me, so… you decide how you want to handle it."

"What do you mean?" Agnes said. "What kind of trouble?"

The kind of trouble I'd tasted on the horizon from the first moment Rory had looked around the scion lounge and told us she wanted all of us not just now but always. The memory sent a little thrill through me, even if it came with a twist of my gut.

I couldn't tell her I wanted to stand by her, to fight for the right to keep her as a lover as well as a colleague and friend, and keep kowtowing to my father's demands. Sometime soon she and him would openly be on opposite sides again, and I'd have to side with her. I didn't need a fortune teller's prediction to know he wasn't going to be pleased about that.

Fuck him. Jude and Connar had cut themselves off from their parents already. Why the hell should I keep playing along? But I'd had reasons, and one of them was sitting right there across from me.

"Dad and I are going to have some… differences of opinion," I said. "Ones that'll make him pretty angry. I can keep myself out of the range of his wrath, but if you're still at home, you'll be an easy target. If he can't punish me, he'll punish you. I don't want to see that happen. If you give me the go-ahead, I've got an apartment set up not too far from Blood U. You can hide out there for the first little while until we figure out a more permanent solution."

Agnes stared at me. Her hands clenched even tighter. "You don't have to act like some kind of bodyguard. I'm not *that* weak. If he comes at me, I can deal with it, just like you already have."

She was trying to be as tough as my parents had always taught us to be. Her defiance brought a swell of affection into my chest even though it wasn't at all the reaction I'd wanted. But I had other angles I could use.

"What if you look at it this way?" I said. "I'm not asking so I can protect you. I'm asking so *you* can protect *me*. If Dad can threaten to hurt you… it'll be a whole lot harder for me to go through with anything. I don't want that on my conscience. So actually I'm being selfish by asking for this."

Her eyes widened as she considered my words. Her jaw worked. "You really think it'd be that bad?"

I let out a hoarse laugh. "I've never openly defied him before, and you've seen what he's capable of even when we're trying to appease him. Do you really *want* to stay in that house any longer?"

Her gaze slid to the windshield. She peered into the darkness beyond it for a minute as if searching for the answer there.

"No," she said. "I don't. Not if there's someplace else. What would we need to do?"

I let out an inward sigh of relief. "I've already transferred all my funds over to an account Mom and Dad can't touch. I think we can do the same for yours in the morning, if we get in there quickly enough before they realize what's happened. If not, I've got enough to cover both of us no problem. Anything that's not that important—clothes and whatever—we can buy new. But I'm going to swing by the house and grab a few things I don't want to leave behind. If there's anything you want me to get from your room, I'll pick that up too. Nothing big and not a lot, you understand."

"Of course." Before my eyes, she was switching into fugitive mode as if it were the most natural thing in the world. She straightened up in her seat with a thoughtful frown. "I don't know. I mean, there's stuff I *like* there, but not worth risking you getting caught over. I've got my phone and my wallet in my purse. There is… if you're going to go back anyway…"

"What?" I prodded gently.

Her hand rose to her neck. "That necklace with the rubies that was Grandma's. It's the only thing she gave specifically to me." She paused. "Well, maybe you should grab my whole jewelry box. Some of the other stuff in there is expensive. If we ever do need more money…"

I had to laugh again, with more humor this time. "I don't think it'll come to that, but if it makes you feel better, I can handle one jewelry box."

"And also—there's that rare book on illusion magic Mom got me for my birthday last year. I don't know where I'd find another copy of that. It's not too big."

"Got it. That's everything?"

Her chin firmed. "Yeah. The rest can be replaced."

I started the car again. "Are Mom and Dad at home?"

"Mom had some dinner she was going to be a special guest at. It sounded like she'd be home late. Dad was working in his office when I left, so he'll probably still be there."

Typical. And thankfully not too tricky to work around. No, the real challenge would be after they realized both of their kids had flown the coop.

"Okay," I said. "I'm going to park out of the way and slip in on foot. I need you to stay in the car while I'm gone, all right? It shouldn't take me more than half an hour. Even if you wanted to help, it'll be easier for me if I only have to worry about covering my own tracks."

She made a disgruntled sound, but she knew how much of an advantage I had when I could use magic and she hadn't come into hers yet. "Fine."

The house was only twenty minutes away. I left the car and Agnes in it near the start of the drive and jogged the rest of the way to the gate on foot. With a whispered spell, it opened silently. I slunk across the asphalt and the lawn to the front door.

That door opened just as quickly, the security spells recognizing me as a Nightwood. I cast more magic around me to soften my footsteps as I slipped inside.

A peek down the first floor hall showed me that Dad's study door was closed. There was no sign of him elsewhere in the house. With a little luck, he'd stay there until I'd gotten what I needed and left.

Upstairs, I started with Agnes's room, figuring I owed it to her to make sure I got at least the little bit she'd asked for. The jewelry box had heft but fit inside the backpack I'd brought along; the leather-bound book slipped into an outer pocket with no problem at all. Since I was there anyway, I grabbed a few changes of clothes out of her closet so she wouldn't need to replace her entire wardrobe immediately.

I'd brought pretty much everything that was important to me to my dorm room on campus before now, but I'd never seriously considered not coming home. There were a couple books on my shelf I didn't want my parents reclaiming, an ancient stone conducting piece I'd never been bold enough to use that had been passed on to me by my grandfather, and, because I was already here, my favorite headphones that I'd forgotten during my last visit.

The whole scavenging run took five minutes at most. My spirits started to lighten as I crept back down the stairs. I was almost home free.

Then a door creaked in the hall below. I froze on the third step from the bottom and crouched down, casting another spell to blend my form into the shadows.

A low laugh carried to my ears—a woman's laugh, but it didn't sound like my mother's. My body tensed. What the hell was Dad up to now? I could criticize a lot about him, but he'd always appeared fully united with his wife.

His voice reached me next, with that coaxing tone he took on when he was talking to someone he wanted to impress. "It hasn't changed much since you were last here, has it?"

"It really hasn't. You'd think you might have changed a thing or two in the last seventeen years."

The voice and the words struck me with a chill straight to my gut. I had to see, to confirm what my mind was telling me, even if it was risky. Braced to run if need be, I eased the rest of the way down the stairs and edged into view of the hallway.

My dad was standing across from his study door, leaning over a woman who'd propped herself against the wall with her arms folded loosely over her chest and a coy smile curving her lips. A woman with the same dark brown hair and elegant bearing as the one I'd left back on campus. He'd brought Rory's mother over to visit.

Not just to visit. That in itself might not have been so strange, but before I could dismiss it and back away, he leaned even closer, letting his lips brush the line of her jaw. She closed her eyes and tipped her head to the side to allow him access to her neck. One of her hands came up to trail over his chest.

"We have time," he murmured. "Don't think I'm done with you yet."

"Maybe I'm done with you," Baron Bloodstone said with a teasing tone.

Dad grasped her waist and pulled her flush against him, gazing down at her with a hunger I'd never seen on his face before—and never wanted to. "We both know that's not true. There never was anyone who could satisfy you like I can. That dolt Pierce certainly never came close."

Rory's mother shrugged, her eyes gone heavy lidded. "He was useful for a few things. He did as he was told. That's what I needed."

Dad's voice dropped to a growl. "Not all you needed. Let's not forget how well I took care of you. Now we've got seventeen years of catching up to do."

His hand dropped down her thigh to slide between their bodies, and I *really* didn't want to watch that. My stomach lurching, I pulled away. At least he was well distracted at the moment.

No one called after me when I snuck out the door. Still, nausea chased me past the gate and up the drive. The comments I'd overheard spun in my head. I stopped just before I reached the road, my hand to my stomach, a much more horrible idea than that of my father cheating coming over me.

He and Rory's mother had a thing. It probably wasn't the first time two barons had dallied on the side. But... they'd clearly been dallying before her supposed death. He'd suggested they'd been seeing each other while she was married.

How careful had they been, if they'd been careful at all? Because if they hadn't, then Rory Bloodstone, perfect Rory with her four magical strengths and spirit to spare, might just be the product of the two most powerful barons currently living.

Which would also make her my half-sister.

# CHAPTER TWENTY-SIX

*Rory*

At night, the campus garage was even gloomier than usual. I walked to Connar's car with him, noting the empty spot where Malcolm usually parked. He'd let us know that he'd gotten his sister safely to the apartment, but he had to lay down more protections to stop anyone from locating her there, so it might be a while before he got back.

And now the Stormhurst scion was heading out too, with a similar mission. We stopped at the car, and he turned to me, setting his hands on the sides of my shoulders. "I'll let you know everything that's going on," he said quietly. "And I won't get close to the house until my parents are definitely gone." He paused. "Did Viceport say how soon that doctor might be able to see Holden?"

"She didn't want to tell him the details ahead of time, but it sounded like he could fit it in quickly as long as the situation seems secure enough. Hopefully whatever happens in the next couple days won't change that."

"I guess waiting is a heck of a lot better than not being able to heal him at all."

"Yeah." I leaned into him for a second, soaking up his solid strength. Despite what he'd already said, I had to add, "Be careful out there."

"You be careful here," he said. "You'll be closer to the line of fire than I am."

He lowered his head to kiss me, and I kissed him back as if I could pour enough emotion into the gesture to make up for however long we had to spend apart. Connar was going to stake himself out near the main Stormhurst home and wait until the joymancers attacked. His parents would almost definitely race off to help, and that would give him the perfect opportunity to get his brother out. He'd already arranged an apartment in the same town where Malcolm was setting up his sister.

And then none of the barons would have an heir under their direct control, other than Killbrook's unborn daughter. How they'd respond to those moves, we'd find out in the aftermath.

I didn't really want to let Connar go, but he needed to be well away before the attack started if he was going to avoid getting caught up in it. I stepped back and gave him a gentle nudge toward the car. "I'll see you soon."

He gave me a crooked smile. "Let's hope so."

I watched him drive off and then headed back down to the doorway, my steps echoing off the concrete floor. I should probably go back to my dorm and try to get some sleep, but the way my nerves were jittering, I wasn't sure I'd be able to drift off. There was too much uncertainty ahead, too many people I cared about taking dangerous risks. Even if our gambit bringing the joymancers here changed enough minds about revealing ourselves to the Naries, who knew what else the barons might have in the works?

My feet carried me down to the scion lounge instead. Jude was still there, parked on the sofa with a game controller in his hand as the racecar on the screen zoomed through a digital course. He paused it when I came in.

"Not ready to call it a night yet?" he said.

"Don't think I can." I rolled my shoulders. "I wish we'd gotten an ETA."

"That would be too considerate of them." He stretched his arms back over his head with a yawn. "I'm just doing my best not to think about it. You want to join in? Smash a few things up, pretend it's the barons' faces?"

I dropped onto the sofa next to him. "Sure, why not? Although maybe I'll skip the violent imaginings."

"Suit yourself." He grinned and grabbed another controller. As he clicked back to the menu to start a two-player game, he glanced over. "You're still hoping your mom will rise above, huh?"

I grimaced. "She's not one hundred percent horrible. I think she's trying to look after me the way she believes is right. She's stood up for me with the other barons. And she's at least a little conflicted about what they're doing to the Naries too."

Jude scooted closer to kiss my cheek. "You're just too

good at seeing the good in people." His expression turned more serious. "You know that even if we all stay together the way you were talking today—I'm never going to be baron. The confirmation ceremony can't be changed like that. And I really *shouldn't* be if I can barely cast at all."

"In case I haven't already made it abundantly clear, my wanting to be with you has nothing to do with whether you're eligible for the barony." I tipped my head against his. "We'll figure something out. You didn't turn out so bad despite how your dad treated you. Maybe your sister won't be like him either."

"I guess he won't stand a chance even as regent once the rest of you take over." Jude motioned to the TV. "All right, enough depressing talk. Prepare to get your ass handed to you."

Even with all the tension hanging over us, I laughed and launched into the game. Jude did kick my ass in the first few races, but once I got the hang of it, I gave him a pretty good run for his money. I'd just squeaked out my second victory to Jude's playful grumbling when both of our phones pinged with text alerts.

We exchanged a worried look as we groped for them. Declan had sent the text. All it contained was a flame emoji, but we both knew what that signified.

The attack had started.

A chill shot through me alongside a jolt of adrenaline. Without any discussion, we dropped the controllers and hustled upstairs. Other senior students were already milling in the first floor hallway as a couple of the professors hollered orders.

"Anyone who was trained for the town squad or otherwise feels solid in their defensive magic, head to the front of campus now," Professor Crowford called. "We need all the force we can gather."

"And that's my cue to step back," Jude said in a wry tone that was only a little bitter. He squeezed my hand and released me.

I wove between the other seniors to reach Crowford. "What's going on?" I asked him, since I really shouldn't know.

The Persuasion professor's normally suave demeanor had cracked with an aura of panic. He had enough sense of those around him to pitch his voice low when he answered. "Joymancers have converged on the town. They seem to have gotten wind of our activities there. We need everyone who can get down there to help push them back."

I let my face tighten with the anxiety I really did feel. "Shit. Okay."

As I dashed out the door, I tapped on my mom's number in my phone. When the call went through, the hum of a car engine sounded through the line. "Persephone?"

"Mom! I just heard the town is under attack—by joymancers?"

"I'm on my way there right now," my mother said, her voice even but strained. "Thankfully I was spending the night at one of our closer properties. I'll meet you there. We need to show our solidarity more than ever."

"Of course. I'll do whatever I can."

I had the urge to reach out to Connar and Malcolm too, but Declan's text had gone to all of us. They'd know what was happening.

Cars honked in the garage as students clashed trying to get their vehicles out at the same time. I opted to skip that step and jogged along the shoulder of the road toward town. The forest stood darkly still on either side of me, no sign that a battle was raging up ahead.

Car after car roared by. Then one pulled onto the shoulder near me. Declan shoved open the passenger door. "Come on."

I dove in, and he took off again. A magical light flashed against the night up ahead. My stomach knotted.

"If this doesn't work—if it just screws things up more—"

"We'll do our best," Declan said firmly. "If the blacksuits are struggling to fend the joymancers off, that means we've already proved this 'project' is impossible to sustain. Even if we send them running the second we get into town, no one can deny this was a catastrophe. Then all we need to worry about is the impact on the locals."

I nodded, trying to hold onto that certainty.

The cars were coming to a halt at the edge of town, parking all across the road. Blacksuits there waved us out and pointed toward the east end of town. "They've broken through some of the wards. Don't let them get any farther into town—and don't let any of the townspeople leave!"

A group of us hurried through the streets lit by streetlamps and lights flaring on as the locals stared from their windows. Farther ahead, something screeched and glass shattered. Shouts rang out, so blurred together I couldn't tell which side they were from.

No matter what deal we'd gotten the joymancers to agree to, things were going to be broken tonight. People would die. Just not anywhere near as many as might have otherwise, I had to hope.

I didn't want to be part of the breaking and killing, though. As we reached the defensive line where more blacksuits were yelling spells, I drew my own magic onto my tongue. Push them back, block them off, sure. I wasn't out to draw blood.

"Bolster the wards!" someone shouted nearby. "We can't let them completely break through."

That I could do. I rolled a casting word that fell right off my tongue and propelled my magic into the splintering barriers that surrounded the town. Opposing magic slammed into that invisible wall at the same time, the impact shuddering right into my body. Other voices muttered spells all around me.

A figure dashed by beyond the wards—a joymancer, presumably. A blacksuit hurled a spell their way that knocked them off their feet and sent them sprawling on the road. The man swung around and blasted back, and someone on our side shrieked. Our deal to avoid deadly force didn't count when their own lives were on the line.

I cast more magic toward the wards, sweat beading and cooling on my forehead. The ground shook beneath our feet. As I struggled for balance, several of the mages around me toppled completely.

A hand caught my arm before I could fall too. I

glanced around to see Maggie had found me, my mother just a few steps behind us. My newly-discovered cousin gave me a quick nod as Baron Bloodstone came up at my other side. My mother's eyes were wild, her face nearly white in the hazy light, but that didn't stop her from stomping her foot with a sharp word that settled the magical quaking in an instant.

Not fast enough. In the chaos, with our castings interrupted, the joymancers must have launched a major battering of the wards. Even as I opened my mouth, the energy shattered, rippling across my skin.

"You're free," someone bellowed through a loudspeaker. "Don't let these monsters torture you anymore. Leave town to get help if you can, or call for it. They can't stop you now."

My mother swore under her breath and rattled off a casting word to start reforming the wards. But it had taken a dozen or more blacksuits at least a day to build them up in the first place. Car engines gunned in the distance. In the buildings all around us, people might already be dialing emergency services on their phones.

"We can't block them all in time," Maggie gasped out. "What are we going to do if they call the police in to help? The fearmancers won't even be able to set foot in town again. We're not set up to engage all the cops and whoever else they'll send in."

"We're not," my mother agreed grimly. Her gaze shifted toward the end of the street where the joymancers were attacking, and a tremor racked her body. Guilt twisted through me. How awful must it be for her to find herself facing the people who'd kept her imprisoned and helpless for so long?

Whatever distress she was feeling fell back behind a flash of fury. Her jaw tightened. "If we all put everything we've got into it, we can stop the bastards from ruining this too." She raised her voice. "Everyone, cast all the magic you have into rebuilding the wards, *now*."

A chorus of contrasting voices rose up. I added mine to the mass. But with every layer we conjured up, the joymancers kept battering at it, forcing us to patch the cracks rather than build it thicker.

More vehicles raced out of town down the other roads. And as I paused after who knew how many minutes to pant for breath, the wail of sirens reached my ears from somewhere far away—but growing louder.

That wasn't the kind of Nary interaction the barons wanted. Who knew what crazy-sounding stories the locals had already reported, but while any fearmancer could avoid arrest, we weren't prepared for all-out war against the entire population.

My mother didn't need any further prodding to realize we'd lost. Her jaw clenched, but she swept her arm through the air to draw attention to her. "Forget the wards. We need all the feebs here to forget everything that's happened—any magic cast around them and who did the casting. If we work together, we can send a cloud of energy over the whole town. Follow my lead."

The blacksuits near us passed those orders on through their phones. My mother lifted her voice loud enough to carry with a surge of magic that crackled like electricity. I wasn't very practiced with memory spells, but I thought I had enough of an idea to carry this one out. If the Naries forgot all the horrors they'd been through in the past week at our hands, I was all for it.

*No magic*, I thought as I cast the energy from behind my sternum into the air to flow through every wall across the town. *No threats, no danger. It's just been a regular week. No reason to need the police. Nothing unexpected or frightening. Everything is okay.*

A sort of lull settled over even me. My chest loosened, more breath rushing into my lungs. I cast out the spell again alongside so many of my classmates, like the fairies in Sleeping Beauty putting the entire court to sleep. Except what we were really doing was erasing what should have been nothing more than a nightmare.

My throat was hoarse and the sirens pealing loud enough to make my pulse jump when my mother sliced her hand through the air. "Enough. We've done it. Fall back to wherever you're meant to be."

The joymancers appeared to have eased off with the arrival of the Nary reinforcements too. No more spells hurtled our way. They must have felt their immediate job was done.

My mother grasped my arm as we strode away down the street amid the scattering students and blacksuits. "I'll see you to your car. Better you don't take the chance of any officer of the law spotting you."

"It's not here." I jerked my head around, scanning the darkness. "Declan drove us. I'm not sure where he ended up."

The baron let out a sneering laugh. "I'd better get you back to the university then. I can't imagine we can count on him for anything. He's probably celebrating his victory."

My gaze shot back to her with a lurch of my heart. "What are you talking about? What victory?"

She clicked her tongue. "Do you really think this could all be a coincidence? The exact same tactic his mother used all those years ago? It couldn't be more obvious. The only one we have to blame for this disaster is Mr. Ashgrave—and you'd better believe I'll make sure he pays the way Baron Ashgrave never had to."

# CHAPTER TWENTY-SEVEN

*Connar*

Word traveled fast among the fearmancers. When I got Declan's text, just halfway to my family's primary home, I only dared to drive another fifteen minutes before I pulled off into a small lane that branched off from the highway. The house was still an hour distant, but this was the only road it'd make sense for my parents to take if they headed toward Blood U.

I cast a concealing spell around the car to ensure no one would notice it and sat back to wait, but it was only twenty minutes later that my mother's Jaguar zoomed by at what must have been nearly twice the speed limit. She'd gotten the word before Declan had even had the chance to notify us. I was just close enough to make out my father's face in a flash of the streetlamps where he was sitting next to her. Then they were gone, tearing on down the road with a droning sound like a fighter jet.

Rory was probably in the fray now. I didn't want to risk texting her when her mother might be nearby. Willing back the thudding of my pulse, I forced myself to wait another ten minutes to be completely sure my parents wouldn't randomly turn back around. Then I turned back onto the highway and gunned the engine.

Even taking into account my parents' current speed, I'd make it to the house before they arrived at the town. I should have plenty of time to get Holden out, and then we'd take a roundabout route to his temporary living space so we wouldn't risk running into them on their way back. So very simple. Except for the fact that I was going against a baron in the way most guaranteed to infuriate her.

Well, if everything worked out with this doctor Professor Viceport was going to set us up with, by the time my mother found us, she'd have two heirs to contend with—both of whom would have every reason to fight back.

When I reached the looming stone mansion, my chest tightened. I activated the spell to open the gate and drove onto the property with my hands clutching the steering wheel.

I hadn't been back here since my parents had cast that awful mind-warping spell on me. I'd have preferred to never set foot in the place again. It was the building where they'd pushed me and my brother around, where they'd tortured us until I'd given in and attacked him, where he'd been kept as a virtual prisoner both behind a locked door and locked in his body for nearly six years. Nothing about it was welcoming.

Someday it would be mine, I reminded myself. Mine and Holden's, to do whatever we wanted with it.

Maybe we'd raze it to the ground and build something new.

At this time of night, the few staff who lived on the property would have gone to bed. To avoid turning on any lights, I murmured a softly glowing ball into being as I stepped into the foyer. It gave me enough illumination to make my way up the stairs and through the halls to Holden's rooms at the far end of the house.

No sound carried through my brother's door. He was probably asleep too. From the little time I'd been able to spend with him since our catastrophic fight, I'd gathered he was still a morning person.

It seemed better not to give my parents anything at all to worry about back home, as distracted as they had to be by the joymancer attack. I took the time to curl my magic around the ward that would alert them if broken or if the door was opened and shifted it into the wall. It could stay there from now on for all I cared.

The spells keeping the door locked I could break with a few words. I turned the knob and eased inside.

Moonlight streamed through the sitting room window. Holden had left it a smidge open—he'd always preferred a cooler temperature than my parents kept the house at—and the drawn curtain whispered in a faint breeze. I crossed the room to the inner doorway and hesitated there.

I'd never actually gone into his bedroom or the other more private areas of his quarters before. He might not have shown me any obvious resentment, but it felt wrong to march in without invitation or acknowledgement.

I didn't have a whole lot of choice, though. I squared my shoulders and walked onward.

The little hall just off the sitting room led to a bedroom on one side and a bathroom on the other. I paused on the threshold of the bedroom. Holden's wheelchair stood beside his bed where he must have leveraged himself onto the mattress. His prone form lay sprawled under the covers, his chest rising and falling with a soft rasp that was barely a snore. He looked so fragile like that.

How did I wake him up without risking him startling and rousing the staff? He might not have a great grasp on his words anymore, but he could certainly yell loudly if he thought he was in danger. And honestly, I didn't want to put him through any more anguish than he'd already faced because of me, even a tiny bit.

Maybe if I did it gradually, as if it was simply the morning sun coming up. I waved my glowing orb past me into the bedroom until it hovered over the bed. With a murmured command, it started to brighten, slowly and surely.

The whole room was filled with a pale but sharpening light when Holden stirred. He turned his head with his arm shielding his eyes to peer at the light.

"Holden," I said quickly. "It's me. Connar." As if he

wouldn't recognize my voice. I took a step toward his bed. "I'm getting you out of here."

"Con?" He peered at me, blinking. His mouth worked with the words he couldn't quite transmit from his mind to his vocal chords. "W— D— Why?"

"There's a lot to explain. The most important part is, Mom and Dad left you like this on purpose. They never had a doctor even try to heal you." My throat constricted. "It was my fault, so I'm making it right. And I'm not letting them get at either of us again."

"Con." The same syllable, made totally different by his hushed tone. The knitting of his brow told me he was trying to tell me he didn't blame me. That was all the more reason he didn't deserve the hobbled state he'd been forced into.

"I'm taking you with me and then I'm getting you help," I went on. "They might come after us, but the other scions are on our side. If you're okay with taking that risk?"

His jaw flexed, and he stopped bothering with trying to speak. Instead he just nodded in his slightly lopsided way and pushed himself into a sitting position on the bed. With practiced motions, he pulled his limp lower half across the mattress and sank into the wheelchair. His body and face might have thinned during his long isolation, but his arms and shoulders were ropey with lean muscle.

He was only wearing an undershirt and boxers. "It's cold out," I said. "We should get you into some warm clothes, and grab some more for later. I guess you can handle that?"

He nodded again and flicked his wheels to cruise to the dresser. In a few brisk movements, he'd pulled out a sweater and loose slacks. He tossed a few more outfits onto the bed and motioned to the closet while he pulled on his clothes.

I found an old suitcase in the closet that would work fine and stuffed the extra clothes in it. By the time I'd finished, Holden was finished dressing and had tossed a couple of records into the suitcase for good measure.

He careened into the sitting room. When I followed him, he gestured for me to set the suitcase on the floor. He snatched his tablet and some books off the shelves and tossed them in on top of the clothes. After one last quick look around, he sighed. "'Kay."

"Does this fold?" I asked, tapping the wheelchair. I could carry his slender body no problem if I needed to, but I'd rather let him keep his mobility from the start.

He gave me a thumbs up and glanced apprehensively toward the door. "Par— Mom?"

"She's out. They're both out. But we'll want to be quiet so we don't run into any issues with the staff."

I cast a spell to muffle the sound of the wheelchair rolling over the hardwood floor. We slipped down the hall, Holden's expression tensing as he took in the wider world that he hadn't been allowed to venture into in years. A shiver ran down his back. I wasn't sure how much of it was emotion and how much his permanently frayed nerves. What could I say to make this moment any easier?

I was here—I was doing everything I could for him now. Eventually that might feel like enough.

At the stairs, I hefted him as considerately as I could and carried him down and right out to the car. The fall chill closed tight around us, turning my breath into a puff of condensation, and it occurred to me to think about coats—but why would my parents have gotten Holden a coat that fit him when they hadn't let him leave the house since he was fourteen? We'd buy him a new one tomorrow.

I set him in the passenger seat and started the engine for warmth. Holden fumbled with the seatbelt but managed to click it in on his own. He hadn't needed to do that since his injuries either.

"Good?" I checked.

He gave me another thumbs up. I hurried back to get his wheelchair and hefted it to the trunk. With a little fiddling and some magical assistance, I figured out how to collapse the frame so I could tuck it inside.

I'd just shut the trunk with a whisper of magic to mute that thump too when my phone vibrated in my pocket. I tugged it out.

Rory had texted me, an urgent rush of words.

*Are you still at the house? Please tell me everything's okay.*

*We're good,* I wrote back. *Just about to leave.*

*Thank God. We need you.*

There were few words more guaranteed to grip my attention. My stomach flipped over. *What's going on?*

*My mother is convinced that Declan called in the joymancers. The only way I can see to stop her from prying until maybe she uncovers the whole thing is to point her toward someone else. We wanted to destabilize the barons' alliance. Your mother is the one she knows the least. Can you set something up at the house or bring something back that would give the impression she was conspiring?*

Like what? My mind went blank. I was the brute force; I wasn't the schemer. My attempts at deceiving my mother in the past had proven that pretty well.

But the other scions were hours away. If we were going to frame Mom for something, I was the only one in a reasonable position to do it.

Another text popped up as I grappled with the idea. *I'm sorry. I shouldn't have asked you something like that. It's your *mom*. We'll see what else we can figure out.*

So compassionate even when one of our lives could be on the line. I tapped out my response as quickly as I could. *No. If it gets them fighting each other instead of us, I'm all for it. I'm just not sure what to do.*

*You've got time. She's in a meeting with the other full barons here at the university now. You know her better than any of us. I know you can do this.*

Her faith rang through every word. I swallowed thickly. I could do *something*, at the very least.

*I'm on it.*

I spoke a word to hide the car's lights and another to block the rumble of the engine so no one from the house should notice them. Then I came around to Holden's seat.

"I'm sorry," I said. "There's something else I need to do before we can go—but it should help make sure Mom and Dad stay off our backs for a while. I can leave the car running so you have heat—and music if you want to put on the radio. Are you okay to wait?"

"Do—" Holden started, and lost his grip on his words as he so often did. His mouth twisted before he finally spat out. "Fine." He gave me the warmest smile he could manage to show he hadn't meant it as aggressively as it had sounded.

I headed back into the house, doing my best to focus my whirling thoughts. What could I take from here or arrange that would make it look as if my mother had been consorting with the joymancers—and that she wouldn't notice in time to cover it up?

I did know her. I'd been forced to cater to her my entire life. *Think*, Connar.

We couldn't claim she'd gone to visit the joymancers recently, not even in New York. She'd have witnesses who'd be able to account for her real whereabouts. How would she have set up an agreement with them if they couldn't magically seal it in person? There was no way she'd ever have risked that kind of treason without something to cover her ass…

Wait. My head jerked toward her home office. Sometimes even with in-person deals, she wanted the terms committed to paper. She had a whole file full of contracts, the paper magically imbued by her to only accept a signature if the signer was acting in good faith. A spell could confirm her magic had acted on it, but if it was a piece without any clear writing on it, it wouldn't be obvious what the contract had been about.

It took me several excruciating minutes to break the spells protecting her office door, my heart racing faster as each second passed. I hustled inside and went straight to the filing cabinet.

There. Dozens of them. I rifled through the recent ones and tugged out an agreement with our current chef. She wasn't likely to go looking for that any time soon to notice it was missing.

I folded it and tucked it into my jacket pocket. But that one piece didn't feel like enough. A single shred of evidence against a baron was pretty much nothing.

If the other barons investigated my mother, they'd probably come here. Where would they think to look? What did my mother actually have to hide?

I frowned, thinking back to the accounts the other scions had given me of the gala here, the last time the barons had been in this building. Declan had found it odd that my parents had insisted on getting the new bottle of wine together. That action might have caught the other barons' attention too. If they went looking for secrets, there was a decent chance they'd search down in the basement.

As far as I knew, my parents didn't keep anything traitorous anywhere in the house. But they *did* have a survival stash concealed in one of the basement walls—my mother had shown us once when Holden and I were little. Supplies in case we needed to carry out a task under the radar or even completely disappear for a little while. There was cash, a few magical artifacts I wasn't entirely clear on the function of, pills to increase alertness… and a burner phone that wasn't connected to any of us by name.

If she'd been conspiring with joymancers, she'd have needed to get in touch with them somehow.

I dashed down to the basement and swiveled around, dragging up the memory from years ago. Where was the spot? If I reached out with my magic to seek the hum of energy disguising it…

An illusion of the blank wall hung in place over the door to the safe, so subtle I barely picked up on it. I drew it aside and compelled the dial into the right notches. The door swung open—and there were all the supplies I remembered, thank the Lord.

I grabbed the phone. I didn't often use my physicality skills on electronic devices, but now that I had a plan, putting it into action was the easy part. I concentrated on the tickle of the battery, using my magic to charge it until the screen lit up and the bar gleamed full.

No messages showed up from previous conversations. If anyone had used it before, they'd deleted their history. That was fine. Let whoever found this think Mom had obtained it specifically for this plot.

I concentrated on the thin strands of energy flowing through the device and murmured to myself as I drew messages into being from a source that showed as a concealed number. With another whisper, I twitched the date of the exchange to yesterday. Just a handful of comments back and forth, nothing over the top, but clearly passing on information about the town and what was happening there, as well as confirmation about the supposed contract.

When I was done, I slipped the phone back into the

safe, locked it, and tugged the illusion back into place. A shaky breath tumbled out of me.

I'd done it. Let's hope I'd done enough to keep all the scions' necks off the chopping block.

Without a backward glance, I loped up the stairs and out to the car where my brother was waiting.

# CHAPTER TWENTY-EIGHT

*Rory*

My mother made getting into the evidence room look easy. She peeked around the corner of the low-ceilinged hall, spoke a couple commands under her breath, and the cop who'd been sitting at the desk by the door got up. He stepped out, considerately leaving the door ajar for us, and hurried off to carry out whatever task she'd sent him on. His gaze slid right past us as he went by, not even seeing us.

"We should have plenty of time," my mother said, but she didn't sound relaxed about it. Her voice was fierce and her eyes were lit with a furor that made my skin creep. She stalked down the hall to the evidence room with a sharp clack of her heels on the cement floor.

I followed her under the humming florescent lights, their yellowish glow matching the faint lemony scent that hung in the cool air. The county's police department was hardly posh.

"What exactly are we looking for?" I asked as we stepped inside between the stainless steel shelving units with their crates of envelopes.

"Anything the dead had on them that could connect them to Mr. Ashgrave. He must have been in communication with them. *He* might have covered his tracks well, but they won't have had the same concern." She glanced at a note on her phone and rattled off a few numbers. "Those are the ones we need to find."

"The barons haven't found anything connecting Declan to the joymancers yet, have they?" I said cautiously as I slipped down the aisle. I *needed* to find those envelopes first—but I couldn't look as if I were overly desperate. Not when my mother was already so hyped up on her suspicions.

"No," she muttered, browsing the shelves opposite me. "But he clearly didn't like the changes we were making. The Ashgraves have been far too soft on the feebs as long as I've known them. And it's rather fitting that he'd follow his mother's footsteps in every possible way."

"There've been lots of fights between us and the joymancers on our territory, though, right?" I said. "Malcolm told me they come poking around up here trying to interfere with our business all the time. It's possible *no one* tipped them off and they just realized on their own that something odd was going on in the town."

"Perhaps. I find that doubtful. You'll get a sense for these things the longer you spend in our community,

Persephone. Someone was meddling. Someone benefitted from this. I know Mr. Ashgrave helped you with transitioning into student life some, but you don't understand all the history there. We can't take anyone at face value."

Well, she was right about that much. I just had to hope she didn't realize her comment extended even to me.

"I'd rather not think someone who's part of the pentacle would sabotage us like that."

My mother's jaw tightened. "He'll regret it—you can be sure of that. Him and the joymancers he roped in." A quiver ran through her fingers as she nudged a box that had been turned to the side.

I picked up my pace, turning down the next aisle. My pulse kicked up a notch as my gaze skimmed over the combinations of letters and numbers printed on the boxes. Come on, come on. Before she found an excuse to let out all that fury on Declan…

There it was. I had to clamp my mouth shut against a sigh of relief. Tugging out the box I'd spotted, I found the three plump envelopes stuffed next to each other at the front, which made sense considering the three dead joymancers would have been brought in as part of the investigation together and only last night.

My mother had moved to the far side of the room to check the shelves there. I tucked my hand into my pocket and grasped the portion of smooth linen paper that Connar and I had doctored early this morning after he'd gotten back to campus.

Most of the aggressive spells flung back and forth in

the fight had involved searing energy, so it seemed reasonable that a paper a joymancer had been carrying might have gotten burnt. We'd conjured a flame on one corner and directed it so it ate away all of the text except a few vague words around a mention of a contract and the beginning of Baron Stormhurst's signature. Only about a fifth of the original page remained, but it should be enough to point the way.

As long as I got it into place without setting off more suspicions. I checked to make sure my mother's back was turned and then flicked open the middle envelope. My heart thudded even faster as I shoved the fragment of paper inside. I closed it with a murmured spell as I lifted all three envelopes out.

"I found them! They're all here together."

"Well, I suppose the feebs can be efficient on occasion." My mother strode over. I took the first envelope and set the other two on an empty section of shelf. As I'd intended, she picked up the one on top—the one I'd planted my false evidence in.

"I guess a phone would be useful," I said with forced nonchalance, digging into the envelope I'd picked. "Of course, if someone was tipping the joymancers off, we don't know whether any of the ones who died was a contact person."

"Let's just see what we have here," the baron said, her attention fixed on her own envelope.

I glanced around and ended up crouching down on the floor so I could spread out my findings there. My mother stayed by the bare section of shelf, laying out her own envelope's contents. Mine held a watch, a partly opened roll of breath mints, a wallet with IDs and a few twenties but nothing out of the ordinary, a restaurant receipt from what must have been yesterday's dinner—

At the edge of my vision, my mother's body stiffened with a sharp inhalation. I looked up at her, willing my lips into a frown. "Did you find something?"

She had the burnt scrap of paper pinched between her fingers. "There's magic in this," she said, with an urgent but eager tremor in her voice. Her brow knit. "That looks like… No."

She couldn't be all that familiar with Baron Stormhurst's signature in the few weeks they'd had to work together. It would take more than that for her to draw conclusions. I stood up. "Can you tell who cast the magic in it—if it's someone you know like Declan, at least?"

"I should be able to. It's a contract of some sort, obviously magically enforced. A little of the mage's identity will be twined with the spell." Her fingers tightened around the paper. Her casting words came out tightly. Then for a second, her eyes glazed. When they cleared again, her jaw had clenched. Her hand jerked down to tuck the evidence into her purse.

"What?" I said, resisting the urge to fidget. "What did you sense? Was it him?"

"No," she said. There was a hollowness to her tone. Then her hands balled at her side, and she snapped, "It's treachery of another sort. Pretending to share the same goals, and then— We can't let this stand. Not when there's a snake right in our midst."

She swung around, tossing the envelope on the shelf. "We have to go to her, quickly, to see if there's any more proof she hasn't yet destroyed. As soon as the others see— The fucking traitor."

Her entire demeanor had gone icily vicious. I stuffed the bits I'd taken out of my envelope back in, did the same with hers, and shoved them into their box, not wanting the cops to realize their evidence had been tampered with even if my mother no longer cared. She'd already marched all the way to the door before I caught up with her.

"Who's the traitor?" I whispered as we burst out into the hall. She didn't seem to care whether the cops in this place noticed us now either. I cast a hasty distraction spell around us to deflect the notice of anyone we passed as much as I could.

"You'll see. You'll be able to hear it from her own mouth—if she's even got the backbone to own up to it."

She didn't say much more on the way out to the car or after we'd jumped inside. The Lexus tore down the highway, weaving around the other cars so swiftly my stomach lurched to the bottom of my throat more than once. My mother muttered to herself here and there—sometimes what sounded like castings, sometimes fragments of sentences that made me think she was going back through her memories: "That time when—" "She never *said* it wasn't—"

In between, she lapsed into stretches of silence

punctuated by periodic shivers that made me even more nervous about her driving. Her face pinched with a wince of pain. The encounter with the joymancers must have stirred up even more awful aftereffects from her imprisonment, even more so with the thought that one of her colleagues had called them to our doorstep all over again.

I kept my mouth shut, wary of interrupting her stream of thought, braced to leap in with a spell if her erratic behavior was about to put us in danger. Despite her shakes and her anger, she kept the car on the road and didn't so much as clip any of the other vehicles, although a few times it looked like a near thing.

This was all going as well as I could have hoped when I'd suggested the vague shape of this plan to Connar. If she discovered the phone he'd doctored at the Stormhurst residence, I didn't think there'd be any room left for doubt, no matter what Baron Stormhurst said. But watching my mother, a chill crept through my gut that I couldn't will away.

I might have set in motion more than I'd realized. I wasn't sure where it would lead.

I still had my part to play. When we roared up to the gate outside the Stormhurst residence, I widened my eyes. I had been here once before for the gala.

"Isn't this…" I started, trailing off when my mother motioned to the gate with a harsh sound. I couldn't tell whether she'd convinced someone on the other end to open up or shattered the gate's protections just like that. Either way, it yawned open to admit us.

"This is why we never completely trust anyone, Persephone," the baron said through gritted teeth. "And this is how we deal with treason."

The car screeched to a stop a few feet from the front steps. The engine had barely cut out when my mother was throwing open her door. I scrambled after her as she hurtled up the steps.

Someone inside had clearly alerted the residents. Baron Stormhurst yanked open the door just before we reached it. Her face was sallow and drawn as if she hadn't gotten much sleep—which I supposed she might not have. How long had it taken her to discover her other son's absence after she'd returned home in the early hours of the morning?

Strength still rippled through her sinewy frame. She eyed my mother with a flex of her square jaw. "What the hell are you doing here, barging onto my property like this, Bloodstone? A little advance notice would be appreciated."

"I'm sure it would," my mother said tartly, and added a casting word that shoved the other baron to the side so she could step into the hall. "Then you'd have more time to conjure up your excuses. I'm not giving you the chance."

Confusion flickered through Stormhurst's expression. "Excuses?" she repeated, grabbing my mother's arm. "I think you'd better watch yourself and remember whose—"

"I know perfectly well who I'm dealing with," my mother shot back. "A woman who'd murder her way through her family for a chance at power. If you're willing to do that, we certainly can't expect you to have any concern for the rest of us, can we?"

Any bewilderment Stormhurst had felt over the intrusion fell away behind a surge of anger. "Get the hell out of my house!"

"Not until I see what you have holed away here." My mother's eyes narrowed. "You were awfully eager to sneak off to the basement with your husband the other night."

She spun on her feet with a quick casting word that broke Stormhurst's hold on her wrist and sent the other baron skidding a few feet backward. With a curse, Stormhurst barreled after my mother, but whatever spell she cast at her crackled into nothingness against a protective shield.

My stomach twisting, I forced myself to follow them. I'd made this happen—I had to see it through, even if watching the confrontation was making me queasy.

Even if I wasn't sure I could avoid getting caught in the crossfire.

I kept a careful distance back from the barons as they charged down the stairs to the basement. My mother fended Stormhurst off with another casting and then swept her arm toward the hall with what I guessed was a seeking spell. She took several steps forward and then cast it again.

"You have no right to intrude on our home like this," Stormhurst sputtered. "You're *insane.* The other barons will hear about this."

My mother glanced back over her shoulder, her face turned so hard and gaunt in the thin light that she looked almost like the skeletal woman she'd been when we'd first rescued her from the joymancers. "You'd like to be able to simply call me crazy, wouldn't you? You wanted to send me right back where I was. I will *never* let that happen again—not to me or my daughter. If you've got nothing to hide, it shouldn't matter to you how much I go looking."

"I can expect my own home to stay mine!" Stormhurst retorted. Her stance went rigid when my mother's next spell blasted through an illusion farther down the wall to reveal the door to a safe. "Get the hell away from that!"

What did she have in there that *she* knew would be incriminating? What would it incriminate her of? Nothing Connar had recognized, obviously.

My mother was already wrenching open the safe with a shock of magic. Connar had left the phone right at the front. She snatched it up and tapped it on.

"That won't even—" Stormhurst started, and lost her words when the screen lit up.

My mother's thumb skimmed over the screen. Her mouth curved into a grimace. Her shoulders tightened. When she looked up at the other baron, the force of her rage blazed from her eyes. She hadn't said another word, but the thrum of her magic rose, potent enough that I could feel it even from several feet away.

"I don't know what's on there," Stormhurst said quickly, "but I swear, I haven't—"

"More fucking *lies*," my mother rasped.

Stormhurst stepped toward her, and my mother let out a hissing sound. She dropped the phone and whipped her hand toward the other woman with a blast of magic that rattled my eardrums and blanked my vision.

I stumbled backward with a flinch. There was a fractured cry and a thump. When I looked again, my mother was standing with a heaving chest over Baron Stormhurst's slumped body.

Stormhurst's mouth hung open, and her eyes stared blankly. Her limbs sprawled limp against the floor. Her entire chest had become a blackened crater.

Oh, God.

For one stunned moment, my mind stumbled back to the session at the shooting range. To the honed bolts of energy my mother and I had flung at the targets. Even for a fatal blow, she'd put ten times more force into this than she could possibly have needed.

She'd murdered a *baron*.

"You—you killed her," I mumbled in my shock. That wasn't what—I hadn't meant—

My mother's fathomless gaze raised to meet mine. "And justice is served."

# CHAPTER TWENTY-NINE

*Rory*

After the driver my mother had called in dropped me off back on campus, I didn't know what to do with myself. She was still back at the Stormhurst residence, showing the blacksuits the evidence of Baron Stormhurst's supposed treachery and maybe spinning a story about how her fatal blow had been as much self-defense as she'd claimed her murder of Professor Viceport's sister had been way back when. The other barons, I assumed, had been informed, but no one else.

I'd reached for my phone at least a dozen times during the drive, wanting to say something to Connar, but texting or even calling him didn't feel like the right way to deliver the news. The news that *I'd* been responsible, if indirectly, for his mother's death. When I owned up to that horrible fact, it should be face to face.

But as far as I knew, he was still off discussing his

brother's treatment plan with Viceport's doctor friend. None of the students wandering by me on the green had any idea their pentacle of leaders had been broken. Nausea kept churning through me from gut to throat.

The worst part, though, was the whisper of a thought in the back of my head. Maybe this was the only way we could have won, for us and the Naries and a fearmancer society that wasn't totally villainous. How could we hope to change anything in the right direction when the pentacle was made up of barons who ruled through brutality and massive superiority complexes?

That question led to all sorts of other places I didn't want to consider.

On the threshold of Ashgrave Hall, I wavered on my feet and decided to head down to the scion lounge. The thought of facing my unknowing dormmates made me feel even sicker. At least in the lounge I'd have the space to sort through the whirling emotions inside me and figure out what I was going to say to Connar.

I opened the lounge door and discovered I wasn't alone in seeking refuge there. At the squeak of the hinges, Malcolm turned where he was standing by the bar cabinet. He was holding a glass, but it was empty, not even a ring of liquid at the bottom to suggest he'd already finished off his drink.

I got a hold of myself enough to acknowledge his own concerns. "Did you get your sister settled in okay?" I asked. He must have gotten back while I was out with my mother.

I could have sworn he flinched, just slightly, at the

question. Before I could worry about what that meant, he gave me a smile. "Honestly, I don't think I've ever seen her happier. Apparently being a fugitive agrees with her."

He set down the glass on the counter area and walked over to meet me, stopping a few feet away. His smile faded. There was something so unusually uncertain in his stance and his expression that my stomach balled even tighter. His gaze bore into me as if he were searching for something vital in my face.

"Malcolm?" I said, my voice coming out rough. Did he already know—had it tainted his opinion of me?

Whatever he'd been looking for, he seemed to find it. He touched my cheek, just as intent as before but with all the confidence I'd usually expect from him, and leaned in so his forehead grazed mine.

"I love you," he said—almost defiantly, as if I'd accused him of the opposite. "Nothing anyone says or thinks is ever going to change that."

Despite the turmoil inside me, my heart lit up at his words. "I love you too."

My fingers curled into his shirt of their own accord, brushing the solid muscles of his chest beneath, and he crossed the last short distance to claim my mouth. His kisses had always been passionate, even when the passion had been partly fueled by resentment, but this one seared through me in an instant. The press of his lips marked me and offered himself up both at the same time.

"You're mine," he added when he drew back. "*Mine*."

I couldn't help raising an eyebrow at him, even though my voice came out breathless. "Not *just* yours."

One corner of his mouth curled upward. "No. But still mine."

Something still felt off about the moment. *Did* he already know what had happened to Baron Stormhurst? I peered up at him, trying to understand what had come over him. "What's this about, Malcolm?"

He opened his mouth and closed it again, a hint of his earlier uncertainty flickering in his eyes. Then he set his jaw. "I—"

The swing of the door cut him off. Declan strode in, with an approving nod when he saw the two of us there. "Connar's just gotten back. He and Jude are on their way down. I think we should discuss right away how we're going to handle the situation going forward." He caught my eyes. "Did your mother pick up the trail you meant her to?"

The older barons hadn't even looped *him* in. My previous horror came rushing back. My grip on Malcolm's shirt tightened as if I needed it to hold me up. "I—I think I'd better wait to get into that until Connar's here."

Malcolm's face darkened with concern. He guided me over to the sofa and sat me down with his arm around me. I couldn't relax quite enough to lean into him and enjoy the comfort he was trying to offer. Declan glanced from us to the door and back, his mouth tightening.

Jude and Connar came in together a minute later. Jude was chuckling about something, and relief showed all through Connar's posture. "The doctor made progress just in the first session," he announced the second the door had closed behind them. "Holden was able to get out some complete sentences—he even moved his legs. His control isn't good enough for him to try standing yet, but the doctor said that should only take a couple more treatments."

He beamed at us—at me, the one who'd arranged through Viceport to get that doctor in the first place—and my heart sank with the knowledge that I was going to have to snuff out that joyful light. I couldn't put this off, though.

"Connar," I said. "There's something I have to tell you. My mother—and your mother— I—"

I grappled with the words for a few seconds before the story came tumbling out: the evidence room, the drive to his house, the confrontation with his mother, my own mother's raging outburst when she'd discovered the second piece of proof. By the end, my throat was raw. I looked down at my hands. "I'm so sorry. I didn't know—I never would have suggested it if I'd thought she'd go that far…"

Stunned silence filled the room as my voice fell away. Then a firm hand clasped my shoulder. Connar tugged me up and into his arms, embracing me so wholeheartedly that my eyes teared up.

"It's not your fault," he said, a little raggedly himself. "I'm the one who set everything up. I know what the barons are like, and I still thought your mother would just call for her arrest."

"It isn't either of your faults," Declan broke in, his voice taut. "Baron Bloodstone *should* have brought the matter to the pentacle, or the blacksuits, or both. She made the decision to take matters into her own hands—and that violently."

"I knew how messed up she was about the joymancers," I mumbled. "Maybe I should have realized she wouldn't be thinking totally straight."

"Rory." Connar eased me back so he could look straight at me. His light blue eyes were serious now, but there was only sympathy in them, nothing remotely accusing. "We're talking about a woman who tormented my brother and me for our whole lives, who forced Holden to live as a prisoner in his own body and her house for years when she could have had him cured in a matter of days… I wasn't out to see her dead, and I'm sorry you had to be part of it, but I'm not going to grieve her either."

I let out a shaky breath. The other guys had gathered around us.

"So," Jude said after a suitable pause, "does this mean Connar is Baron Stormhurst now? It's not as if your mom left anyone else in the family alive to stand in as regent until you graduate."

I blinked at him, and then Malcolm let out a sputter of laughter. Connar's mouth twitched as if he couldn't quite allow himself to smile just yet. "I guess… once Holden is recovered, he and I will have to hash that out. He's missed his whole schooling, but that shouldn't mean—if Rory could be allowed to catch up—"

He looked to Declan, our expert on political policy, who rubbed his mouth. "Most likely the spot on the table will stay vacant until you graduate, the way the

Bloodstone point did before Rory's mother returned. You'd be first qualified, of course, but if you and Holden decided he should take the position, you could simply hold it until he's ready."

For the first time since I'd stared at Baron Stormhurst's blasted body this afternoon, the anguish in my chest loosened. "The barons can't make any more policy changes, then, can they? Not while they're missing one. Even if they manage to work around you again, they can't make some huge shift in approach with only the three of them and your aunt."

A small smile crossed Declan's face. "That should be true. From what I understand, the blacksuits are withdrawing from the town as they confirm that none of the locals are saying anything incriminating. The fearmancers I've spoken to are talking about the experiment as a total failure. I don't think we need to worry about them restarting that. And with that failure, it'll be a lot easier to push back against continuing to expose the Nary students on campus to magic."

We'd won ourselves major ground—at immense cost, but still. I inhaled deeply into my lightening chest. "All right. I guess that's where we'll start once the dust settles. I don't know how the other barons are going to react to my mother taking 'justice' into her own hands… There might be plenty of conflict just within what's left of the pentacle in the next little while."

"Less chance they'll come up with new ways to screw *us* over," Malcolm muttered with a wry note. "Connar can focus on getting his brother better, and I can figure out what my sister can do with herself for the next year or so until she comes into her magic, and…"

"And I was thinking," Jude put in, "what with extended family recently coming out of the woodwork and all—maybe I should see where my uncle—well, Baron Killbrook's brother—would fit into all of this. I know the baron has been worried about him having designs on the barony, but I don't think he's ever done anything horrible. If his values are closer to ours than my not-actual-father's are, he could turn out to be a decent ally. Especially if we have the opportunity to expose the current baron for the crap he's done."

"That's a good idea, if you're comfortable with reaching out," Declan said.

As I nodded my agreement, my phone chimed. My pulse hitched with the thought that it could be news from —or about—my mother. I dug it out of my purse.

The text was from Maggie. *Need to talk to you ASAP. Can we meet? I'm already near campus.*

She could know what was going on, and it sounded urgent. I glanced up at the others. "Speaking of the extended family, Maggie wants to talk to me about something important. It might be good if you all hear it too. Can I tell her to come here?"

Malcolm shrugged. "Why not? We've had guests in the lounge before. She's been all right since she sorted things out with you. As long as she doesn't have designs on replacing you as scion, I'm good with her."

With the other guys' agreement, I texted back that Maggie should come down to the lounge. My emotions whipped up with fresh anxiety as I paced the rug, waiting for her to arrive. What if the other barons had decided to arrest my mother for her attack on Stormhurst? The entire leadership would end up in chaos—and Lord knew what it'd do to her to find herself imprisoned again.

Maggie knocked rather than coming right in. When Declan opened the door, she hesitated for a second, seeing all five of us gathered around. Then her chin came up. "I guess it's good that you all hear about this as soon as possible. I can't stay very long—Baron Bloodstone is waiting on me—but I didn't want to risk passing this on over the phone."

My mother was waiting for her—then she couldn't be in *that* much trouble. "What's going on?" I asked.

Maggie crossed her arms over her chest, her mouth flattening into an uncomfortable line. "I know you thought the attack on the town would interrupt the barons' plans for dominating the Naries. They *are* abandoning that experiment… so they can escalate their tactics in a different way. They've decided they went about it in the wrong direction, that they've got to destabilize the Naries on the highest levels behind the scenes and then they'll be able to swoop in and take over. And crush the joymancers out of existence too, if your mother has any say in it."

My mouth had dropped open. It took me a second to get my vocal chords working again. "Take over *what*?"

Maggie gave me a grim look. "Everything. The whole damn country. And they're figuring out their first step in that plan right now."

# ABOUT THE AUTHOR

Eva Chase lives in Canada with her family. She loves stories both swoony and supernatural, and strong women and the men who appreciate them. Along with the Royals of Villain Academy series, she is the author of the Moriarty's Men series, the Looking-Glass Curse trilogy, the Their Dark Valkyrie series, the Witch's Consorts series, the Dragon Shifter's Mates series, the Demons of Fame Romance series, the Legends Reborn trilogy, and the Alpha Project Psychic Romance series.

*Connect with Eva online:*

www.evachase.com

eva@evachase.com

Made in the USA
Las Vegas, NV
16 March 2024